Val M[illegible] on the east coast [illegible], then read English at Oxford. She was a journalist for sixteen years, spending the last three years as Northern Bureau Chief of a national Sunday tabloid. Now a full-time writer, she divides her time between Cheshire and Northumberland.

Booked for Murder is the fifth of six novels featuring journalist-sleuth Lindsay Gordon, and was shortlisted for the Lambda Award. Val is also the author of the Kate Brannigan series and four tense psychological thrillers featuring criminal profiler Tony Hill. The first of these, *The Mermaids Singing*, was awarded the 1995 Gold Dagger Award for Best Crime Novel of the Year, while the second, *The Wire in the Blood*, lends its name to the acclaimed ITV series featuring Robson Green as Tony Hill. She has also written three stand-alone thrillers: *A Place of Execution*, *Killing the Shadows* and *The Distant Echo*.

For more information see Val's website
www.valmcdermid.com

By the same author

The Distant Echo
Killing the Shadows
A Place of Execution

TONY HILL NOVELS
The Torment of Others
The Last Temptation
The Wire in the Blood
The Mermaids Singing

KATE BRANNIGAN NOVELS
Star Struck
Blue Genes
Clean Break
Crack Down
Kick Back
Dead Beat

LINDSAY GORDON NOVELS
Hostage to Murder
Union Jack
Final Edition
Common Murder
Report for Murder

NON-FICTION
A Suitable Job for a Woman

V.L. McDERMID

Booked for Murder

HarperCollins*Publishers*

This novel is entirely a work of fiction.
The names, characters and incidents portrayed in it are the work of the author's imagination. Any resemblance to actual persons living or dead, events or localities is entirely coincidental.

HarperCollins*Publishers*
77–85 Fulham Palace Road
London, W6 8JB

The HarperCollins website address is:
www.harpercollins.co.uk

First published in Great Britain by
The Women's Press Ltd 1996

This paperback edition published 2005

1

The author asserts the moral right to be identified as the author of this work

ISBN 978-0-00-785806-4

Set in Meridien by Palimpsest Book Production Limited,
Polmont, Stirlingshire

Printed and bound in Great Britain
by Clays Ltd, St Ives plc

For Jai and Paula. They know why.

ACKNOWLEDGEMENTS

Readers often wonder how much research writers do in the pursuit of our plots. I used to think that the only way to do it was over a beer or a meal. That was before I discovered the Internet and the wonders of e-mail.

This time around, I'd like particularly to thank Kathryn Skoyles, whose knowledge of the seamy side of commerce was invaluable, and Janet Dawson and Chris Aldrich, who kindly prevented me from committing an assortment of trans-atlantic solecisms. Others who contributed in varying degrees, wittingly or unwittingly, were Lee D'Courcy, Frankie Hegarty, Brigid Baillie, David Byrne, Chaz Brenchley, Jai Penna and Sharon Zukowski.

Setting a book in the publishing industry holds certain dangers for an author. In a bid not to become what the Americans now term 'dis-published', I'm bound to say that none of the editors, agents or publishers depicted in these pages bears the slightest resemblance to the people I actually work with. Except the dog.

PROLOGUE

Murder, she felt fairly sure, was not the kind of 'Purpose of Visit' calculated to speed her through the notoriously difficult US immigration channels. 'Pleasure', she ticked, deciding it might not be entirely a lie. At least no one would suspect the truth that lay behind the occupational description of 'systems consultant'. In spite of the books and films that indicated otherwise, hers was not a job people expected to be carried out by a woman.

She finished filling in the form and looked out of the windows of the jumbo jet. They had chased the sunset west across the Atlantic, and now it was firmly dark blue night out there. Streetlights formed a glittering web when they passed above small towns. Over bigger cities, the lights seemed to be enclosed beneath a dimly glowing bowl that held them trapped, the highway lights leading away from them like chains of refugees. Somewhere out there, her target. Watching TV, eating dinner, reading a book, talking to her lover, gossiping on the phone, composing e-mail. Whatever it was, she wouldn't be doing it tomorrow. Not if the woman was successful in her mission.

She turned away from the window and pulled her paperback novel out of the seat pocket. She opened it where she had carefully dog-eared a page to mark her place and carried on reading *Northanger Abbey*.

A change in engine note signalled the start of the descent into San Francisco. It was a sign she noted with relief. A transatlantic, transcontinental flight was quite long enough for her body to feel permanently realigned into the shape of the aircraft seat. That might be just about bearable in first class, but back in anonymous economy it provoked the irresistible fear that she might never walk properly again. The woman stretched her spine, thrusting shoulders back and chest out. The sleeping man next to her snorted and shifted in his seat. Thankfully, he'd been like that for most of the flight. She never liked talking on public transport unless she had instigated the conversation, usually for professional reasons.

She couldn't believe how quickly she cleared immigration. It had been half a dozen years since she'd last set foot in America, and her abiding memory of arrival had been spending the thick end of an hour shuffling forward foot by foot in an endless queue that snaked across the concourse while sadistic immigration officers with faces impassive as hatchets questioned every new arrival. As she collected her luggage, she wondered idly what had brought about the change. It couldn't be that the Americans had become less xenophobic or less paranoid about terrorism, that was for sure, especially after Oklahoma. She only had to think about the drop in the numbers of American tourists to Britain in the wake of the IRA's abandoning of their precarious ceasefire.

Slinging her suit carrier across her shoulder, the woman headed for the taxi rank and gave the name of the hotel where she hoped a room would be waiting for her. Even though she'd been up all night, she feared that sleep would abandon her as soon as her head hit the pillow. It didn't matter. She had time. According to her briefing, the best opportunity she'd have wouldn't come before six in the evening of the following day.

She'd heard about the fog rolling in across the bay in the late afternoon, but she'd never quite believed it could be so tangible a phenomenon. She sat among the Sunday tourists in one of the Fisherman's Wharf cafés and watched the bank of fog envelop the rust-red curve of the Golden Gate, leaving the twin towers stranded above and below. She stirred the last inch of her cappuccino. It had been about the only thing she'd recognised on a list of beverages. They didn't have iced mocha latte in the coffee bar where she picked up her morning carton of steaming pale brown liquid that smelled mostly of its polystyrene container. She supposed this was what they called culture shock.

She'd spent the morning on a whistle-stop sightseeing tour of the crucial highlights. None of her clients had ever sent her to San Francisco before, and she always liked to make the most of her trips at other people's expense. Her one regret was that she hadn't had time for Alcatraz. Now she was reading through her brief one last time, making sure there wasn't something important she'd failed to notice. But it was all as she remembered it. The photographs – well, snapshots really. Directions to the target's home. Suggested lines of approach. And the number to call when she'd achieved her mission.

The woman swallowed the dregs of her coffee and headed back to her hire car, shivering as the damp air hit her. She was wearing only a light cotton shirt over the linen shorts she'd bought for last year's Greek island holiday. It had seemed an appropriate outfit for the warm sun that had beaten down on her earlier. It was California in July, after all. Now the weather had turned into English autumn, she was hopelessly underdressed. She wondered whether she had time to slip back to her hotel, but decided against it.

Ten minutes out of the city, and she was as glad of her decision as she was of the car's air conditioning. The fog that had chilled her was so localised that half a dozen miles away people were still sweating in the same heat that had engulfed her earlier in the day. But at least the air conditioning meant she was clear-headed enough to pay attention to the road signs, making sure she ended up heading down the coast on Highway 1. She drove cautiously, aware that a speed limit lower than the UK's would be easy for her to breach without realising. Attracting the attention of the Highway Patrol would definitely not be a good idea.

The road curved across the peninsula past the vast suburban tract of Daly City, then swerved towards the ocean, the blue swell coming properly into view as she rolled down the hill and past the boxy condos of Pacifica. According to the map she had unfolded on the passenger seat, she was nearly half-way there. Once the map ran out, she had a hand-drawn map of her exact destination, courtesy of her client.

She appreciated the need for the detailed map as soon as she turned off the highway into Half Moon Bay. She found herself in a grid of streets between highway and ocean, quiet residential streets where a strange car cruising slowly and making wrong turns would probably be noticed before too long. Following her directions, she turned on to a road fronting the Pacific. The houses were detached, two storeys high, covered in either carefully tended white or pastel siding or natural wood protected from the climate by heavy coats of sealant. Several had verandas along the front that looked out across the calm ocean towards the eventual sunset. The houses looked like money. Not excessive, obscene, vulgar amounts, but substantial, two professional income levels. As she approached the house where her target lived, she was careful neither to speed up nor to slow down, but she slewed her eyes left as she passed and registered a battered black convertible in the drive. According to the client, that was the target's car. As expected, she wasn't home. But this wasn't an appropriate place. Too easy for her target to avoid what came next.

The woman carried on to the end of the road and turned left on to the rough, unmetalled track that led across the few hundred yards of greenish-brown scrub that lay between the houses and the dunes that edged the beach. As she drew nearer, she could see what had looked like a gentle swell breaking on the sand in a white frothing surf. Where the track ended there was a clear area, and, as instructed, she parked her hire car there, a short distance from the two other vehicles already facing the pounding waves.

She got out of the car and ignored the hard-packed path that led from the car park to the beach. Instead, the woman walked about half a mile north across the scrub before she chose another route down to the beach. She didn't go all the way down, halting at a point where, if she hunkered down, she would be invisible both from the beach and the flat scrubland above. She settled behind an outcropping of gritty sandstone and surveyed the long sweep of the strand. She'd never seen so spectacular a beach that wasn't scarred with serried ranks of sun loungers, parasols, cars and bars. The beach was wide and flat, sweeping round in a long white arc. From the air, it would look more like a crescent than a half moon, scything a thick line between the dark blue sea and the brown land.

She took a small pair of green rubber binoculars from her satchel and scanned the beach from north to south. Luckily for her purpose, there were surprisingly few people, and those there were clearly didn't belong to the bucket and spade brigade. Every time the woman's binoculars picked out a dog, she paused and took a careful look at the animal and its owner. There was no sign of her target.

The woman lowered her binoculars and waited five minutes before repeating the exercise. On the third sweep, she picked out the black Labrador frolicking in the waves. In spite of his playfulness, he was clearly no puppy. She felt a frisson of excitement. Forcing herself to be patient, she continued her slow scan. A couple of hundred yards behind the dog, a figure jogged slowly. A finger nudged the focus wheel and the face came into sharp focus. There was no doubt about it. It matched the pictures supplied by her client. The dog was a six-year-old Labrador cross called

Mutton. The woman was a thirty-seven-year-old journalist with a reputation for stirring up trouble. Her name was Lindsay Gordon. If the observer was successful in her mission, tomorrow someone else would have to walk the dog.

With infinite care, the watcher returned the binoculars to the backpack. It was time to do the business.

1

Lindsay Gordon jogged gently along the hard sand at the edge of the Pacific surf on Half Moon Bay. Against the rhythmic beat of Air Nikes on wet sand and the thud of blood pulsing in her ears, the waves crashed less regularly. Ahead of her, Mutton chased the foaming surf as it retreated across the sand to be sucked back into the vast body of water, occasionally pausing to bark a deep protest as some bubbles he'd been particularly attached to disappeared. Other joggers might have Walkmen clamped to their heads, shutting out everything except their chosen sounds. Lindsay preferred a more natural music, particularly on a day like today when she had death on her mind.

The day had given no indication that it was going to bring tears before bedtime. She'd got up with Sophie and they'd eaten breakfast on the deck together – peaches, bananas, grapes and walnuts chopped up and sprinkled with Grape Nuts, freshly squeezed orange and grapefruit juice and, for

Lindsay only, the industrial-strength coffee she still needed to kick-start her day. It didn't matter how healthy her diet and her habits became; she had grown up on a high-voltage caffeine jolt first thing in the morning, and herbal tea was never going to boot her synapses into activity. Later than usual, because it was Sunday and she was only on standby, Sophie had headed north to the hospital in the Bay Area where she worked with HIV-positive mothers, leaving Lindsay to her computer. She preferred to work when Sophie was on duty so she could enjoy their time off together without guilt. Consequently, she didn't mind settling down with more coffee and a pile of photocopied newspaper cuttings next to her keyboard.

Six years before, she'd stopped practising journalism and started teaching it. Not a day had gone by when she hadn't congratulated herself on her decision. Now, thanks to the 'publish or be damned' demands of her boss at Santa Cruz, she'd been catapulted into her past life. A persuasive editor had talked her into a publishing contract for a book on the decline of British tabloid journalism from 1980 to 1995. It was supposed simultaneously to be a penetrating political analysis and an entertaining romp for the general reader. 'Define oxymoron,' Lindsay muttered as her machine booted up with its usual mechanical grumbles. 'The demands of a publisher's editor. On the one hand, deep and insightful. On the other hand, shallow and superficial.'

Today, the Falklands conflict. Not the battles between the Argentinian and British soldiery, but the rows that raged between government censors and militant journalists betrayed by proprietors who caved in under pressure. And the *Sun*'s shameful 'Gotcha!' headline on the sinking of the *Belgrano*. It was more than enough to keep her absorbed in her screen until late afternoon, apart from a quick break at noon to walk Mutton around the scrubland and eat a chicken Caesar salad.

By five, she'd had enough. Whistling the dog, Lindsay had fired up her battered black Caddie and headed inland to a grocery store a few miles away that carried a stock select enough to satisfy the most discriminating California foodie. Lindsay's freezer was empty of bread, and she needed to stock up on ciabatta with olives, with artichokes, with sun-dried tomatoes and just plain. The challenge was always to get it home without tearing lumps out of it *en route*. While she was there, she raided the deli counter for grazing material for the evening. It was that once-a-month night when Sophie would be out with her doctor friends putting the world to rights, so Lindsay could veg out on the sofa and watch the *Inspector Morse* episode she'd taped the week before, with occasional trips to the kitchen to stack up another plate of nibbles. Bliss.

Her plans died when she got back to the house and finally got round to opening the morning paper. She idly flicked over the front page, breaking off a piece of artichoke ciabatta. *Darkliners Author Dies in Freak Accident* seemed to separate itself from the rest of page three and rise towards her like a macabre magic carpet.

'No,' Lindsay breathed as she started to read.

(London, AP)

Penny Varnavides, best-selling author of the Darkliners series of novels, died yesterday as the result of a freak accident while on a trip to England. She was killed when a bottle of beer exploded in the kitchen of the apartment in London, where she was living temporarily.

The body was discovered by a neighbor, alerted by the open door of her apartment. It is thought Ms Varnavides had just returned home when the accident occurred.

According to police sources in London, Ms Varnavides bled to death when a shard of glass from the explosion penetrated her carotid artery. The unusually prolonged hot summer weather this year in England, where some areas have not had rain for over five weeks, is being blamed for the accident.

A police officer said, 'The beer in question was apparently a kind which contains live yeast. In the warm weather, it must have started a secondary fermentation, and so the pressure inside the bottle would have increased enormously. The slightest vibration could have triggered the resulting explosion.

'It was a freak accident. Ms Varnavides was alone when it happened. If someone else had been present, it's possible she might have survived. But there are no suspicious circumstances.'

Ms Varnavides was in London to complete research on her latest book, said to be a departure from her award-winning Darkliners series of fantasy novels for adolescent readers. She was rumored to be working closely with her British publishers, Monarch Press, on a 'women in jeopardy' thriller aimed at the adult audience.

A member of the Monarch editorial team said, 'We're all devastated by Penny's death. She was in the office only hours before she died. It's a tragic loss.'

Ms Varnavides, 42, grew up in Chicago and studied at Northwestern and Stanford. After graduating, she worked in the computer industry. Her debut Darkliners novel, The Magicking of Danny Armstrong, *was first published in England because she couldn't find a US publisher. But its runaway success was repeated all over the world and she became a full-time novelist ten years ago. She was unmarried and lived in San Francisco.*

The apartment where the tragedy took place is the home of a British academic who exchanged it with Ms Varnavides' duplex in Noe Valley for the summer.

The piece of bread never made it to her mouth. Lindsay sat down suddenly on a kitchen chair and reread the article, tears pricking her eyes. Mutton slumped against her leg, butting his head against her sympathetically. Lindsay's hand went to the dog's head in an automatic movement, rubbing her fingers over the silky ears. Her other hand traced the outline of the newsprint. Penny was dead.

The tears spilled over and trickled down Lindsay's cheeks. Less than five weeks before, Penny had been sitting on their deck knocking back Sierra Nevada amber ale and bemoaning the end of her relationship with Meredith Miller, the woman she'd been seeing for the previous five years. It had been a shocking conversation. If anyone had asked Lindsay who were the couple most likely to make it work, she'd have answered without hesitation, 'Meredith and Penny.' They'd always seemed entirely compatible, a marriage of equals. Even Penny's need to remain in the closet because of her huge market among teenagers in middle America hadn't been a bone of contention; it was matched by Meredith's own requirements. A computer scientist with a defence contractor, she had top-secret clearance, a grading she'd lose immediately her sexuality became known to her professionally paranoid bosses.

The two women had shared a tall Victorian house that had been divided into a duplex; Meredith lived in the two lower floors, Penny above. But the terraced garden at the back was common, allowing them to move freely from one section of the house to the other without being overlooked. So they'd effectively lived together, while maintaining the fiction of being nothing more than friends. In San Francisco, Lindsay had realised a long time ago, it wasn't always easy to tell who were lovers and who merely friends. It was so easy to be out that everyone assumed anyone who wasn't had to be straight and sadly lacking a partner.

Although it had been clear from the tone of the conversation that it had been Penny who had given Meredith her marching orders, she had spoken with deep regret about the ending of the relationship. 'She left me with no choice,' she'd said sadly, head leaning against Sophie's shoulder as Lindsay tended the barbecue. 'Right from the start, we always had borderlines, you know? We had common concepts of what was acceptable in a relationship and what wasn't. Fidelity was an absolute. She must have known she was leaving me no option, doing what she did.' She took another pull on her beer and stared into the sunset.

'Maybe she was testing you,' Lindsay had tried.

'I don't think so,' Penny said. 'I think she was in self-destruct mode. And you can't stop somebody who's that determined.'

'No, but you don't have to give them a shove in the wrong direction,' Lindsay muttered, knowing she wouldn't be heard over the hissing of the marinade she'd just used to baste the salmon.

By the end of the evening, Penny had had enough bottles of the dark golden ale for Sophie to insist she stayed the night and Lindsay had had enough of Penny's grief to slip away on the excuse of checking her e-mail. 'Tactless toerag,' Sophie had muttered as she'd slid into bed beside her later.

'How can I be tactless from my study?' Lindsay asked plaintively.

'Have you forgotten who taught you to be computer literate? Who showed you how to surf the Internet?'

'Oops,' Lindsay said.

'Oops is right. You going off to collect your e-mail was the signal for Penny to slide right over into maudlin tears and reminisce about Meredith turning the lesbian community cyberpunk.'

'But only if they let her wear a bag over her head,' Lindsay responded. 'You know, I couldn't do a job where I had to stay in the closet.'

'No,' Sophie sighed. 'You have many fine qualities, Lindsay, but discretion isn't even in the top forty.'

And now Penny was dead. Lindsay kept staring at the newspaper. She had no idea what to do next. She supposed she should call Meredith in San Francisco, but she didn't have any enthusiasm for it. It wasn't that she didn't want to be supportive, rather that she knew she was more use at the practical rather than the emotional side of things. In their partnership, it was Sophie who did emotional support.

Impatient with herself, Lindsay wiped the tears from her face. She'd take the dog for his evening run, then she'd call Meredith. 'Penny would have taken the piss mercilessly,' she told Mutton as she walked up to the bedroom and changed into her running uniform of shorts, T-shirt and cross-trainers. '"Whatever happened to the tough journalist?" she'd have said. "Thought you could face out anybody? You scared of a bit of raw emotion, Lindsay?" She'd have been a proper monkey on my back, dog,' she added as Mutton licked her knee.

Lindsay jogged up the street, then cut across towards the beach, avoiding the wiry grasses that would whip her legs raw within minutes. Once on the sand, she headed for the water's edge, turned her back on Pillar Point and let her rhythm gradually build to a place where it became a part of her she didn't have to think about. There were fewer people than usual on the beach that evening but Lindsay didn't notice. Penny Varnavides was at the centre of her mind's eye, caught in a slo-mo memory replay, playing beach volleyball with Lindsay, Sophie, Meredith and half a dozen other women last Easter. Lindsay could see the ponytail of glossy black hair switch across Penny's tanned shoulders as she leapt for the ball, the sun glinting on dark eyes and white teeth as she soared into the sky, fingers stretched to the limit to nudge the ball upwards again for one of her team-mates to sweep back over the net.

Never again, Lindsay thought, bitter and sad. Next time they all trooped down to the beach, they'd be one short.

Although she wasn't consciously checking out her surroundings, part of Lindsay's mind was on alert. Her evening routine with the dog had been going on sufficiently long for her to be familiar with other locals who ran or walked by the ocean. A stranger was enough in itself to register with her. A stranger walking a north-westerly line that looked as if it were chosen to intersect inevitably with her southerly one was enough to take her mind momentarily off Penny. Lindsay slowed slightly and stared at the approaching figure.

A woman. Height around five six, hair shoulder length and mid-brown. A large leather satchel slung over one hip. Shorts, lightweight shirt and sandals, but the skin too pale to be a Californian. Mutton bounded up to the woman, barking cheerfully. At once, she stopped and crouched to pat him. 'English,' Lindsay grunted to herself. She slowed till she was barely faster than walking pace. The woman looked up, met her eyes and straightened up. By then, only a dozen yards separated them.

'Lindsay Gordon.' It was a statement, not a question. Two words were enough to confirm Lindsay's presumption that those pale limbs didn't belong to an American. Mutton dropped on to his stomach on the sand, head down between his front paws.

Lindsay paused, hands on hips, breathing slightly harder than she needed to. If she was going to have to take off, better that the other woman thought she was more tired than she was. 'You have the advantage of me, then,' she said, a frosty imitation of Mel Gibson's proud Scottish dignity in *Braveheart*.

'Meredith Miller sent me. I . . . I'm afraid I have some bad news.'

The accent was Estuary English. It had never been one of Lindsay's favourites, always reminding her of spivvy Tory MPs on the make. Distance hadn't lent it enchantment. She wiped away the sweat that had sprung out on her upper lip. She cocked her head to one side and said, 'I know Penny's dead, if that's what you mean. It made the papers. Who *are* you?'

The woman opened her satchel and Lindsay rose on to the balls of her feet, ready for fight or flight. The past she'd tried so hard to bury in California had conditioned her responses more than she liked to admit. Especially when she was dealing with people with English accents. But nothing more threatening than a business card emerged from the bag. Lindsay took it and read, 'DGM Investigations. Sandra Bloom, senior operative.' There was an address with an East London postcode that would have rendered the whole card a joke before Canary Wharf started to fill up. Now, it signalled that Sandra Bloom's company thought they were out at the leading edge of private investigation, light years away from the bottle of bourbon and the trilby.

'DGM?' Lindsay asked.

Sandra Bloom's mouth twisted in a wince. 'Don't get mad?'

Lindsay nodded. 'Must have seemed like a good idea at the time. So what's all this about, Ms Bloom? What are you doing here? What's your connection to Meredith? And why are we standing in the middle of a beach when we live in a world that has more phones, faxes and modems than hot dinners?'

Sandra looked faintly embarrassed. 'I don't know exactly what it is that Ms Miller does for a living . . .'

Lindsay interrupted with a snort of ironic laughter. 'Join a very large club.'

'. . . but whatever it is, it's made her rather paranoid about normal methods of communication,' she continued regardless.

Lindsay nodded. 'Right. I remember the lecture. Menwith Hill, Yorkshire, England. One of the biggest listening posts in the world, run to all intents and purposes by the US government. Who routinely monitor phone calls, faxes and computer traffic. I've always found it hard to get my head round the idea. I mean, the sheer volume of it. Some days I don't have time to read my own e-mail. The thought of ploughing through everybody else's . . . Anyway, yeah, it's starting to make sense. Okay, I understand why

Meredith wouldn't want to entrust anything sensitive to any form of telecommunication. And given the news in today's paper, I don't have to be what's-her-name with the crystal ball on the national lottery to figure out it must be something to do with Penny. So what's going on?'

Sandra pushed her hair back from her face in what was clearly a regular time-buying gesture. 'Ms Miller and her lawyer have sent me over from London . . .'

'Hang on a minute,' Lindsay butted in again. 'What's with the "lawyer" bit? I didn't even know Meredith was *in* London, never mind that she'd got herself a lawyer.'

'Ms Miller has a lawyer because she seems to think she's about to become the police's number one suspect in their inquiry into the murder of Penny Varnavides,' Sandra blurted out in a rush, clearly deciding it was the only way to tell Lindsay anything without interruption.

Lindsay found herself staggering slightly at the abrupt news. Mutton scrambled to his feet and thrust a wet nose into her hand. 'Can we walk while we talk? My muscles need to warm down properly or I'll cramp up,' she stalled, turning so she and Sandra faced back up the beach. Sandra fell in by her side. A few steps further on, Lindsay said, 'The paper here said there were no suspicious circumstances. What changed?'

'The police found out about the murder method in Ms Varnavides' new book.'

'Which is?'

'The killer reads a warning in the newspaper from a chain of – is it "convenience stores" they call them over here?'

'That's right, if you mean off-licences.'

'This warning tells customers to keep wheat beer refrigerated in prolonged spells of warm weather to prevent secondary fermentation and possible explosive accidents. So the killer puts half a dozen bottles of wheat beer on top of the fridge at head height. Then he knocks one to the floor, where of course it breaks explosively. He snatches up a shard of glass and when his victim comes rushing through to see what's going on, he thrusts it into her neck. Then he pulls it out, wipes it clean of his fingerprints and lets her bleed to death. Then he shakes up another bottle and opens it so that she's sprayed with beer as if she'd been caught in the actual explosion.' Her delivery was precise and measured. That made it easier for Lindsay to tune out the thought that it was her friend who had been killed in this ruthless way. She imagined Sandra's reports would be masterpieces of concision.

'Yeah, right,' Lindsay sighed. 'I can see why they might have changed their minds. But that still doesn't explain what you're doing here, stalking me like some trainee assassin,' she added, trying to get rid of the sinking feeling in her stomach with smart-mouthed defiance.

'I'm here to bring you back to England,' Sandra said baldly.

Lindsay shook her head. 'No way.' She'd been right to feel apprehensive. For once, being right didn't make her feel any better.

'Ms Miller has hired me to persuade you to come back and help her,' Sandra said woodenly.

'So far, you're not doing too well. What does she need me for? She's already got a private eye.'

'We don't do this kind of work. Our speciality is white collar fraud. I wouldn't know where to begin on a murder investigation. Ms Miller seems to think you would.'

Lindsay shook her head. 'I'm not a hired gun. I'm a journalist, not a private eye. Besides, I've been away from England a long time. I'm not what Meredith needs.'

'She thinks you are.'

Lindsay shook her head violently. 'No way. You've had a wasted journey, Ms Bloom.' Then she turned away and started to run back towards the safety of her own four walls.

2

The high whine of the jet engine dropped a little as the plane hit its cruising height and levelled out. Lindsay pressed a button in the armrest and exchanged the operatic aria in her headphones for contemporary Irish music. At least flying Aer Lingus meant there was a decent choice of in-flight music, she thought. And the music was the perfect distraction to avoid having to think about why she had agreed to a marathon journey back to London, changing at Dublin, in the charmless company of Sandra Bloom.

Ten minutes after Lindsay had made it back home, the dogged private eye had rung the doorbell. Lindsay had tried to ignore it, continuing on her journey to the fridge for a cold beer, but Mutton refused to play. He ran to the front door, snuffling eagerly round the edges, then barking loudly, tail wagging as he scented his newest friend. He turned to look expectantly at Lindsay, uncapping her beer and ostentatiously ignoring the dog. He gave a soft whimper then turned back to the door, outlining its edges with anxious snorts and anguished yelps.

'All *right,*' Lindsay sighed. She took a long swig of beer, then crossed to the door. She yanked it open and immediately said, 'I told you no, and I meant it.'

Sandra Bloom nodded agreement. 'I know. But Ms Miller is adamant that you're the only person who can help her. She stressed that she wants you to come not only because of your investigative skills but also because you're a friend and that means she can trust you with things she'd be wary of explaining to a stranger.'

Lindsay cast her eyes upwards. 'Emotional blackmail now, is it? I suppose you'd better come in. The neighbours think we lower the tone enough as it is without having private eyes leaning on the doorbell.'

Sandra Bloom had been an investigator for long enough not to care how ungracious an invitation might be as long as it was forthcoming. She followed Lindsay inside and took in a living area with polished wood-block floors, dark squashy sofas and brilliantly coloured Georgia O'Keefe prints splashed across white walls. She decided not to comment on its attractiveness, knowing instinctively her target would dismiss it as merely another ploy. 'I realise you feel pressured,' she said as Lindsay threw herself down on the nearest sofa, scowling.

'Good.'

'But Ms Miller is in a very vulnerable emotional state. Her lover –'

'Former lover,' Lindsay interrupted.

'Her lover until very recently,' Sandra Bloom corrected her precisely, 'has been murdered in a particularly calculated and cold-blooded way. She's on her own in a strange city, thousands of miles from her friends. And as if that isn't enough, she's a suspect in the murder inquiry. And you're the only person she thinks can help her.'

'But I'm not,' Lindsay protested. 'What has she told you about me?'

'Very little. She did say that although you weren't a detective, you'd solved murders before.'

Lindsay took another long pull at her bottle of beer. 'Look,' she said. 'I'm a journalist by trade. I don't even do that any more. I teach kids how to be journalists because I realised I couldn't do the job any more. It was costing me too much to burst into people's lives and turn them upside down. Yes, I got caught up in murder investigations a couple of times and managed to uncover some stuff that the police didn't. But none of that makes me competent to sort out Meredith's problems.'

'You're probably right,' Sandra Bloom said sympathetically. 'It takes a lot of skill and experience to be a good detective. You might have the rudiments of the skills, but you certainly haven't got the experience. Frankly, I think Meredith

Miller would be better off hiring almost any private investigator in London. That's what I told her lawyer. But Ms Miller wasn't having any. It was Lindsay Gordon or nobody.'

Lindsay's scowl deepened. 'I told you, emotional blackmail doesn't work.'

'Fair enough.' Sandra Bloom's smile was placatory. 'And I fully appreciate why you don't want to get involved. It can get hairy out there on the streets. You don't want to be out on the front line unless you really know how to handle yourself. No, better Ms Miller has nobody out there batting for her than she has somebody who doesn't know what the hell to do next.'

The smile was starting to make Lindsay feel patronised rather than soothed. 'I didn't say I was totally clueless,' she muttered.

'Of course not,' Sandra continued blithely. 'But you said yourself, you're a long way off being a pro. But you appreciate I had to come and double check.' She took a step towards the front door. 'I can go back now with a clear conscience. Once she realises that she can't count on having an investigator who's one of her closest friends, I know she'll settle for a regular firm of private investigators. I know a couple we can recommend to her. Thanks for your time, anyway.' Another step towards the door. 'I'll tell Ms Miller that you fully sympathise, but you're unable to help.'

Lindsay dropped her empty bottle on the floor with a clunk. She sighed. 'OK. You win. I'll come back. You can stay here tonight, and first thing tomorrow, we'll sort out a flight.'

Sandra Bloom's smile quirked upwards at one corner. It was the only sign that she'd succeeded in a carefully worked-out plan. 'Not quite,' she said. 'I've got reservations for an overnight flight.'

Lindsay looked at her watch. 'Tonight? No chance. I've got to discuss this with my partner, I've got to pack, I've got arrangements to cancel . . .'

'And Ms Miller could be under arrest by morning.'

Lindsay stood up and glowered at Sandra Bloom. 'Have you ever met my partner? Sophie Hartley?'

Sandra Bloom shook her head, puzzled. 'Why? Should I have?'

'I think the two of you took the same guilt-tripping course,' Lindsay growled, picking up the bottle and stomping through to the kitchen.

Five hours later, she was in flight. Because college had broken up for the summer, she had no teaching burden to rearrange. Writing the book could wait; she'd reached the point where any distraction was welcome. It had taken less than half an hour to pack the assortment of light and heavy clothes an English summer normally demands. Lindsay's attempts to contact Sophie had taken rather longer since Sod's Law – anything that can go wrong will go wrong – was the only exception to itself, operating like clockwork as usual. Inevitably, Sophie and her cronies hadn't been in their usual restaurant, so Lindsay hadn't been able to speak to her lover. She'd ended up leaving a written explanation stuck to the tin of camomile tea that she knew Sophie would hit as soon as she came home. Hopefully, Sophie wouldn't be too upset, given that their own summer trip to the UK was due to start in a week's time anyway.

As the night slipped away under the plane's wings, Lindsay wondered what she would find at the end of her journey. One thing was certain. Her own mourning had to go on hold if she was to be any use to Meredith at all. And in spite of her initial resistance to Sandra Bloom, Lindsay wanted to do what she could for Meredith. She'd always had a soft spot for her, not least because of Meredith's response to her techno-fear.

It had happened after her last brush with murder. She and Sophie had been telling the story to Meredith and Penny one weekend when the four had been camping down at Big Sur. By lantern light, Sophie had revealed how, without her computer expertise, Lindsay would never have uncovered the truth behind the death of trade union boss Tom Jack. Both Meredith and Penny had been open-mouthed with astonishment to discover that someone who worked in the communications industry was a virtual electronic illiterate.

'Doesn't make me a bad person,' Lindsay had mumbled uncomfortably.

The others hooted with laughter at her discomfiture. 'You don't have to be a nerd to know a bit from a byte,' Meredith told her. 'Hey, it's only scary because you don't understand it.'

'I've tried to teach her,' Sophie said.

Meredith snorted. 'That's like husbands teaching their wives to drive. Never try to teach your beloved anything technical. It's the fast lane to divorce. Nah, Sophie, leave it to me. I'll have her writing code by the end of the year.'

It had never gone that far, but Meredith had taught Lindsay more about hardware, software, hacking and net-surfing than she'd ever needed to use. The only question it had left unanswered was what exactly Meredith did for a living that meant she had all this stuff at her fingertips. There was no secret about who she worked for – a software and electronics complex in Silicon Valley, south of San Francisco, whose income, everyone knew, came from the Pentagon. Whenever Lindsay or anyone else asked for something approximating a job description, Meredith would simply smile and shake her head. 'I kill bugs. You want more details, you have to need to know, babe,' she'd say. 'And just being curious don't count as a need.' Lindsay had sometimes wondered if even Penny had known.

Somehow, though, Meredith's silence about that crucial area of her life hadn't been a barrier between her and Lindsay. While Sophie was undoubtedly closer to Penny, Lindsay and Meredith forged a complicit bond where they played the childish role to the other pair's sensible maturity, running off to play computer games or to chase the dog along the beach when the conversation grew too serious for their mood.

But it wasn't all frivolity between them. Meredith regularly printed out obscure snippets and articles from the Internet that she thought might interest Lindsay, and often as they walked along the sand the two had debated the thorny issues around freedom of information and the preservation of personal privacy. From theoretical debate, their dialogues had moved to the personal, each sharing issues in their relationships with lovers, friends and colleagues. While Lindsay was unequivocal in her conviction that Sophie was her closest friend, she knew too that Meredith had an important place in her life. 'I have to have somebody to whinge about Sophie to,' she'd said once, only partly joking. She might have few complaints about her partner, but she knew herself well enough to realise that the way to keep them in perspective was to release them to someone who could point out that she was overreacting. For Meredith, coached in a life of secrecy both professionally and personally, talking to Lindsay, no matter how sparingly or obliquely, was often her only outlet. It wasn't so surprising that she had sent Sandra Bloom after her.

Remembering what Meredith had taught her about the relentless logic of computers, Lindsay sifted through the little she knew about Penny's death. She sighed and shifted in her seat. 'How did the police get on to the idea that it wasn't an accident after all?' she asked Sandra Bloom.

The detective looked up from her copy of *Sense and Sensibility*. 'The murder method was identical to the one outlined in Ms Varnavides' new book,' she said, her tone patiently condescending.

'Yeah, I got that first time around, thanks. What I mean is, what tipped them off to the fact that Penny died the same way as her fictional victim? I'm having some trouble getting my head round the idea of some cop sitting down with Penny's laptop and scrolling through her files on the off chance of finding something that would turn an accident into a murder inquiry. It's usually the other way round, isn't it? Ignore the suspicious circumstances, call it an accident, it doesn't half cut down on the paperwork.'

Sandra Bloom breathed heavily through her nose as she listened to Lindsay's irony. 'According to Ms Miller's solicitor, Ms Varnavides' agent called the police. She'd read a synopsis of the book and she believed it was more than coincidence that her client should die in an identical way.'

'Her *agent*? Bloody hell, that's one way to make sure you maximise your ten per cent!'

'I think that's a pretty harsh judgement,' Sandra said stiffly.

Lindsay snorted. 'Easy seen you've not encountered many literary agents. Think about it. Penny's death is going to increase sales anyway. But murder? That's a whole different ball game. Tie your dead author in to a gruesome murder mystery that's linked in turn to her books and you've hit the jackpot. Penny Varnavides is probably going to sell more books dead than she ever did alive. But I don't suppose any of that even crossed her agent's mind when she rushed off to perform her civic duty.' Her Scottish accent intensified with her sarcasm.

'It was bound to come out sooner or later,' the detective said. 'I expect her publishers will be doing their bit to cash in too. Somebody will presumably have to finish her final book so they can publish it. So they'd have been bound to make the connection.'

'I suppose so.'

'And by that stage, the waters would have been muddied by the passage of time and it would have been that much harder to nail the killer,' Sandra observed calmly.

Lindsay nodded. 'You're right. In fact, you seem to be pretty good at this being right business. I don't suppose you'd want to stick around, help me out with the investigation?'

Sandra Bloom gave the first spontaneous and open smile Lindsay had seen so far. 'With someone as awkward as you? No offence, Lindsay, but life's too short.'

Put in her place as firmly as few had ever managed, Lindsay grunted and squirmed round in her seat, tucking her pillow under her head and pulling her blanket over her shoulders. 'Wake me for breakfast. Not before,' she said firmly.

You could never confuse the approaches to San Francisco and Heathrow, Lindsay thought as she stared down at the chequerboard of small fields and housing estates. Having dozed fitfully some of the way across America and the Atlantic and read the rest of the time, she'd been stupefied with lack of sleep during the transfer at Dublin Airport. At one point she'd found herself wandering dreamlike into a Doc Marten's shop and trying on a pair of shiny gold boots. If it hadn't been for Sandra Bloom looming over her at the crucial moment, she might even have bought them. But now she was grittily awake, feeling faintly sick and aware that the long flight had just been a way of putting things on hold. In a few minutes, they would land, and she'd be in the thick of things. Penny's death, Meredith's grief and someone's guilt would have to be dealt with. She wished she'd waited for Sophie.

Baggage reclaim, customs and immigration were swift and painless. The two women emerged into the main concourse, Lindsay apprehensive, Sandra relieved. Straight ahead, Meredith bent one arm at the elbow in a half-hearted wave. The forlorn gesture knocked Lindsay on her heels with its pathos. Then she surged forward, leaving Sandra to take charge of the abandoned luggage trolley, and swept Meredith into her arms.

For a long minute, the two women rocked each other back and forth wordlessly. For Lindsay, who knew the pain of losing a lover to death, it was as if Meredith's agony was seeping into her by osmosis, taking her back to a place she thought she'd left far behind. All Meredith was aware of was the comfort of a familiar face, a familiar shape in her grasp.

It was Meredith who pulled back first. 'You'll never know how much this means,' she said, her voice cracking.

'Couldn't just abandon you,' Lindsay said. As soon as the words were spoken, she knew they were the truth. There had never really been any chance of Sandra Bloom coming back empty-handed. 'I'm so sorry,' she added.

Meredith nodded, biting her lip, clearly battling tears. Lindsay put her arm around her and they moved away from the incoming passengers and their meeters and greeters. Out of the corner of her eye, she was aware of Sandra Bloom conferring with a woman in a dark trouser suit, a mac thrown with stylish lack of care over her shoulders. Where Lindsay and Meredith moved, they followed.

Lindsay steered Meredith into a chair in a quiet corner away from the crowds. 'Okay?' she asked anxiously, watching Meredith blow her already red nose and dab at puffy eyes with a crumpled tissue.

The woman in the suit stepped forward. 'I'm Geri Cusack,' she said, the soft blur of an Irish accent still evident enough almost to swallow the vowel on the end of her first name. 'Meredith's solicitor.'

More sexily slurred vowels, Lindsay couldn't help noticing. She'd also taken in the straight shoulders and the gentler curves below, the reddish hair and hazel eyes set in a face shaped like a Pre-Raphaelite maiden. The features, though, were far too strong to appeal to any painter whose idea of womanhood fell on the submissive side of the fence. Geri Cusack, Lindsay decided, was not a woman to mess with. Wherever Meredith had found her, it hadn't been first pick in the *Yellow Pages*. 'It was good of you to bring Meredith to meet me,' she said. 'We'll manage now.'

'I don't think you appreciate the gravity . . .' Sandra Bloom started. Geri Cusack raised her hand in a warning gesture and the detective's words trailed off.

'Sandra, would you wait with Meredith a minute? Me and Ms Gordon need to have a word.'

Lindsay, half in love with the lawyer's voice, followed her meekly for a few yards. 'I meant it,' she said. 'We'll manage now.'

'That's fine. I understand you need to ask her things it would be as well I didn't know the answers to. That's the way it goes in difficult cases like these. I don't have a problem with it. I just wanted to fill you in on where we're up to. Saturday evening, she was arrested and taken in for questioning. They were concentrating on establishing that she knew about the murder method in the book, and on where she was at the time they think Penny was killed. She doesn't have anything approaching an alibi. But they've got nothing on her except the thinnest of circumstantial evidence so they've released her on police bail.'

'They wouldn't want the custody time to run out without enough evidence to charge her,' Lindsay said sourly.

'You know how the Police and Criminal Evidence Act works? That might come in handy. Anyway, she's been advised not to attempt to leave the country and to report back to the police station on Friday morning. Just so's you know.'

'And you want what, exactly?'

Her wide mouth twitched in what looked like a half smile, half grimace. 'My client's instructions were to get you here so you could establish her innocence. I think I'd settle for that.'

'Nothing too difficult, then,' Lindsay muttered.

'Not for you, according to Meredith.' Her eyebrows rose momentarily. If it hadn't been a wildly inappropriate moment, Lindsay would have been convinced she was flirting. As it was, she decided, it was simply part of a formidable armoury Geri Cusack dedicated to the greater good of her clients. 'I'll let you get on,' the lawyer said.

Lindsay stayed where she was for a moment, watching Geri Cusack say farewell to her client and scoop Sandra Bloom up in her wake. Then she moved across to Meredith and sat down beside her, taking her hand and squeezing it gently. Meredith stared bleakly at Lindsay with the red-rimmed eyes of a sick and bewildered child. 'I didn't kill her,' she said. 'God knows, I felt like it, but I didn't do it.'

3

The service flat in St John's Wood was a reminder to Lindsay that Meredith and Penny inhabited a different financial dimension from her and Sophie. While Meredith was making coffee, Lindsay prowled the room, noting the deep pile of the carpet and the expensive brocade of upholstery and curtains. The weekly rate was probably about double the monthly mortgage on the house in Half Moon Bay. Whatever had brought Meredith to England, it was clearly something she valued.

It hadn't been difficult to persuade her that the arrivals lounge at Heathrow wasn't the best place to deal with her grief. Stifling her Calvinist conscience at the thought of the expense, Lindsay had followed her to the cab rank, secretly grateful that she wouldn't have to lug her bags any further than absolutely necessary. They hadn't said much on the stuttering journey through west London's heavy traffic, contenting themselves with superficial conversation about

San Franciscan acquaintances and Lindsay's flight. It had been a relief to escape from the stuffy cab and feel able to talk openly.

Meredith carried through a tray with mugs and milk jug grouped around a steaming cafetière and placed it carefully on a footstool large enough to accommodate a pair of seven league boots. As she poured, Lindsay looked at her more closely. Meredith's dark blonde hair was ratty, pulled back into a ponytail held by an elastic band. Her eyelids looked bruised and puffy, and dark pouches had appeared under eyes whose grey irises swam in a background of red and white craquelure. The skin on her face and neck seemed to have sagged and crêped overnight, and her lips were chapped and split. Passing her in the street, a casual observer would have assumed the expensive clothes, carefully chosen for their flattering cut and colour, belonged to someone else. Lindsay had always thought Meredith attractive; now she understood that it was only the spark of her liveliness that had made her so. With Penny dead, the light in Meredith's face had died, leaving her damaged and ordinary.

'I appreciate you coming,' Meredith said. 'I didn't know if you would.'

Lindsay felt a pang of guilt that she'd even considered refusing. 'Yeah, well, we've been friends a while now.'

'I haven't behaved much like a friend since

Penny and I split up. I didn't return your calls, I didn't come round.'

Lindsay shrugged. 'I assumed you weren't ready to talk about it. I wasn't offended.'

Meredith sighed. 'It wasn't just that I wasn't ready. I knew Penny was seeing Sophie. I saw Sophie pick her up one night around dinnertime and drop her off a couple of hours later. I figured you'd have heard Penny's side of it. Which would not have been a pretty story. I didn't expect you'd be too bothered about the case for the defence.'

'You should know me better than that.'

Meredith acknowledged her reproach with a sad smile. 'I know. But I haven't been thinking too straight.'

'That's what I'm here for now. But if you're serious about wanting me to investigate this, you're going to have to give me a free hand.'

Meredith nodded, cradling her coffee in her hands as if it were precious and fragile. 'You got it,' she said.

Lindsay nodded, her lips tight in anticipation of awkwardness. She pushed her hair back from her face and said, 'It means I have to ask difficult questions. You probably aren't going to want to answer some of them, but it's important that you tell me the truth, okay? Even if it's something that makes it look bad for you, you have to tell me. I'm not going to misunderstand the way your lawyer might, because I *know* you couldn't have killed Penny.' Well, not like that, she added mentally. Not with that degree of premeditation.

Meredith stared into her coffee. 'I don't have anything to hide,' she said, her voice flat as a synthesised answering machine. She looked up, her eyes blank. 'I didn't kill Penny. I don't know who did. That's what I need you to find out.'

'I'll do my best. So, when did Penny actually arrive in Britain?'

'She'd been here a day or two under three weeks.'

Lindsay jotted a note on the fresh pad she'd dropped into her backpack in Half Moon Bay. 'I knew she was coming over, of course, I just wasn't sure exactly when she'd left. It was Sophie who spoke to her last. And you were due to come too, is that right?'

'I guess you remember how carefully she liked to plan things, and she'd been organising us both for this trip for months.' Meredith sighed. 'Originally, the plan was that I was going to join her for a couple of weeks near the beginning of her stay, then I was coming back towards the end for another ten days. After we split up, she decided it would be good for her to go ahead with the trip anyway, only alone.'

Lindsay nodded. 'But you decided to come regardless?'

'I couldn't leave it be. It meant too much for us to walk away from it. Hell, you know how much we loved each other. You and Sophie, you were there right from the start. Ruby's birthday dinner at Green's. The lights shining on the bay, only all I had eyes for was Penny . . .' Meredith's voice tailed off and two fat tears spilled down her pale cheeks.

Lindsay leaned forward and put an awkward hand on Meredith's arm. 'I remember. She was the same. I couldn't get a word of sense out of either of you. If there hadn't been a table between you, you'd have been arrested for indecency in a public place.'

A sad smile curled the edges of Meredith's lips. 'Yeah. Feels like ancient history now, though.' She rubbed the tears away with an impatient hand. 'That said, I still cared about Penny too much to want to let her go. I figured I had a chance if I could only get her to listen to me. So I came on after her. I'd already booked the vacation time, it was just a matter of arranging a base for myself.'

'And when did you get in?'

'Exactly a week ago.'

Lindsay gave the room a quick scrutiny. 'You dropped lucky with your digs.'

'Pardon me?' Meredith looked puzzled.

'Sorry. Soon as I get back on British soil, I become more idiomatic than the natives. I was saying, you lucked out with the apartment.'

Meredith looked round her vaguely. 'This place? The company has a deal with the management here. This is where we always stay when we're over on business. It's easier to be private for meetings and stuff in an apartment like this than in a hotel. I just asked our travel department to book me a place and bill me direct.'

Lindsay leaned back, relieved that her ploy had loosened Meredith up a little. 'Going back a bit,' she said casually. 'To when you split up. That was about five, six weeks ago, am I right?'

Meredith's eyes went back to her coffee cup. 'I guess,' she said.

'I'm not entirely clear what went wrong.'

Meredith made a choking sound that Lindsay translated as a bitter laugh. 'The chapter and verse is clear enough. But why it escalated the way it did, that's the obscure part.' She stood up abruptly and walked across to the window to stare out at the canopy of trees. 'Do you have a cigarette?' she demanded, turning back into the room.

'Meredith, you know I quit years ago,' Lindsay protested.

'I know, I just figured you might have brought some in tax-free for somebody. Friend, family, I don't know.'

'You quit too. About six months after me. Don't do it, Meredith. Don't let the bastard kill you as well as Penny,' Lindsay said passionately.

With an impatient gesture, Meredith freed her hair from the elastic band and let it fall around her face in a limp curtain. 'Oh, fuck it!'

'You going to tell me what happened?' Lindsay said quietly, not taking her eyes off Meredith's face.

She threw herself into a large wing chair opposite Lindsay. 'It all started with Penny deciding it was time she got out of the closet on her own terms before some smartass decided to out her.'

'Was that likely?'

'You better believe it. There are a lot of militants out there who think that people like Penny owe it to the lesbian sisterhood to be out and proud. No compromises accepted. Never mind that Penny's been doing more good by keeping her sexuality to herself and providing positive images in her books. The politically correct know there's only one way to be and that's in people's faces.' Meredith shook her head angrily. 'Don't they understand that when you out somebody like Penny, all it means is that every right-wing parent in the country stops buying her books? As long as she looks as straight as a Midwest momma, they're never going to look inside the covers to see what their kids are reading. Soon as she's out, they'll be burning her books regardless, because she's a dangerous dyke poisoning the minds of their children.'

Meredith's tirade left Lindsay momentarily without words. Compulsory outing was one of the few subjects on which she didn't have definite and strong views. She was for it when it came to hypocrites who abused their power over the lives of others, like politicians who failed to support gay rights issues and churchmen who preached one thing and practised another. But when it came to people who merely happened to have become celebrities, she was considerably less certain. She'd heard all the arguments about role models, but what message was being sent by a role model who had to be dragged kicking and screaming into the daylight? Clearly not one Meredith relished. 'Mmm,' Lindsay eventually muttered. 'And Penny thought it was going to happen to her?'

'She'd already been threatened. We were at a party about three months back at Samoa Brand's house. Samoa has this new baby dyke lover, just graduated from college. And since she's twenty years younger than Samoa, she gets indulged all she wants. So this moron comes up to Penny and starts in on her with, "My kid sister's read all your books. Don't you think it's time to pay back? People like you should be outed, don't you think? Shouldn't we show the world we've got a middle class too?"'

Lindsay raised her eyebrows. 'That's just one motor-mouth kid, though,' she said. 'Surely Penny wasn't getting herself in a state over that?'

'She didn't think the kid was going to do anything, but it made her start to wonder how long it would be before somebody did. So she decided the best way to deal with the fallout was to take control and out herself. She knew there would be a lot of publicity round the new book, with it being her first adult novel. She figured that would be a good time to spread the word.'

Meredith rubbed the palms of her hands over her face.

'And you didn't think it was a good idea?'

Meredith sighed. 'This is really difficult for me. No, I didn't think it was a good idea. I knew it would hurt her sales, but that would've been her price for her choice. That wasn't what it was about for me. I told Penny she was forgetting something important. She was forgetting there were two people in this relationship.'

'But her coming out wouldn't automatically implicate you, would it? You didn't technically live together. You have separate postal addresses, separate front doors. Your lives are legally detached,' Lindsay protested.

Meredith shook her head. 'You don't understand the kind of job I do. Every damn year, I get vetted. That's why you never see me the second half of March and the first half of April. That's when it's my turn, so I have to look like Little Miss Prim around then. I *need* top security clearance to do my job. Soon as it became public knowledge that the person who lives in the other half of the house is a lesbian, they'd start to look a lot more carefully at me. If you know what you're looking for, you'll find it. Besides, you know what it was like for Pen. She wasn't some literary writer that nobody's ever heard of. She was a celeb. There isn't a literate teenager in America who hasn't read a Penny Varnavides Darkliners novel. She comes out and there's going to be media interest. And they're going to want to know exactly who her lover is. I had no chance of surviving if she came out.'

Lindsay closed her eyes momentarily. 'I'd avoid saying that to the police, if I was you,' she sighed. 'So, Penny was talking about coming out and you were trying to dissuade her. That about the size of it?'

'I guess.'

'So how did you get from there to splitting up?'

Meredith looked away. 'The whole thing was so dumb.' Her voice was bitter.

'It usually is,' Lindsay said.

'We were fighting a lot. That's something we'd never done before. Things never used to escalate like that between us. But it seemed like every time we were together we ended up fighting about whether she should come out.' Meredith ran her hands through her hair in a gesture of frustration. 'It was driving me crazy. I need to be clear-headed at work, I need to be able to think straight. And Penny was making me nuts. She just wouldn't be logical about the situation.'

Lindsay waited. Eventually she said, 'It's a lot of pressure, when things start going wrong between you and your lover. Something's got to give.'

Meredith nodded. 'It did. I slept with somebody else. I was out of town, we had dinner together. She was all the things Penny used to be with me – warm, funny, sympathetic. And I slept with her. I didn't even need a few drinks to get me there, I went sober and willing.'

Lindsay thought back to a time when infidelity had been something infinitely casual to her. It was so alien to her relationship with Sophie, it felt like a past life experience. But memory helped her construct a glimmer of what that urge to betrayal felt like. 'You're not the first and you're not going to be the last. There are other kinds of treachery that cause just as much damage. I take it Penny found out and confronted you?'

'I told her,' Meredith said bleakly.

Oh, great, thought Lindsay. Why couldn't she have been a Catholic and off-loaded the guilt to a silent priest? 'You didn't think she'd take it badly?'

'I knew she'd take it badly. That's why I told her. I figured it would make her realise how upset I was about her plan to come out. I guess I thought she'd realise that if I felt backed into a corner so far that I had to do something that went so fundamentally against everything our relationship was about, it was real serious and she should think again about what she was doing.'

'And that's not what happened.'

Meredith snorted ironically. 'You got it. She could not see past her own concerns. All she could see was that I'd been unfaithful to her. She didn't stop to think why I might have felt driven to do that. She just didn't get it. Far as she was concerned, I'd committed one of the cardinal sins against the relationship. She was judge and jury and there was only one sentence she could pass. Had to be the death sentence. No mitigation.'

'Didn't you try and explain?'

Meredith leaned forward, elbows on knees, hands clasped. 'What do you think?'

Lindsay gave a wry smile. 'I think you showered her with flowers and cards, filled her answering-machine tape with messages and kept a constant watch on the deck so that if she so much as stuck her nose out the door of an evening, you'd be able to saunter casually up to her and throw yourself at her feet and beg for mercy. That's what I think.'

'Not far off the mark.'

'And she ignored all your messages, dumped the flowers on your doorstep and didn't set foot outside from the moment you came home from work to the minute you left again in the morning?'

'She tell you all this?' Meredith asked, resigned to embarrassment.

'She didn't have to. Like you said earlier, I've known the pair of you right from the start. So you followed her over here to try and change her mind?'

Meredith nodded. 'Waste of time and money. She'd have no more to do with me over here than she would back home. I guess she just about wore me down. The day she died, I left her another message on the answering machine. I swore it was going to be the last, and I told her so. I said it was her last chance to put it back together, otherwise I was going to assume she meant what she said and take appropriate action.'

'Ah.'

'Exactly.'

'I was wondering how the cops got to you so fast.'

'Wonder no more,' Meredith said wryly. 'I left the number, of course.'

'And you knew all about the plot?'

'Oh, sure. Penny used to discuss her plots with three people – her agent, her editor and me.'

'Is that all?' Lindsay asked, dismayed at seeing her circle of suspects shrink towards zero.

'She ever talk about them with you and Sophie?'

Lindsay shook her head. 'She once asked Sophie for some background information about HIV, but even then she didn't explain why she wanted to know. We had to wait till the book came out before we knew what it was all in aid of.'

'Exactly. She always said if she talked about it too much, she got bored with the story, then she couldn't be bothered to write it.' Meredith's words clearly jogged a painful memory, for her eyes glittered with tears again. 'I can't believe it, you know? It's like some sick joke. Like the phone's going to ring and she's going to say, "Hey, have you suffered enough yet?"' She clenched her eyes shut, but tears still seeped through.

Unsure what to do for the best, Lindsay stood up and crossed to Meredith's side, putting a careful arm round her shoulder. 'I know,' she said softly. 'Just when you think you've learned everything there is to know about pain, something creeps up on you and lets you know you're only a beginner. And everybody tells you you'll be all right, that time's a healer. I'll tell you something, Meredith. I don't think it ever gets better. It just gets different.'

Meredith half turned and buried her face in Lindsay's chest, her body jerking with sobs. As she wailed, Lindsay simply held her close, one hand rubbing her back, trying not to think about Penny. Or her own Frances, all those years ago. It couldn't last for ever, she told herself.

Eventually, cried out, Meredith pulled away and blurted, 'I miss her so much,' her voice choked with emotion. She pulled herself upright and staggered across the room into the hallway. Lindsay, hesitantly taking a step or two after her, was reassured by the sound of running water. She went back to her seat and waited. Long minutes passed, then Meredith returned, her eyes even more bloodshot, her face glowing from the scrubbing she'd clearly given it.

'Okay,' she said briskly. 'This is not getting you any closer to finding Pen's killer. What do we do now?'

'Who had a motive?' Lindsay demanded. 'Apart from you, that is?'

4

Lindsay hadn't expected London temperatures to be nearly as high as California's. She was still dressed for the air-conditioned coolness of the plane, she thought, shrugging her shoulders to unstick shirt from skin. In this heat, jeans and cotton twill were not the ideal outfit for climbing four flights of narrow, dusty stairs with the smell of urine from the entrance still pungent. She wondered how many prospective clients were put off by the approach to Catriona Polson's office. Then she remembered that those climbers would be pre-published authors full of hope. 'None,' she muttered under her breath as she rounded the curve of the stairs and reached the final landing.

In contrast to the understated brushed-steel plaque on the downstairs wall and the ambience of a stairway which clearly doubled as a hostel for the homeless, the offices of Polson and Firestone indicated that somewhere on their client list there were some major earners. Even when Lindsay had left Britain, before Soho went up-market and sexually ambivalent, office suites in the area had commanded high rents. Now that the district was almost chic, it must take a sizeable bank balance to secure the whole top floor of a building with a view of Soho Square.

The offices lay behind tall double doors of pale grey wood and brushed steel. Lindsay opened the right-hand door and walked into a reception area that was still lurking in the previous decade. The bleached grey wood was the keynote, looking like the ghost of trees. What wasn't wood was leather or brushed steel. Including the receptionist, Lindsay thought grimly. She was glad she'd employed a ruse to ensure Catriona Polson would be in. Looking at hair blue-black as carbon steel and a jaw with a higher breaking strain than a girder, she knew she was about to be given the brush-off for having the temerity to arrive without an appointment or three chapters and a synopsis. The sweat on her forehead from the sudden transition to air conditioning didn't make her feel any more confident of success.

Lindsay had felt slightly guilty about ringing up and pretending to be an American publisher's assistant breathlessly booking a noon phone call to Ms Polson, but not guilty enough to miss making sure she wouldn't have a wasted journey. The receptionist's grim glare gave her immediate absolution. She smiled. Nothing altered. The receptionist continued to stare at the screen of her computer. Lindsay cleared her throat. The receptionist's plum-coloured mouth puckered. Lindsay found herself irresistibly thinking about cat's bottoms. Then the lips parted. 'Can I help you?' haughtily, in a little girl voice that would have shattered crystal.

'I'd like to see Ms Polson. No, I don't have an appointment. I know she's in the building and I'm absolutely positive she's not in a meeting.' Lindsay's smile grew wider as her voice became more honeyed.

The receptionist's whole face tightened, eyeliner and mascara almost meeting in a smudge of black. 'I'm sorry,' she said smugly. 'She's expecting an important phone call.'

Lindsay assumed her Southern belle accent. 'I know, cher. I was the one booked the call. I just wanted to be good and sure Miz Polson would be here to see me.' Then she grinned. 'Would you tell her I'm representing Meredith Miller?'

The receptionist did her cat's bottom impression again. But she condescended to pick up the phone. 'Name please?' she demanded as she keyed in a number.

Resisting the temptation to respond with her Sean Connery impersonation, Lindsay simply gave her name. The receptionist spoke into the phone. 'Catriona? I've got a person here called Lindsay Gordon who says she's representing Meredith Miller. She also says she made a hoax phone call to us earlier, booking your call from

New York . . . She says she wanted to make sure you'd be here . . .' She flicked an ostentatious glance up and down Lindsay's outfit. 'No, she's definitely not from the tabloids . . .' A malicious smile crept across her face at those final words. She replaced the handset. 'Ms Polson will be right with you.'

Lindsay perched on the edge of the desk to irritate the receptionist while she searched her business card wallet for something appropriate. When she found it, she slipped it into her breast pocket for later. Just then, the inner door opened. Now Lindsay realised why all the doors in Polson and Firestone reached right up to the Victorian ceilings. Any lower and Catriona Polson would have been perpetually banging her head. She was one of the tallest women Lindsay had ever seen, and she must have been aware of the effect she had on people meeting her for the first time. Yet there was nothing apologetic or clumsy about the way she carried her six feet plus. Lindsay imagined with relish the effect on some of the more effete males of the publishing world whom she'd met. She wore a swirling skirt of Indian cotton, flat strappy sandals and a loose embroidered cotton camisole. Flyaway blonde hair was cut in a twenties bob and framed a round face that looked as if its normal expression was cheerful and welcoming. Right now, wariness was the predominant aspect.

She peered down at Lindsay without stooping. 'Ms . . . Gordon, was it?'

Lindsay nodded. 'Catriona Polson?'

'That's me. When you say you represent Meredith Miller, in what capacity are we talking here?' Her voice was firm and clipped, her accent straight out of a girls' school story.

Wishing she had a discreet card saying, 'Private Investigator', Lindsay said, 'I think it would be better if we conducted our business in private.'

Catriona frowned. 'I'm not at all sure we *have* any business. All I know about you is that you perpetrated a time-wasting hoax on my company and you claim to "represent" someone who is not one of our clients and who, as far as I am aware, has nothing to do with publishing.'

It was hard not to feel intimidated by the whole package. Lindsay struggled to maintain any sense of control over the confrontation. Just then, the outside door opened and a middle-aged man in a leather jacket came in. Shit or bust, she thought, dredging up an ancient memory of an interview with a private eye. 'I'm a legal agent acting on Ms Miller's behalf,' she said firmly. 'I'm trying to conduct this matter discreetly, but if you prefer to discuss business matters in the lobby, that's fine by me. You are Penny Varnavides' literary executor and my client is her residuary legatee. My client wants to know what exactly . . .'

Before Lindsay could say more, Catriona had stepped back and was holding the door open for her. 'This way,' she said, her voice ten degrees frostier than the air conditioning.

Once she'd ushered Lindsay inside, Catriona stepped in front of her and led the way down a corridor lined with framed book covers. A couple were prize-winning Penny Varnavides Darkliners titles. At the end of the corridor was another steel and wood door which led into a small boardroom. The table and the chair frames were the now familiar ashen wood. Lindsay began to wonder if they'd taken over the offices from some failed financial consultancy. More book covers lined the walls, interspersed with author photographs. Penny was still there, in the centre of one of the side walls. Catriona walked determinedly to one end of the table and sat down, stretching her long legs in front of her and crossing them neatly at the ankles. 'So,' she said. 'Why are you really here?'

Lindsay pulled out a chair a couple of seats away from her and sat down. 'What makes you think I'm not here to talk about your executorship?'

'Pointless before probate's granted,' she said dismissively.

'So why march me in here?'

'When people waltz into my office intent on causing trouble, I prefer not to give them the satisfaction of an audience.' She dug into a pocket of her skirt and pulled out a packet of the mild cigarettes Lindsay had only ever smoked when she was kidding herself she was about to give up. As she lit one, she kept an eye on Lindsay.

'So who are you, and what are you really doing here?'

The best lies, Lindsay knew, were the ones closest to the truth. 'I'm an investigator. Meredith Miller is innocent, and she's engaged me to make some inquiries about the death of Penny Varnavides. I'm here to talk to you about Penny,' Lindsay said, watching the smoke curling upwards and remembering how the business of smoking had always made her feel much better than the physical sensation.

'What makes you think I've got anything to say?'

'You had plenty to say to the police. And you were quick enough to say it.'

Catriona leaned back in her chair and stretched for an ashtray sitting on a sideboard. 'The police are the appropriate people to talk to when one believes a crime has been committed. And given Meredith's status as prime suspect, I'm not at all sure it would be appropriate for me to talk to you. Besides, there's an issue of client confidentiality here. Penny was my client, and I'm not inclined to breach our professional relationship.'

'As soon as probate is granted, it'll be Meredith who benefits from your work even more than you will yourself. She will, in effect, be your client. Don't you think it would make life a little easier for everyone if you cooperated with me?' Lindsay tried.

'If Meredith did kill Penny, she won't be

earning a shilling from the estate, will she?' Catriona inhaled, then released what was left of the smoke from her nostrils. It was hard not to read self-satisfaction into the gesture.

It was clear that Catriona and Lindsay were never going to become friends. With nothing to lose, Lindsay went on the attack. 'But you will, won't you? Ten, twenty per cent of what Penny earned must have made you a lot of money while she was alive. Dead, she's going to generate a small fortune, isn't she? Even if it was just an accident, her sales are going to climb. But if it's a particularly gruesome and mysterious murder, using the very method outlined in her next book, her sales figures are going to go through the roof.'

Catriona's eyebrows furled together in an angry frown. 'That's an outrageous suggestion. You take my breath away, Ms Gordon.'

'You're not the first woman who's said that,' Lindsay said suggestively, gambling that Catriona was straight.

'How dare you!' Catriona said with contempt.

'Penny used to say it all the time,' Lindsay continued blithely. 'I wasn't entirely candid with you, Catriona. I live in California, you see. Penny and Meredith are very old friends of mine. I know a lot more about you than you do about me. I know, for example, how much you'd hate a story in one of the middlebrow newspapers that pointed out how much you stand to gain from your little trip to the police station. And how, when it actually comes down to it, you knew much more than Meredith about the murder method. She'd only heard Penny talk about it, but you'll have read it. And if we're talking *cui bono . . .*'

'My God,' Catriona said, voice dripping contempt, 'I didn't know private snoopers like you knew *cui bono* from Sonny Bono. Ms Gordon, to kill Penny Varnavides for the income generated by one short burst of sales would be akin to killing the goose that laid the golden eggs in the hope of pushing the market price of gold higher. I stood to earn a lot more cash from Penny Varnavides alive than I could ever hope to gain from her death.'

'Maybe so. But it would still make a nice tale in the tabloids. I'm not asking you to breach commercial confidentiality. All I want is some answers to a few innocuous questions. I'm not the one who got heavy here.'

'I despise blackmail,' Catriona said, lighting a second cigarette.

'Me too,' Lindsay said cheerfully. 'It doesn't half get results, though.'

'You must go down like a cup of cold sick in a euphemistic society like America.'

'They love it. Penny used to call me a breath of fresh effluvium. They think all the Scots are brutally frank. They've been watching too many historical Hollywood epics. So, are we going to talk to each other, or am I going to talk to the tabloids? Did I mention I used to be a national newspaper journalist?' Lindsay's smile alone would have been accepted by any court in the land as sufficient provocation for GBH.

Catriona fiddled with her cigarette. 'There's so little to say that it's not worth arguing over. I'm far too busy to have to deal with muck-raking journalists as well as interfering busybodies.'

It wasn't a graceful climbdown, but Lindsay wasn't proud. 'Thanks,' she said. 'I know Penny would have wanted you to help.'

Catriona looked as if she'd bitten into a profiterole and found a slug. 'Such convenient knowledge,' she muttered.

'You've been Penny's agent right from the start, am I right?'

'Since before she was ever published. She brought *The Magicking of Danny Armstrong* to me after it had been rejected by all the major American houses and her agent in New York had let her go. I was able to place it for her over here, and the rest, as they say, is history.'

Lindsay took out her notebook, more for show than necessity, and scribbled a note. 'This latest book? Very different, I hear.'

'Penny decided she wanted a challenge. She was doing three Darkliners titles a year, and she wanted to break out of what had started to feel like a rut. *Heart of Glass* was going to be her first adult thriller. It was very *noir*, very passionate and very powerfully written. I had great hopes of it.'

'How much of it was actually finished?'

'Penny had written about three-quarters of it. She came over here to do some research she needed for the last part of the book, and to finish writing it. I read what she'd completed before she arrived. But within days of getting to London, she announced she was doing a major rewrite. I was surprised, because what I saw was very good. But Penny was adamant that it needed some substantial alterations.'

Lindsay frowned. 'She wasn't going to change the murder method in the book, was she?'

'Not as far as I'm aware. From what she said to me, it was the characters she planned to work on, not the plot or the structure.'

'Was there anything in particular that she mentioned?'

Catriona stubbed out her cigarette. 'Nothing specific,' she said.

'Have you got a copy of the manuscript?'

Catriona sighed heavily. 'Unfortunately not. Penny took it away with her. She said she wanted me to come to the rewrite with as fresh an eye as possible, not to be able to compare it with what had gone before. She was always quite fussy about retrieving first drafts. Almost neurotic.'

'She was a perfectionist,' Lindsay said sadly, stricken by memory of her friend. 'She hated the idea of anyone revealing her early drafts to the world after she'd gone. I remember her talking about it one night.'

'I don't even have a current synopsis,' Catriona said, sounding more cross than sad. 'If Meredith should come across the manuscript of *Heart of Glass*, or the computer disk it's on, I'd really appreciate it if she could pass it on to me.'

'Why?' Lindsay asked, suspecting she already knew the answer.

'The 300 pages I saw were publishable quality,' Catriona answered, confirming Lindsay's guess. 'If they came with a synopsis, her editor could probably cobble together an ending in an appropriate style.'

'Oh, great, just what Penny would have loved,' Lindsay said sarcastically. 'A load of cobblers.'

'I think I have more right to be the judge of that,' Catriona said stiffly. 'If Penny had doubted my judgement, she would hardly have granted me so much power as her literary executor. Penny wanted to show the world that she was more than just a writer of teenage fiction. What I've seen of *Heart of Glass* demonstrated a formidable talent, and she deserves to have that credited to her reputation. That's what she really wanted, Ms Gordon. She wanted it so badly she could taste it.'

Lindsay looked away, realising that Penny had wanted it so badly she had even been prepared to jeopardise Meredith's career just to generate more publicity. That indicated a raw ambition Lindsay had never recognised in Penny before. She could understand her desire for acknowledgement; what she couldn't relate to was her willingness to sacrifice her emotional happiness and security for the fickleness of reputation. 'Yeah, well,' was all she said.

'I'm not really the person you should be talking to about this,' Catriona added casually as she lit another cigarette. 'Penny spent a lot more time with her editor than she did with me this trip.'

'And her editor is?'

'Belinda Burton. Baz to her babies. Baz would have had a much clearer idea of where she was up to and where she was going. They were very close. It was a large part of the reason behind Penny's success. The relationship between an editor and a writer is crucial. Different people work in different ways. When you link an editor and writer whose minds run along the same tracks and who like to work at the same level of detail, you've got a match made in heaven. A mismatch and everybody's life is an absolute bloody misery. It's part of my job to marry up writers with appropriate editors. Baz and Penny fit like a matching plug and socket,' Catriona said expansively.

'You wouldn't be trying to divert me, would you?'

Catriona laughed. 'No. But if you're still fixated on the profit motive and you think that Penny dead is an appealing moneymaker, you really would be better employed talking to Baz. Penny's royalty is ten per cent, so my cut is around one and a half per cent of the retail price. Monarch

Press, on the other hand, are picking up between ten and forty per cent on every book sold. As they say on your side of the Atlantic, go figure.'

Lindsay stood up. She wasn't entirely convinced she'd got everything out of Catriona Polson that there was to be had, but she didn't have the right questions to elicit more. Perhaps after she'd spoken to Baz Burton, she'd have more ammunition to fire at the agent. 'Fine,' she said. 'I'll talk to her. Now, wasn't that painless?'

'Painless but not a terribly productive use of my time,' Catriona said dismissively, leading Lindsay out of the room and down the corridor. 'I'm bound to say, I hope your client is paying you up front. I suspect she may end up wasting all her available cash on defence lawyers. I think you're backing the wrong horse, Ms Gordon. Always a mistake to let sentiment stand in the way of reality, however unpalatable that may be.'

For once, Lindsay refused to let herself be wound up. She contented herself with, 'As Arnie says, hasta la vista, baby.' On her way out of the front door, she took out the card she'd put in her shirt pocket earlier. It was about ten years old, but that didn't matter. She flicked it across the desk to the receptionist. 'Have a nice day, cher,' she said in her best Bayou accent. She didn't wait to register the response to a card that read, 'Lindsay Gordon, Staff Reporter, *Daily Nation*'.

5

When she left Catriona Polson's office Lindsay felt a strange sense of dislocation, a combination of sleep deprivation and an awareness that there had been changes in the street ambience of Soho in the six years she'd been away. Seedy sex tourism had given way to café bars with fashion victims spilling out on to pavement tables, braying loudly. Surely, Lindsay thought, there couldn't be *that* many jobs for film critics? What she needed was a space to call her own, somewhere she could spread her things around her and feel grounded. Meredith had offered her the second bedroom in her apartment, but Lindsay didn't want to be constantly bound to Penny's death.

She found a phone box near Tottenham Court Road, checked her personal organiser and punched in a local number. 'Watergaw Films, how can I help you?' she heard in a bright Scottish accent.

'I'd like to speak to Helen Christie,' Lindsay said. 'The name's Lindsay Gordon.'

'One moment please.' Then what sounded like *Eine kleine Nachtmusik* played on penny whistles. Lindsay gritted her teeth and waited. It would be worth the assault on her eardrums if this call gave her what she needed, and she didn't anticipate denial. Helen had lived with Sophie for years, but she'd been Lindsay's friend long before that. The two women had linked up years before at Oxford, the only two working-class women in their college's annual intake. The recognition had been instant, forging an immediate friendship that time, distance and lovers had never threatened. They had discovered their common sexuality in tandem, been paralytically drunk and terminally hung over together, wept over broken hearts and celebrated famous victories by each other's side. No matter how long the gap between their encounters, Lindsay and Helen invariably fell straight back into the easy camaraderie that had marked their relationship right from the beginning.

'Lindsay?' It was Helen's familiar voice, Liverpudlian crossed with Glaswegian, untouched by anything south of the M62. 'How're you doing, girl?'

'Off my head with jet lag, but otherwise okay. Listen, Helen, I need a bed a few nights sooner than we anticipated.'

'What do you mean, jet lag? Are you here in London already?'

'Yes. Just me. I'll explain when I see you, it's

too complicated over the phone. Is your spare room free?'

'Course it is. The whole house is a total tip, though, on account of I wasn't expecting the pair of you till next week, but if you don't mind a bit of chaos and no milk in the fridge, move on in. Sophie'll go nutso when she sees the state of the place, but I've had more important things on my mind than tidying and Kirsten wouldn't notice if the council started emptying bins into the living room, bless her,' Helen gabbled.

'Sophie's not with me,' Lindsay cut in as soon as Helen paused for breath.

'Aw, Lindsay, you've not done one, have you? I know you, first sign of trouble and you're off over the horizon. You should stay and talk it over, you know you should. You're a million times better for her than I ever was.'

Lindsay laughed. 'Give me some credit. I have grown up a wee bit in the last half-dozen years. There's nothing wrong between me and Sophie, I swear. The reason I'm here early is something else entirely. Look, I'll explain when I see you, okay? I'm running out of money here.'

'All right. Listen, can you get yourself round to the office? Only I've got to leg it to an important meeting, but I can leave the spare set of keys with reception, and you can sort yourself out, is that okay?'

'That's fi –' The money ran out and Lindsay found herself talking to dead air. She hailed the first cab that passed and asked him to wait outside the warehouse in Camden occupied by Watergaw Films while she picked up the keys. They stopped at Meredith's to collect Lindsay's luggage, then carried on to Helen's terraced house in Fulham. As the black taxi juddered through the early afternoon traffic, Lindsay pondered her next move. Collecting keys and luggage had reminded her that she needed to check out the flat where Penny had been living.

Dredging her memory for details of a half-forgotten dinner conversation with Penny and Meredith, Lindsay recalled that Penny had swapped her house for a flat in Islington belonging to a friend of Sophie. An academic, Lindsay recalled. A philosopher? A psychologist? A philologist? Something like that. The Rubik's cube of memory clicked another turn and the pieces fell into place. A palaeontologist attached to the Natural History Museum. Called . . . She pinched the bridge of her nose in an attempt to awaken her protesting brain as the taxi rattled along Fulham Road. They turned into a side street wide enough for cars to double park without obstructing the road, then rounded the corner into a street of three-storey terraced villas, their stucco in varying states of repair that reflected whether they were single residences or split into rented flats. As the taxi squealed to a halt, Lindsay suddenly realised she didn't really need to remember his name. He was the man living in

Penny's house, at the end of a phone whose number she knew almost as well as her own.

Feeling triumphant, she paid off the taxi and staggered wearily up Helen's short path with a bag that felt heavier with each step. She unlocked the three mortises that fastened the front door of the sparklingly painted house and keyed the last four digits of the phone number into the alarm pad to silence the high-pitched squeal of the warning klaxon. Then she stumbled into a living room that could have been sold to the Tate Gallery under the title of *Installation: Millennium Chaos*. There were piles of newspapers and magazines in a haphazard array by the chairs and the sofa. The coffee table was invisible under an anarchy of used crockery. A spread of CDs was strewn in front of the stereo and tapes were tossed randomly on the shelves to either side of it. Books teetered in tall pillars against the wall. The only remotely ordered area in the room was a cabinet of videos that seemed to be arranged according to some system, though there were gaps in the rows and half a dozen unboxed tapes were piled on top of the TV. A tabby cat sprawled on one of the two video recorders, barely registering Lindsay's arrival with a flicker of one eyelid.

Lindsay closed her eyes briefly. She'd had her moments in the untidiness rankings, but she'd never come close to this. Helen had been right. Sophie would go absolutely nutso. Grinning, she gripped her suitcase and staggered upstairs. The spare room was considerably clearer than downstairs. On the floor next to the ironing board was the biggest pile of clean but crumpled clothes Lindsay had ever seen, but that apart, the room could have been almost anyone's guest room. What marked it out as belonging to Helen were the framed TV and film stills featuring actors she'd placed in her previous career as a casting director. Though she'd progressed to producer/director in her own independent production company, it was clear she hadn't forgotten how she'd started in the business.

Lindsay dumped her case on the floor, not even bothering to open it, and headed back downstairs. There had to be a phone somewhere. She tracked it by the flashing light on the answering machine. A glance at her watch told her it would be just after eight in the morning in San Francisco. She didn't even have to feel guilty about calling too early. On the third ring, a voice said, 'Hello?'

Foiled in her hope that he'd identify himself, Lindsay blundered on regardless. 'Hi,' she said cheerfully. 'It's Lindsay here. Sophie's partner?'

'Oh, hello,' said the precise voice she remembered from phone calls she'd answered previously. 'How are you?'

'I'm fine. And you? Settling in okay?'

'Well . . . Everything was going splendidly and then I had some rather terrible news about . . . well, about our flat and the woman we swapped with.'

'I heard about that,' Lindsay said sympathetically. 'That's actually why I was ringing, Brian.' Brian! It had suddenly come to her in mid-sentence. Brian Steinberg, married to an anthropologist called Miriam. Grinning with relief, Lindsay said, 'I know this probably sounds a bit weird, Brian, but did you happen to leave a spare set of keys with anybody when you left?'

'Keys?' he echoed.

'Yeah, for the flat.' When in doubt, gabble. It was a lesson Lindsay had learned from Helen years ago, and she'd just had the refresher course. 'The thing is, Penny's girlfriend, Meredith, is in a bit of a state, as you can imagine, and I'm over here in England with her trying to get things sorted out. You know what it's like, all the bureaucracy. Anyway, I'm just trying to sort out the practical stuff, and Penny's agent is desperate to get hold of the manuscript of Penny's last book, and it's stuck on the hard disk of her computer, which of course is in the flat, and the police are being really difficult about letting anyone in, so I thought if I could get the keys and just nip in and out . . . I mean, you know me, you know I wouldn't be doing anything I shouldn't be doing . . .'

'I don't know,' he said hesitantly. 'If the police don't want you to go in . . .'

'There's no reason for us not to go into the flat. It's not as if the police have any objections, it's just that they're being really awkward about fixing up a time when we can go and sort it out. I don't have to tell you about bureaucracy, you're dealing with American academia.'

'Yeah,' he said, with feeling. 'Oh, I suppose it'll be okay. I can't see any real problem, and the police have had days now to do whatever it is they have to do. I left a spare set with Miriam's sister. She lives up in Hampstead.' Brian gave Lindsay the address and promised to phone his sister-in-law right away to warn her Lindsay was on her way.

What felt like a lifetime later, Lindsay emerged from the rancid stuffiness of the tube into sunlight at Highbury Corner. Even though it was laden with traffic fumes, the air was still fresh enough to rouse her from the virtually catatonic state she'd reached underground thanks to the combination of heat, jet lag, lack of oxygen and lack of proper sleep. She hoped her exhaustion wouldn't make her miss anything in the flat. Probably it could have waited till the following day, but Lindsay had never liked leaving till tomorrow what could be thrashed out today. Besides, this was a good time to make an unauthorised entry. At the end of the working day, all sorts of people were going in and out of buildings where they didn't necessarily live.

To guard against her potential for carelessness, she stopped at a chain-store chemist for a pack of disposable latex gloves. A few minutes later, she turned into the street where Brian and Miriam occupied the middle flat in a converted Georgian terraced house. Even though she was pretty certain the police would have finished by now with the scene of crime, that was no reason to take chances. She walked right to the end of the street, then kept turning right till she'd done a circuit of the block and was back where she'd started. She'd seen no sign of any police officers, nor did there seem to be any twitching curtains or faces at windows as she strolled down the street for the second time.

Deciding it was clear, she turned nonchalantly into the entrance of Brian and Miriam's house. She climbed the four steps up to the front door and hastily sorted through the bunch of keys until she found the ones that fitted the two locks on the heavy street door. Inside, she closed the door smartly behind her. Ahead lay a dim carpeted hallway, a flight of stairs at the far end. Cautiously, Lindsay made for it and climbed to the first landing. There was a sturdy door facing her, criss-crossed with yellow plastic tape that proclaimed Police. Keep out. The flat was still officially a crime scene.

Pulling a face, Lindsay pulled on the gloves, then fumbled with the locks until the door swung free. Then, with a quick look round the corner to check the stairs above were still clear, she ducked under the tapes and into the flat. This long after the killing, she couldn't believe she was going to affect any crucial forensic evidence.

She found herself in a corridor which opened out into a large, high-ceilinged room whose walls were hung with richly coloured fabric panels. The soft furnishings were low, squashy and oatmeal-coloured, coordinating with what could be seen of the room's paintwork. Face down on a low table whose legs were carved African fertility goddesses was an open paperback of a Robertson Davies novel. Beside the nearest chair was a bowl of grapes starting to go mouldy, a thick A3 pad of scrap paper and, inevitably around Penny, a couple of autopencils. Caught momentarily off guard, Lindsay was ambushed by her grief. Suddenly, she couldn't see through tears, and the lump in her throat threatened to choke her. Subsiding into the nearest chair, she set her sorrow free, her shoulders shaking with sobs as memory flooded her.

Eventually, the wave of pain receded, leaving her beached in a corner of the enveloping sofa. She rubbed a hand across her face, forgetting about the gloves until the latex skidded across her tear-streaked cheek. With a watery grin, Lindsay pushed herself out of the sofa and forced herself to work.

There wasn't much more in the living room to mark Penny's presence, apart from a postcard of the Golden Gate bridge from Meredith, wishing her a safe arrival. Interesting that she hadn't binned it, Lindsay thought. Perhaps Penny hadn't been as adamant in her dismissal as she had seemed to be.

Lindsay crossed the hall into the kitchen. While the lounge looked as if its resident had popped out for a minute, the kitchen made it plain that she wouldn't ever be coming back. On the cork-tile floor was a reddish-brown stain like a giant Rorschach test. Spatters of dried blood afflicted everything else in the room, from cupboard doors to kettle, their sizes ranging from pinpricks to bottle tops. There was even what looked like a thin drizzle in one corner of the ceiling. On every surface, the bloodstains were half obscured by fragments of glass and fingerprint powder. Looking at the room, it was hard to imagine how it had got like this. Logically, Lindsay knew that when an artery was pierced, blood spurted and sprayed like an out-of-control fountain. But this was beyond that. It looked as if someone had shaken a jeroboam of blood-coloured champagne and sprayed it joyously round the room, like a driver winning a murderous Grand Prix. And then thrown the bottle after the foam.

She took a deep breath. There was a faint metallic smell of blood but it was overlaid by the sour smell of spilt beer. Lindsay looked around at the arena of death, taking in the outline marked on the floor like a scene from a bad Saturday Night Mystery Movie. She noted the fridge, tall for a British one, its top standing just under five feet above floor height. On top of it, three bottles of German *Weissbier* remained standing. In spite of her reputation among her students and former colleagues as a cold-hearted bastard, Lindsay didn't expect to drink wheat beer ever again.

It was easy to see how the first assumption was of accidental death. A bottle exploding under pressure at that height could easily drive flying glass slicing through soft tissue. To have imagined it was murder would have seemed perverse without Catriona Polson's information. Even so, there were no signs of another's presence. No alien footprints, no tell-tale bloody handprints on the door jamb. Nothing that didn't tally with the hypothesis of accident.

Sighing, Lindsay backed away from the kitchen and started to search the rest of the flat. In the bedroom, she found nothing unexpected. Penny's suitcases were under the bed. Her clothes occupied one half of the wardrobe, Brian and Miriam's, presumably, the other half. The chests of drawers told the same story. In one, Lindsay recognised Penny's T-shirts and swimsuits. In the other, unfamiliar clothes were stuffed into overcrowded drawers. The bedside table held a notepad and autopencil, a battered copy of W. H. Auden's *Collected Poems* and an alarm clock.

She had higher hopes of the study when she saw the papers strewn across desk and table, but even a casual scrutiny told her there was little of interest there. There were a couple of scribbled lists of Stuff To Do along the lines of 'Imperial War Museum, tampons, Tabasco, *Brewer's*

Dictionary, ???video store???, bread, grapes, ???Calistoga???' Under a paperweight there was what looked like a reading list – *The Ghost Road, The Invisible Man, The High Cost of Living, The Information, Crime and Punishment*. An odd selection, but other people's reading tastes never seemed normal, in Lindsay's experience. Most of the rest of the sheets contained single handwritten paragraphs of description of individual characters. These ranged from highly stylised and polished pen portraits to scrawled sentences like 'looks like Larry, broods on imagined slights, has the dress sense of a color-blind hobo in a thrift shop'. Lindsay couldn't help a smile escaping as she skimmed them.

Eventually, she found a dozen pages with the header *Heart of Glass*. Judging by the page numbers, they were from the first couple of chapters, though not all the pages were present. She searched those of the desk drawers that were unlocked, but found no more of the supposed 300 pages that Penny had completed. As she shifted the desk away from the wall to search more thoroughly, she discovered something more chilling than the missing papers. The power socket behind the desk contained a plug with a cable that led into a transformer which stepped down the voltage from 240 to 12. A second cable led from the transformer to nowhere. But Lindsay knew what would normally be attached to that particular cable.

'"The curious incident of the dog in the night-time,"' Lindsay muttered as she cast around the room for any possible remaining hiding place for a laptop computer and a fistful of floppy disks. It was conceivable that the police might have taken the manuscript away with them for further scrutiny once murder had been alleged. But she found it hard to believe that even the most dim-witted of detectives would have taken the laptop away for further study without the source of its power. Admittedly, it ran off batteries too, but not for long enough to scrutinise every file on the hard disk.

The absence of the laptop was a serious problem. Lindsay had hoped it would still be here, not least because Penny and her computer were virtually joined at the hip. Unlike most authors, who seemed content to use their machines merely as word processors on which to write their novels, Penny fed everything into her machine – accounts, diary, notes, scanned photographs of Meredith, her friends and her beloved garden. Lindsay had expected to find answers to almost all of her questions nestling somewhere in the massive memory of a machine that weighed little more than a bag of sugar. To find it gone was more than a setback; it was a puzzle.

Whoever had taken it was no petty thief; the printer, for example, was still sitting on the floor under the table. Lindsay decided the chances were it had been taken by someone who knew a little about computers, since there wasn't a floppy disk in the place. After a painful episode in the early days of her computing life when a hard disk had crashed and Penny had lost seventy pages of a new book, she had been particular to the point of paranoia about making copies of all her material on floppy disks. Given that her motto when working was 'Back up early and back up often', it was inconceivable that there were no floppies to be found.

The only reasonable conclusion seemed to be that the killer had known Penny's habit of storing every piece of her personal and professional data on her computer and had needed to make sure some incriminating piece of information was gone for ever with the absence of her hard disk and every floppy in the place. Whoever killed Penny Varnavides had not only known about the murder method outlined in her book. They had also had to possess a considerable amount of information about her life. Lindsay rubbed her tired eyes and sighed. If she hadn't been representing Meredith, she'd have been her prime suspect.

She had a last trawl round the flat, checking she hadn't missed the laptop and the back-ups. Finally, she was forced to admit failure. Wherever they were, it wasn't in the flat. And there was nothing else to be found here.

Dispirited that she had learned so little, Lindsay made sure she'd left nothing tell-tale behind, then let herself out of the flat. As she turned the top mortise lock, she heard footsteps coming up behind her on the stairs.

'Excuse me,' a man's voice said officiously, 'But what exactly do you think you're doing?'

6

Limited options flashed across Lindsay's mind as cold sweat sprang out along her spine. Her escape route was cut off by the man filling the stairwell behind her. She could whirl round and catch him off guard, banking on one swift push toppling him and being able to get clear by jumping over him. She could pretend to be connected to the police, mutter something obscure, finish locking up and leave. Then she remembered Sandra Bloom's briefing what felt like weeks ago. The murder had been discovered by the upstairs neighbour. Since this was probably the man who had found Penny's body, she realised that whatever she did, she needed to find a way to talk to him.

Lindsay swung round and gave an alarmed smile to the man, who stood frowning a couple of steps below the landing. A thatch of greying, mousy hair jutted out above a high forehead that narrowed to a pointed chin. Round, intelligent blue eyes flanked a beaky nose that overhung a small, feminine mouth whose lower lip bore the indentations of two front teeth. He reminded Lindsay irresistibly of a cartoon octopus.

'God, you nearly gave me a heart attack,' she said as lightly as she could manage while desperately dredging her memory for his name.

'Sorry,' he said automatically. 'I just wondered what was going on. That's a crime scene, you know.'

'That's why I was in there,' Lindsay said, holding up her gloved hands for his inspection. 'Just checking up on one or two details for my boss.' She grinned disarmingly, still reaching for a name.

'You're with the police?' he asked, still an edge of suspicion in his voice.

'How else would I have the keys?' she parried. If she managed to avoid making any firm statement, it would be that much harder afterwards to make a case against her for impersonating a police officer. 'I wish everyone was as civic-minded as you, Mr Knight.' She'd summoned up a mental picture of the names by the bells on the front door jamb; she prayed she'd gone for the right one.

The man relaxed visibly. She'd got it right, and her knowing his name immediately made the rest of the scenario credible, even though it was a picture almost entirely of his own painting. He smiled back at her. 'Well, you can't be too careful, can you? How's the investigation progressing? I heard on the news that you'd released the woman you were questioning.'

'That's right. We need to build a more solid case before we can think about charging anyone.'

'I can imagine,' he said. 'But you're pretty sure you've got the right person, are you?'

Lindsay winked. 'Obviously that's not something I could comment on, sir. But we're not expanding our circle of inquiries any wider just as yet, if you get my meaning.'

'I only wish I'd actually seen her leave, been more help,' he said wistfully.

'You've been very helpful already, sir. Without your intervention, who knows how long Ms Varnavides might have been lying there?'

He shrugged, his expression a cross between smug self-satisfaction and embarrassment. 'I'm a great believer in taking social responsibility.'

Now she remembered another snippet from Sandra's briefing. Derek Knight was a manager in one of the new hospital trusts. As caring as Mr Gradgrind, if what she'd read in her imported *Guardian Weekly* about the new breed of health service bosses was anything to go by. 'I suppose you have to be, in your job,' Lindsay smarmed. 'Actually, I was hoping to catch you. There were just one or two points I needed to clarify with you.'

'Was there some problem with my statement?' he asked anxiously.

'No, no problem at all. It's just that in the light

of subsequent interviews, my boss wanted me to come back and go over some of the details in your statement. Just to check there's no possibility of error.'

He nodded magisterially. 'I understand. Iron out any potential contradictions.'

'I wouldn't say contradictions, exactly . . .' Lindsay hedged. 'Perhaps if we could go upstairs? More private than here?'

'Of course, of course. If I could just . . . ?'

Lindsay squeezed into the corner to allow him to pass her and turn the corner to the upper flight of stairs. She followed him into a flat whose layout was similar to the one below, save that Derek Knight had left the wall of the corridor intact. Combined with the lower ceilings of the top floor, it made his living room seem significantly smaller and more claustrophobic than Brian and Miriam's, an impression compounded by the dark brocade curtains and upholstery. The room managed to be both fussy and impersonal. It looked like the province of a much older person, as if it had been decorated and furnished by his mother and he hadn't dared impose his own personality on it, Lindsay thought.

Knight dropped his briefcase by the door and gestured towards one of two wing chairs facing each other across a gas fire that was the double of one Lindsay had lived with as a student nearly twenty years before. It hadn't been new then. Beside it, incongruously, was a set of antique brass fire irons. Obediently she sat, and he settled in opposite.

'You'll have to bear with me,' Lindsay said. 'I only had the sketchiest look at your statement before the boss whipped it off me, so I'm probably a lot less *au fait* with what went on the other night than you are.'

'Well, as you'll have seen from its brevity, there wasn't a great deal your colleagues considered to be significant,' he said primly.

'You came home at . . . what time would it have been?'

'The usual time. Just like tonight.'

'So . . . around half past seven?'

'Between twenty-five and half past seven. It depends on the tube.'

Lindsay nodded, her notebook out and her pen scribbling. 'And you noticed nothing at the street entrance to indicate there might be any problem, is that right?'

'No, no, that was the first sign that things were not as they should be. I said so in my statement,' he said plaintively, as if dealing with a stupid and recalcitrant child.

Thinking furiously, Lindsay gave it her best shot. 'The lock?' she hazarded.

'Exactly. The mortise was unlocked. It was only the Yale that was engaged. As if someone without a key had just slammed the door shut behind them. Well, I knew the Thomases on the ground floor wouldn't dream of leaving themselves so vulnerable. I had had occasion to mention the importance of it to Ms Varnavides, but since then she'd been quite reliable about it, so I was rather upset.' He pursed his lips and sighed through his nose. 'I assumed she'd just been remiss again. As I think you were today?'

Lindsay looked surprised, recalled she hadn't locked a mortise behind her as she'd come in and smiled sheepishly.

'I thought as much. Of course, I had no idea there was more to it than carelessness.'

'Of course not,' Lindsay said, trying to keep the irritation out of her voice. 'Thinking back, was there anything that struck you as being out of place? Sometimes, with the passage of time, things become clearer to us . . .'

Knight crossed his legs at the knee, revealing an inch of bony, milk-white leg between grey sock and grey trouser cuff. He knitted his fingers together in his lap and pondered, clearly revelling in self-importance. 'Nothing springs to mind,' he eventually said reluctantly.

'Never mind. So you climbed the stairs and saw . . .?'

'The door to the Steinbergs' flat was open.' He gave a tight little smile, as if imagining the impact when he imparted this in the witness box.

'When you say open, do you mean ajar, or standing wide open, as if someone had flung it back?'

A momentary flicker of a frown tugged at the

skin round Knight's eyes. 'Are you sure you read my statement?'

Lindsay willed herself to relax and smiled. 'Like I said, I just had time to glance at it. We like to do these follow-up interviews without too many preconceptions. A fresh eye on the subject, you know?'

'Hmmm. Waste of time, more like,' he muttered. 'I wouldn't stand for a waste of resources like this in my hospital.'

'The door?' Lindsay prompted, biting back a sharp comment about patients being shunted from one hospital to another in the futile search for an intensive care bed before they died in the attempt.

'It was half open. Considerably more than ajar, but not wide open.'

'As if someone had come out in a hurry?'

He pulled a face Lindsay recognised. It was the same one her chemistry teacher had used whenever he'd been asked a question he didn't really know how to answer. 'I wouldn't really have thought so,' he eventually said. 'The Steinbergs have one of those thick-pile carpets in the hall, so the door doesn't swing free. If someone had yanked it open in a rush, it would have been wider than it was.'

Lindsay filed the incongruous detail away for further consideration, marking it with an asterisk in her notes. 'So, being a good neighbour, you went in?'

'I knocked on the door,' Knight corrected her. 'I called out, but there was no reply. I was starting to feel a little concerned.'

'And so you went in?' Lindsay prodded.

He nodded, a prurient gleam in his eye. 'I knew something was wrong as soon as I got inside. The place smelled like a brewery crossed with a butcher's shop. I could see there was nothing amiss in the lounge, but when I got to the kitchen doorway . . . Well, I don't have to tell you what it was like,' he said, an obviously spurious delicacy giving him pause.

'Just for the record?' Lindsay asked, pen poised.

'Blood everywhere. On the floor, on the walls, all over the worktops. And glass. There was broken glass scattered around. And in the middle of it all, Miss Varnavides. It was obvious she was dead. No one could lose that much blood and still be alive.'

There was no compassion in his voice, Lindsay thought bitterly, only the self-satisfied confidence of a man who thinks he knows what he's talking about. 'Indeed,' she said, her voice dry and emotionless. 'Did you actually go across the threshold into the kitchen?'

'Of course not. These days everybody knows you mustn't interfere with the scene of a crime and I could see that something terrible had happened. I assumed some intruder had hit her with a broken bottle. That was the only explanation I could come up with, seeing all the blood and the glass. Your people thought it was an accident. But it turns out I was right after all.' He smirked.

'Mmm,' Lindsay said noncommittally. 'So you came upstairs and called the police?'

'Well, yes. I didn't want to use the phone down there in case the last number Miss Varnavides had called was a clue.'

'Not very likely if she'd been killed by an intruder,' Lindsay said quietly as she made a note.

'She might have been trying to call the police,' he said defensively. 'She might have panicked and rung 911 instead of 999, being American.'

It was, she supposed, a reasonable point. 'And then our lads arrived,' she said.

Knight gave her a curious look. 'Sorry?'

'And then our lads arrived. The police. After your 999 call. The boys in blue.'

'That's right,' he said slowly. 'Very quick off the mark, your detective inspector.'

Lindsay smiled. 'He doesn't hang around.'

Knight got to his feet. 'I'm sorry,' he said. 'I'm being very inhospitable here. I just realised how thirsty I am. You must be too, in this heat. Can I get you anything? Tea? Coffee? Mineral water?'

Lindsay shook her head. 'I'm fine, thanks. I'll need to be on my way soon. I've just got a couple more questions about visitors to the flat . . .'

'I'll be right back, if you'll just bear with me a moment.' He cleared his throat noisily. 'Desperate for a cup of tea. Terrible frog in my throat.' Knight smiled ingratiatingly as he sidled out of the room, closing the door behind him.

Lindsay sat still for a moment, wondering what she'd said to unsettle Knight so obviously. Then, faintly, she heard the electronic exclamations of a touch-tone telephone. 'Ah, shit,' she murmured, stealthily easing out of the chair and edging towards the door. Half-way there, she noticed there was a phone on a side table just within reach of Derek Knight's preferred armchair.

She sidestepped the chair and reached for the phone. One hand gripped the handset, the other wormed its way under the earpiece until it was pressed down over the black plastic trigger that replaced the old-fashioned cradle. She lifted the handset to her ear, still keeping the trigger firmly depressed. She wrestled one-handed with the handset until her thumb was pressed hard against the mouthpiece, effectively cutting off any external sound, then put the earpiece to her ear. With slow and infinite care, Lindsay gently and gradually released the black trigger.

Derek Knight's voice was loud in her ear, waspishly impatient '. . . asked to be put through to Inspector Nicholson.'

'This is Detective Constable Partridge, sir. I'm one of the inspector's team. How can I be of help?' a more distant voice rumbled. Lindsay's chest tightened. If Knight was calling the police, there could only be one reason. He'd sussed her.

'I don't wish to appear rude, officer, but I've already had dealings with Inspector Nicholson on the Varnavides case, and it would save time all round if you'd just put me through to the correct extension.'

Good sense would take her feet out of there as fast as they could go, Lindsay knew. But good sense had never been her first choice when curiosity was one of the other available options. She wanted to know what had triggered Derek Knight's suspicions of her. Then she'd leave, and only then.

'I'm afraid that won't be possible,' DC Partridge said, his voice placatory. 'Inspector Nicholson isn't in the station right now.'

'When will she be back? This is urgent, officer!'

She, Lindsay thought ruefully. What a time for her to be hoist on the petard of sexist assumption. The police had been 'the lads' for so long, it hadn't occurred to her that the officer in charge of a murder hunt could be a woman. And everybody else had been so busy being politically correct that no one had mentioned it to her.

Lindsay was so busy mentally cursing herself that she missed the officer's reply. But she heard Derek Knight's response loud and clear. 'Well, in that case, you'll just have to do. Are you familiar with the Varnavides case?'

'I'm the officer who took your statement, Mr Knight,' Partridge said heavily.

'Fine. Well, I've got a woman in my flat

impersonating a police officer. I caught her coming out of the murder scene and when I challenged her, she claimed to be with the police. She said she had some more questions for me, but I was suspicious. Then I tricked her into revealing that she thought Inspector Nicholson was a man.'

'And this person is still in your flat, sir?' Suddenly Partridge sounded alert and interested.

'Oh, yes.'

'Do you think you can keep her talking until we can get a car there?'

'No need for that, officer. I've locked her in.'

Lindsay closed her eyes and swore silently. Then she gently depressed the phone button and replaced the receiver as silently as she possibly could. She crept to the door and depressed the handle. Nothing happened. Derek Knight hadn't lied. She was locked in his living room three floors above the Islington street.

7

Within minutes, the police would be on the other side of the door. Lindsay doubted whether they could touch her for violating the crime scene since she had the tacit permission of the householder to be there. But from what she'd heard Derek Knight say, he'd be going in hard on the angle that she'd lied to convince him she was a police officer. He'd have to, she realised. She'd barely known him half an hour, yet she knew that in a tight corner, the most crucial issue for Derek Knight would always be saving face.

'This isn't the time to stand about thinking,' she muttered angrily to herself. 'Shit!' She looked round the room in desperation, hoping something would inspire her to find a way out. At a pinch, she supposed, she could use the fire irons to batter the wooden door to splinters, but she didn't imagine she would have time for that. Besides, the last thing she needed was a charge of criminal damage to add to everything else. She swung round and stared at the door, willing it to open. Then she noticed the butt end of the hinges.

Probably as old as the late Georgian building, the hinges were substantial. But unlike the door, they were free of generations of paint. Lindsay stepped closer and scrutinised the polished brass. 'Yes,' she said softly. She hurried over to her chair and grabbed her backpack, delving into the front pocket to emerge triumphantly with her Swiss Army knife. Then she picked up the poker from the fireplace. She crossed back to the door and pulled free one of the knife's blades. It was a narrow spike that extended about two inches from the middle of the knife, forming a T-shape. Lindsay placed the tip of the spike against the bottom edge of the linchpin of the upper of the two hinges. It was difficult to get much of a back-swing on the poker so close to the door, but she did her best. Using the heavy brass knob on the end of the poker as a hammer, she hit the back of the knife in a bid to force the pin free of the hinge. The first blow made the hinge creak, but nothing shifted. The second whack coincided with a screech from Derek Knight of 'What the hell are you doing?' The third bang of poker on knife drove the spike into the centre of the hinge, thrusting the linchpin a good three inches clear of the top of the hinge. 'Yes!' Lindsay exclaimed. She knew she could pull the pin clear easily now.

Turning her attention to the lower hinge, she repeated the process, ignoring Derek Knight's frantic yells. This time, she pulled the pin completely clear, then worked the top pin free. Now, only the lock held the door in place. Gripping the edge of the door with her fingertips, Lindsay inched the hinge side of the door back from the frame. The tongue of the lock creaked against its socket, but she managed to pull the door back sufficiently far to clear the jamb. Then, one hand on the handle, the other on the hinge side of the door, she slid the whole thing sideways, pulling it neatly free of the lock.

Derek Knight was standing in the hall facing her, his mouth open and his eyelids as wide as they could go without surgery. Lindsay stepped through the doorway, leaning down to pick up her backpack. 'Sorry, got to go,' she said.

He lunged at her, mouthing something incomprehensible, but Lindsay sidestepped neatly and rushed for the door of the flat. She took the stairs two at a time, the blood pounding in her ears, obscuring any sounds of pursuit. She didn't even bother closing the street door behind her, sprinting down the street in the opposite direction to the tube station. At the corner, she turned left at random, cutting diagonally across the road and jinking into a mews court that ran between two parallel streets.

At the end of the mews, she stopped running. She wasn't dressed for jogging and no one on the Islington/Canonbury border ran except joggers and muggers. As she turned left into the next street, she heard the whooping sirens of police cars nearby. On the corner was a pub. Lindsay breathed deeply to calm her thudding heart, walked straight through the doors and ordered a pint of bitter.

The first drink had gone down so well, Lindsay hadn't had to work hard to persuade herself that she deserved a second. She'd found an unobtrusive corner, hidden by a raucous group of youths wearing sweat pants, sports shirts and training shoes that had never seen activity more strenuous than the game of darts their owners were throwing. Lindsay kept her head down and thought about the little she'd learned from Derek Knight before she'd given herself away in so embarrassingly inappropriate a fashion.

What stuck in her mind were his comments about the doors. From the moment Sandra Bloom had revealed that Penny's death was murder, Lindsay had recognised it as a carefully planned, premeditated crime, based as it was on the plot in Penny's own book. According to Derek Knight, the flat door was ajar, but not flung wide, which tied in with that supposition. It wasn't left that way in a panic, but deliberately. It also indicated that the killer wanted the body to be found fairly quickly.

However, the mortise lock on the street door had been left undone. That suggested either that the killer didn't know the residents routinely kept it locked or that in his or her haste to get away from the scene of the crime they hadn't been able to find Penny's keys. It was confusing. On the one hand, it had been made to look like an accident; on the other hand, like murder.

Lindsay sighed and finished her second pint. It was nearly nine o'clock, and she felt like she hadn't slept properly for days. In the ladies', she splashed water over her tired eyelids, then set off on the long journey across London to Helen's. Outside the pub, to be on the safe side, she set off on a wide detour that would bring her via side streets to the top end of Highbury Fields, so she could approach the tube station from a diametrically opposite direction to Penny's flat. Better safe than sorry if the cops happened to be keeping an eye open at the station.

Her route took her down the side of the park, past tall, narrow houses that looked out across the variegated greens of trees and grass. It was a view she knew well. There had been a time when she had regarded one of those tall houses as her home. It had belonged to her lover, Cordelia. When Lindsay had moved in with her after their relationship had pushed her into abandoning her old life in Glasgow, she had thought that love was enough and for ever. 'How wrong can you get?' she muttered under her breath as she passed what had been her front door during what she looked back on as the time of the Great Illusion. Neither love nor Cordelia had proved to be what they seemed, and Lindsay still carried the scars. It had been a nice view, though, she thought fondly, wondering who lived there now and if it still belonged to Cordelia, the rent funding her permanent exile.

As the station grew nearer, caution forced nostalgia to the back of her mind. With sinking heart, Lindsay noticed there were a couple of police officers talking to a *Big Issue* vendor on the station approach. Slipping her backpack off her shoulder, she carried it by her side like a bag and walked briskly into the station, looking right nor left. As she turned to go down the stairs, she risked a quick glance back. Neither police officer was looking in her direction. Grinning to herself, Lindsay trotted down to the platform and waited for her train. The only way they were going to catch up with her now was if they still had her fingerprints on file. After all these years, she doubted that. Even paranoia had to call it a day some time.

By the time she made it back to Helen's, reaction had set in, perfect partner to her growing jet lag. Her knees felt disconnected from her legs, her hands had a tremble she couldn't be bothered trying to control and her eyes felt grittier than they did on days when the wind whipped the sand on Half Moon Bay into a hazy cloud. 'Oh, God,' she groaned, closing the front door behind her and leaning against it.

A woman in faded 501s and a white T that told

the world 'My grannie was working class' pressed 'pause' on the video remote control and looked across at her, dark blue eyes crinkling in a smile. 'You'll be Lindsay,' she said. 'I'm Kirsten.' She jumped to her feet and thrust her hand out.

Lindsay pushed off from the door and dragged her weary body across what felt like miles of carpet, dragging Kirsten's details up from the dim recesses of her mind. Freelance radio journalist. A few years younger than Helen, from somewhere in the West Country. They'd met at Pride two years before, had been living together around eighteen months. Sophie and Lindsay had missed meeting her on their last trip home because she'd been off covering some obscure opera festival. 'Good to meet you at last,' Lindsay said, taking Kirsten's hand and letting herself be drawn into a welcoming embrace.

'You look completely shattered,' Kirsten said sympathetically. 'Come on through, have a drink, something to eat. Helen's in the kitchen.'

Lindsay was past independent thought. She let Kirsten lead as they threaded a staggering path through the chaos of the living room into the kitchen.

Helen jumped to her feet and greeted Lindsay with a huge bearhug. 'Hey, Linds, it's great to see you, girl. And now you've met Kirsten in the flesh. Isn't she drop dead gorgeous?' She took one arm away from Lindsay to draw Kirsten into the cuddle.

'Behave,' Kirsten protested. 'You're embarrassing me!'

'Impossible, you're a journo. And she was one for too long to believe in the possibility of another hack getting a red neck over a compliment,' Helen teased. She stepped back, looking critically at Lindsay. 'Where you been till this time? You look like last orders in the dyke bar. We were going to wait to eat till you came back, but we couldn't hang on, we were starving. But there's loads left,' she added, waving a vague arm at an array of foil takeaway cartons that covered half the available worktop space. 'Just load up a plate and smack it in the video cooker.'

'I'm too tired to eat,' Lindsay said, disengaging herself from Helen's arm and slumping into the nearest chair. 'Thanks for letting me stay here. I really appreciate it.'

'I'm made up you're here. I'd have been really brassed off if I'd found out you were staying some place else!' Helen opened a cupboard and took out a wine goblet, picked up a bottle of red that was sitting beside the pile of papers she was working on and glugged out a glassful. 'Get yourself wrapped round that and tell me what you've been up to. Oh, by the way, Soph rang earlier. I don't think you're top of her Christmas card list right now.'

Lindsay took the glass and swallowed a mouthful of something that reminded her of a pit bull terrier – warm but with a bite that didn't let go. 'She want me to call her back?'

'She said she'd ring again.' Helen glanced at her watch. 'In about half an hour. So what have you been up to? What's going on? Soph said something about some friend of yours being murdered. What's the score?'

'Helen,' Kirsten protested. 'Let her get her second wind.'

'It's okay, I'm used to her appalling manners,' Lindsay said.

'Only because I learned them off you!' Helen roared with laughter.

Fortified by the wine, Lindsay gave Helen a succinct outline of recent events. 'I'll colour in the picture when I've had a kip, okay?' she wound up.

'You just can't keep away from it, can you?' Helen said. 'We're two of a kind, you and me. We can't just sit on our hands when something needs sorting.'

'Mmm,' Lindsay grunted, reaching for the bottle and pouring a second glass. 'So how's the film business?' She needed to keep awake for Sophie's phone call, and listening to Helen seemed a less taxing option than doing the talking herself.

'If I'm honest, Linds, it's actually a bag of shit right now.'

'What's the problem?' Lindsay slurred through a mixture of drink and exhaustion.

Kirsten groaned. 'Don't encourage her. We'll be here all night and I need my beauty sleep.'

'If anyone needs their beauty sleep around

here, gorgeous, it's not you. The problem, Linds, is Guy. Well, it's not really Guy as such, it's Stella. You remember the set-up at Watergaw?'

Lindsay remembered. Helen and Guy had set up their independent film-making company three years earlier. Before that, Helen had worked in theatre administration, then run her own casting agency, working for TV and film companies initially in Britain and later across Europe. Guy had been a TV director and producer first of current affairs and later of high-profile documentaries. Together they'd decided to create Watergaw Films to take advantage of new EU funding geared towards community groups who wanted to develop TV and film projects, both dramatic and documentary. 'How could I forget?' she said. 'Straight partnership, down the middle, you and Guy. Best buddies, known each other since school, both gay, both refugees from New Labour, both filled with the burning desire to make meaningful TV.'

'That's what I thought too,' Helen said bitterly. She ran a hand through her mop of flaming red hair. 'Turns out I was well wrong. On pretty much every count. I could just about live with the way he's turned into the worst kind of exploitative capitalist, because I could always weigh in and get the balance straight again. But now he's got that bitch Stella on board . . . I just don't know how much more of his shit I can take.'

It had to be serious for Helen to be badmouthing

another woman like that, Lindsay realised with a jolt. Normally first to the barricades when sisterhood came under threat, it took a lot for Helen even to admit a woman was in the wrong when there was an available male to be blamed. 'Who's Stella?' Lindsay asked as Kirsten moved behind Helen and started to massage the back of her neck and shoulders.

'Oh, that's wonderful,' Helen purred, rolling her head back. 'The bitch goddess from hell joined us about a year ago. We needed someone else on board with directorial experience, and she came highly recommended. Plus she had a bit of capital which we needed right then, so she bought in at twenty per cent of the company. What was supposed to happen was that she would do the bread and butter stuff for Guy and work with me on projects where I was producer. What wasn't supposed to happen was Guy rediscovering his lost heterosexuality and climbing into bed with the scheming little minx,' Helen said. Not even Kirsten's massage was enough to subdue the anger in her voice.

'Oh.'

'Yeah, "oh".' Helen reached behind her and gently disengaged Kirsten's hands. 'Thanks for the thought, K, but you're wasting your energy. That pair have got me so wound up . . .'

'Well, don't talk about them, then,' she said reasonably.

'As well as tell a river to stop flowing downhill,' Lindsay muttered.

'Exactly. And as if it's not enough that he's sleeping with her, he's taking professional decisions with her. To all intents and purposes, she's in control. Whatever she wants, Guy backs her. Whenever there's a difference of opinion, whether it's about company strategy or something as minor as how a sequence should be filmed, Guy sides with her every time, and I'm the one left out in the cold. I feel like I'm being frozen out of my own company, and it's really pissing me off. Things get decided when I'm not even there – like as not between the sheets. But it's more than just being sidelined that bugs me. They're changing the culture of the company, and I'm spending all my time and energy running to try and stand still instead of moving us forward. It's not what I came into this business to do, but I just don't know how the hell to beat this bitch at her own game.' Helen drained her glass and emptied the last of the bottle into it.

Lindsay rubbed her eyes with her knuckles and tried to straighten out of the slump that was spreading her upper body over the table top. 'There's got to be some dirt,' she managed to say.

'You what?'

Lindsay dragged herself upright and yawned hugely. 'You don't get to be queen bitch at your first attempt. If she's such a smooth operator, there's got to be bodies buried somewhere.'

Light dawned in Helen's eyes. 'Hey, why didn't I think of that!'

Those were the last words Lindsay heard as she drifted into a limbo between sleep and waking. 'Mmm,' she murmured as she slipped away.

It didn't last long. Before she could fall far enough for dreams to capture her, the shrill chirrup of a telephone cut into her unconsciousness. 'Huh? . . . wha'? . . . what is it?' she gabbled as her head shot up and her eyes snapped wide open and staring. She registered Helen reaching over to grab the phone that was buried under some papers inches away from where Lindsay's ear had been.

'Hiya, Soph. All right? . . . Yeah, she's here. All seven dwarfs rolled into one – Sleepy, Grumpy, Dopey, Snorey, Guilty, Boozy and Sexy.' Helen roared with laughter.

Lindsay, pitying Sophie's eardrum, said, 'You've been practising that line all night. Gimme the phone.' She stretched her arm out, beckoning with her fingers.

'Here she is. See ya, Soph.' Helen grinned, handed the phone to Lindsay and grabbed a bundle of papers before sweeping out of the kitchen.

Lindsay cleared her throat. 'I know. If I was home, I'd be sleeping with Mutt. In the doghouse.'

'No, if you were home, you'd be where you're supposed to be,' Sophie said, sounding more exasperated than angry. 'How do you get into these things?'

'Natural talent?'

'Natural stupidity, more like.'

'I couldn't just leave Meredith to it, could I?' Lindsay said plaintively.

'I don't see why not,' Sophie grumbled.

Even with a continent and an ocean separating them, Lindsay could tell her heart wasn't in it. 'The woman you fell in love with wouldn't turn her back on Meredith.'

'That was then. Things that are endearing in the first flush of passion can lose their charm, you know,' Sophie pointed out, a warning creeping into her voice. 'This isn't just about Meredith, is it?'

'Yeah, all right. Partly it's for me. I cared about Penny. We both did. I've tried to keep my nose out when people I care about have died before, and I never managed it. I thought this time I might as well be honest right from the start and admit that I know I can find out things the police won't get to hear in a million years.'

'I thought it might be something like that. Is that why you didn't wait until I got home? Did you really think I'd try to talk you out of it?'

Lindsay thought she detected a trace of hurt under the warmth in Sophie's voice. 'I wanted to wait till you came home, but the plane tickets were already bought and booked. I didn't feel I had the right to go wasting Meredith's money. I did try to call you at Crazy John's, but they said you guys weren't in and didn't have a table booked. I didn't know where else to try. I'm sorry if you feel I didn't take you into account. That wasn't what I had in mind.'

Sophie sighed. The silence stretched and Lindsay couldn't avoid filling it. 'Anyway, you'll be here next week. Things'll be sorted by then. We'll have our holiday just like we planned.'

Another sigh. This time Sophie followed it up with words. 'If you're still in one piece,' she said gloomily.

'No reason why I shouldn't be,' Lindsay said. 'Come on, I know how to take care of myself.'

More silence.

'I've done this before, you know. I did it before I had you fussing around like a nursemaid. I'm not a child, Sophie. I'm not helpless.'

'I didn't say you were, my love. I just worry about you, okay? I know it's totally unreasonable of me, but I do worry.'

'You don't have to. I'm too much of a coward to get damaged.'

In her office with its view of the Oakland Bridge, Sophie Hartley grabbed her greying curls with her free hand. Lindsay might have chosen to forget, but she could never lose the knowledge of how dangerous her lover's favourite game could be. 'I hope you're right,' she said softly. 'I really hope you're right.

8

Lindsay stirred the warm grey liquid that passed for coffee in the supermarket café and stared across the car park at the row of converted mews cottages that housed Monarch Press. Nothing was moving so far. But that was hardly surprising of a publishing house at five to nine in the morning. In an ideal world, she'd still be tucked up in bed letting her body recover. But Helen had never mastered the art of rising quietly and unobtrusively. If she was awake at seven, the rest of the house was guaranteed to be awake by five past, their ears possessed by Radio Four at full volume. Helen liked to hear the morning news wherever she was in the house, including the shower.

Lindsay had staggered downstairs at ten past seven, lured by the smell of coffee. She'd found Kirsten reading the *Guardian* in her dressing gown, her short dark hair sticking up in a Fido Dido crest, hands wrapped round a mug of very black coffee. The room was an oasis of relative quiet, the radio there being silent. 'Plenty in the pot,' Kirsten mumbled. 'Croissants in the oven. A couple of minutes yet.'

Lindsay tried moving a mouth that seemed to be lodged in a concrete face. 'I can't believe you got her to switch off the radio in here,' she managed as she helped herself to coffee.

'I don't mind bringing work home with me. But I'm damned if I'm going to wake up to it as well. I told her, it's the *Today* programme or me.'

'It must be love,' Lindsay commented.

Right on cue, Helen bounced into the room swathed in a kimono, her marmalade hair in damp coils to her shoulders. 'Sleep okay, Linds?' she demanded, sweeping past them both and yanking a tray of hot croissants and *pains au chocolat* out of the oven.

'Yeah,' she said. 'Could have done with a few more hours, but . . .'

'Don't be daft,' Helen said, dumping the croissants on to a plate and balancing it on top of the papers she'd been working on the night before. 'Never mind Tulsa, you're back living on Tulse Hill time,' she continued, breaking into song and playing air guitar in a bad imitation of Eric Clapton.

'Helen,' Kirsten groaned plaintively.

'Best cure for jet lag,' Helen persisted. 'What've you got on today, K?'

Kirsten frowned momentarily. Then her face cleared. 'Doing a piece for Radio Bloke about holiday reading. One last interview to do, then I can cobble it all together.'

'Radio Bloke?' Lindsay asked faintly.

'Five Live,' Helen informed her. '"Twenty-four hour news and sport from the BBC,"' she mimicked, helping herself to a croissant.

'I do bits and pieces for them, but mostly I work for Four,' Kirsten said, her warm radio voice re-emerging from the early morning gravel. 'Arts and media stuff.'

'That's handy,' Lindsay said, perking up as the coffee worked its way through to her brain.

'Watch out, K,' Helen cautioned through a mouthful of pastry. 'When this scally starts to take an interest, there's always an ulterior motive. She'll be after borrowing some fancy recording equipment or something, just wait and see.'

Reaching for a *pain au chocolat*, Lindsay shook her head. 'You know me too well, Helen.'

'You can't scam a scammer,' Helen said.

'Is there something I can help you with, Lindsay?' Kirsten asked between mouthfuls.

'I don't honestly know,' she said. 'Maybe. Do you know anything about Monarch Press?'

Kirsten nodded. 'As it happens, yeah. *Kaleidoscope* did a feature on their tenth anniversary. I wasn't producing, but I went along to the party. Lemme see . . .' Her dark eyes focused on the middle distance as Helen leaned across to refill her coffee cup. 'Thanks, love. Now, lemme get this right. The guy behind the company is an East

End wide boy called Danny King. He's a proper cockney, one generation away from a barrow boy. Though that's being a bit unfair. His dad actually got off the barrows and worked as a printer in Fleet Street.'

Lindsay groaned. 'Bigger highway robbers than Dick Turpin.'

'Yeah, well, old man King retired to Spain on his redundo some time in the mid-eighties, leaving his wife behind.'

'How did you find all this out?' Helen demanded. 'I know you're nosy, but that's ridiculous!'

Kirsten grinned. 'I was standing next to his dad during the speeches, which were mostly the kind that can only be improved by talking through them. He told me his entire life story, most of which, thankfully, I have managed to erase from the memory banks.'

'So how did an East End cowboy get to be a gentleman publisher?' Lindsay asked, trying to keep the conversation on track.

'Who said anything about gentleman?' Kirsten said, eyebrows steepling. 'Danny's mum was a great believer in self-improvement, and she was always encouraging her little lad to read. When he ducked out of school, his dad called in a few favours and got him a job in the print works of one of the big publishing houses. From there, Danny parlayed himself a job as a sales rep. Supposedly he was a very good one. Then he won the pools.'

'You're kidding!' Helen exclaimed. 'How much?'

'A mill and a quarter. Which was a lot of cash eleven or so years ago.'

'It's a lot of cash now,' Lindsay pointed out. 'And he set up a publishing house?' The incredulity in her voice was matched only by the expression on Helen's face.

'That's right. He announced to a waiting world that nobody was publishing the books he'd wanted to read as a teenager, or the books he'd wanted to sell, or the books he wanted to read now, and he was going to fill the gap in the market. Everybody laughed at him, of course. Publishing was in a decline, the market was shrinking, there were too many books and not enough buyers already. And of course, he was a toerag from the wrong side of the tracks without the requisite English degree. But he proved them all wrong.'

'So what kind of stuff does Monarch publish? Apart from Penny's Darkliners series?' Lindsay asked.

Kirsten dug a packet of cigarettes out of her dressing-gown pocket and lit up. 'It's a pretty eclectic list. Mostly fiction, mostly by young writers who don't come out of the sausage factory of university and journalism. The keynote is that it's all slightly off the wall, out of the mainstream. Cult fiction. Acid-head dole-ite narrators. Travel guides to places you didn't know you wanted to go to till you read the book. Their slogan is, "Fact or fiction – in your face." Your friend Penny was his first big success, but there have been others since.'

'How did he do it? What made it work?' Lindsay asked. Her curiosity was pricked now, and it was nothing to do with Penny.

Kirsten shrugged. 'He was one of the first to abandon hardback publishing and go for good-quality softback originals that were only a pound or two more expensive than mass-market paperbacks. The books had a strong corporate image, so they stood out on the shelves. He hired people who weren't afraid to back their hunches on new writers. And he marketed the books with a bit of chutzpah. They advertised in music mags, style mags, top-end women's glossies – places where publishers hadn't gone before, except with individual titles. It wasn't any one thing – it was the way he combined ideas.'

'He took the right risks,' Lindsay said.

'That about sums it up. And now Monarch has got a real brand identity with its readers. People read a Monarch title and they like it, so they try another one. Pretty soon, they start to buy the new titles automatically.'

'Sounds a bit too much like a dream come true,' Helen said sceptically.

Kirsten rumpled her hair. 'You're just a twisted old cynic. Not every business has a skunk like Guy and a snake like Stella.'

Lindsay nodded. 'Maybe you should pitch Danny King into the film business, Helen. Sounds like he's got the golden touch.'

Helen snorted. 'Spare me any more boy wonders.' She glanced up at the schoolroom clock on the wall. 'Speaking of which, I'd better get my skates on before I find we're contracted to make a soap for satellite.'

After Helen had gone, Lindsay said, 'Did you happen to meet Baz Burton? She was Penny's editor.'

'Can't help you there. After I disentangled myself from Danny's dad, I was doing the rounds of the authors, trying to see if I could pick up any programme ideas. I didn't actually talk to anybody from Monarch. Sorry.'

Then it had been Kirsten's turn to leave. Even after Lindsay had loaded the dishwasher and put the remains of the previous night's takeaway in the fridge, it was barely eight o'clock. Showered and dressed, she'd been on the street by half past and in the supermarket opposite Monarch's Shepherd's Bush office twenty minutes later. Now all she could do was wait for the publishing day to begin. At least, for the first time in her life, she was on surveillance somewhere with an unlimited supply of coffee and, more importantly, a toilet.

By ten fifteen, Lindsay reckoned that anyone who was planning on coming to work at Monarch was probably there. Besides, the table clearer in the café was starting to become restive, sighing heavily every time she passed Lindsay's table with its coffee cup still half full. She picked up her backpack and strolled out into the car park, where the warmth hit her, a shock after the air-conditioned cool of the store. 'Just like being at home,' she muttered. At least she was dressed for it today, in Bermuda shorts and a sleeveless tunic with a mandarin collar.

As she got closer, Lindsay could see that the ground floors of five of the mews cottages had been knocked together to give a semi-open-plan appearance to Monarch's ground floor. The reception area, in the middle cottage, was decorated in the same sunshine yellow and forest green as the distinctive livery of the imprint's paperbacks. The receptionist sat behind a high yellow desk like an airport check-in. Her acid fuchsia T-shirt clashed magnificently with the decor. Clearly not a place to work if you were prone to hangovers or migraine, Lindsay thought as she approached with a smile. A green sign told the world the twenty-something receptionist's name was Lauren. Somehow, she looked like a Lauren. She had long hair the colour of set honey, big blue eyes and a bone structure that hollowed her cheeks. In spite of the right components, she somehow missed being beautiful. 'Good morning, Lauren,' Lindsay said. 'Is Baz Burton in?'

The receptionist dragged her attention away

from something behind the desk that Lindsay couldn't see. 'Is she expecting you?' she asked, her voice a disappointing nasal south London whine.

'I don't have an appointment. But I'd really appreciate it if she could spare me a few minutes.' She smiled ingratiatingly.

'Can you tell me your name and what it's in connection with?' was the bored reply as the eyes strayed back beneath the counter top.

'My name is Lindsay Gordon and it's in connection with Penny Varnavides. I'm representing Meredith Miller.'

That got Lauren's undivided attention. 'Right,' she said, her voice approving and interested. 'Let's see what we can do, eh?' Her hand appeared above the counter clutching a phone and she keyed in a number. 'Susan? It's Lauren at the front desk. Someone here for Baz . . . No, but I think Baz will want to see her . . . Penny Varnavides . . . No, she's not press, she says she's representing . . .' her voice trailed off and she looked questioningly at Lindsay.

'Meredith Miller.'

'A Meredith Miller . . . Right.' She replaced the phone and gave Lindsay a friendly smile. 'Ms Burton's assistant is going to check if she can see you.'

'Thanks.' Lindsay strolled over to a wall display of book jackets, her eyes automatically seeking out Penny's titles. A phone rang and Lauren answered it. 'Monarch Press, how may I help you . . . You want to leave a message for. . . . Certainly. And you are . . .? Could you spell that . . .? T-a-v-a-r-e? Fine, Mr Tavare, I'll see he gets the message.'

As the phone went down, a scarlet-faced woman with a disturbing resemblance to a hamster marched round the end of a partition and into the reception area. 'How many times do I have to tell you?' she hissed at the receptionist. If it was meant to be out of Lindsay's earshot, she'd failed. 'People who arrive without an appointment get shown the door. You do *not* buzz through and put Susan on the spot, is that clear?'

Lauren flushed. 'But Baz . . .'

'I don't want to hear buts. It's a simple enough procedure, surely you can manage it? Or do I have to talk to Danny?'

Lauren, who had clearly learned her lesson from the Princess of Wales, dropped her head and looked up at Baz from under her eyebrows. 'I'm sorry, Baz, okay?'

'And while I'm on the subject of simple procedures, how come an urgent set of proofs that gets biked round to me yesterday morning doesn't make it on to my desk till ten minutes ago?' The woman's voice rose in pitch and volume. 'Do you know what the word urgent means, or do I have to buy you a bloody dictionary?'

Before Lauren could answer, Lindsay jumped in. 'Excuse me, but am I in the wrong place? I thought this was a publishing house, not a casualty ward. I mean, how urgent can a set of proofs be? You know, every time you get wound up like that, it takes days off your potential life span.' She smiled disarmingly. 'I'm Lindsay Gordon. You must be Baz Burton.'

Baz gave Lauren a final glare, then swung round with a broad smile towards Lindsay. 'Pleased to meet you.' She didn't offer her hand. 'Sorry about that. You know what they say – you just can't get the staff. My assistant tells me you're representing Meredith Miller. Can I ask in what capacity?'

'Can we talk somewhere a little more private?' Lindsay said, stepping to one side to avoid a pair of young men walking through reception deep in discussion about book clubs.

'Is this going to take long?' Baz asked, glancing ostentatiously at a Mickey Mouse watch. 'Only, I've got an important meeting in twenty minutes, so if you need longer, I'd suggest you make an appointment for another day.'

'Let's make a start with that twenty minutes, then,' Lindsay said firmly. 'If we need more time, I can always come back later.'

'Fine,' Baz said curtly. 'Follow me.'

She led the way round a room divider and into a small office partitioned off the larger room, where people sat at computers and piles of manuscripts. Baz settled into a leather executive chair behind a desk cluttered with papers. She didn't invite Lindsay to sit, but she did anyway, noting that the visitors' chairs were significantly lower than the edge of the desk. The room had no door, and Lindsay felt strangely exposed with her back to the entrance.

Baz tilted her head to one side, frankly studying Lindsay. Lindsay returned the compliment, taking in a hennaed urchin cut over straight brows and eyes the same muddy colour as the supermarket coffee. Her plump, jowly cheeks were at odds with a neat frame whose slimness was accentuated by the tight black jeans and vest she was wearing. Her shoulders were as pink as her cheeks and showed all the signs of peeling from too much sun. In her left ear was a single earring in the shape of an axe. In her right, a line of half a dozen silver studs marched upwards from the lobe till they met a pair of ear cuffs. 'Sorry about that business out there. It's not that I didn't want to talk to you. It's just that I am literally snowed under with work, and that idiot girl on reception keeps on funnelling wannabe writers through to me as if I'm running a counselling service for failures,' Baz said to break the silence.

'All the more thanks for giving me some time,' Lindsay said noncommittally.

'You still haven't answered my question, though,' Baz said with a teasing smile that completely altered her face, reminding Lindsay that hamsters could be cute. She leaned forward with her elbows on the desk and gazed at Lindsay.

'At Meredith Miller's request, I'm investigating Penny Varnavides' murder.'

Baz looked incredulous. '*You're* a private eye?'

'Not exactly. But I have had some experience of murder inquiries.'

'And Meredith's hired you to clear her name, is that it?'

'Sort of.' For no reason she could put her finger on, Lindsay was reluctant to reveal how much she knew about Meredith or Penny. Admitting she was working out of friendship would be to give too much away.

'Fine. I'm all for Meredith's name being cleared. It's absolutely ridiculous that she's even come under suspicion.' Baz spoke vehemently, her voice rising. 'Anyone with half a brain could see that Meredith would never hurt a fly. She's one of the gentlest people I've ever met.'

There were a lot of words Lindsay would have applied to Meredith before she got to gentle. 'Have you known her long?' she asked.

'Almost as long as Penny. Which makes it about eleven years. I met her the first time I went to San Francisco. And I've seen her quite a bit over the years, both in the US and here in England. When she's in town on business, we sometimes have dinner. I really hope you can get the police off her back,' she added, beaming a wide white smile at Lindsay.

'You knew right from the start they were lovers?'

Baz's lips quirked in a half smile. 'You know what they say. It takes one to know one. It took Penny about four years to tell me the big secret, but I sussed it from day one. But why all the questions about Meredith?' she demanded, suddenly suspicious. 'I thought you were supposed to be on her side?'

'I am. Just background, that's all. I'm told that you had seen a lot of Penny this trip?'

'I wouldn't have said "a lot",' Baz objected. 'We met a few times to discuss the progress of her new book.'

'Did you normally do that?'

'Not with the Darkliners series, no. Pen could knock them off standing on her head with one arm tied behind her back. She'd just send me a two-page synopsis so the art department could get busy with the cover and we could do the jacket copy. Then twelve weeks later, like clockwork, another fifty thousand words of Darkliners title would drop through the letter box. Then we'd have a meeting to sort out the edits, and that was about it, really. If she was over here anyway, we'd do lunch or dinner, but for pleasure, not work.'

'But this time it was different?' Lindsay prompted.

'Inevitably. *Heart of Glass* was a very different book from anything Pen had attempted before.' Baz gave Lindsay another dazzling smile. 'I wanted to give Pen all the support she needed to complete it.' Sensing her facial expression was inappropriate, Baz swiftly changed to a suitably sad look. 'Tragically, that didn't happen.'

'How was the book progressing?' Lindsay asked briskly, refusing to be sidetracked into a sharing of sorrow.

'Very well. About 70,000 words on paper.' Baz had suddenly become abrupt, her previous chattiness vanishing as if it had never been.

'Do you have a copy of the manuscript?'

'No. I don't have any text. I don't even have a synopsis. Pen was guarding this one with her life.' As she realised what she had said, Baz's mouth fell open.

'So it would seem,' Lindsay said grimly. 'So what exactly was it that her killer didn't want the world to read?'

9

Baz's mouth was moving but no sound was coming out of it. 'There must have been something,' Lindsay persisted. 'Nobody has a copy of the book – not you, not her agent, and certainly not Meredith. Her laptop and her back-up disks have gone missing. There must have been something in there that someone wanted to keep hidden.'

'That's ridiculous,' Baz finally said. 'It's only a novel, for God's sake. Nobody thinks fiction's important enough to kill over it!'

Lindsay shrugged. 'Why else use such an outrageous murder method? It's ridiculous. Who'd go to all that bother when they could just have picked up a bottle and cracked her over the head with it? It's as if the killer was leaving a message: "Anybody else in the know that's thinking about messing with me, don't do it!"'

'You're wrong,' Baz said desperately. 'You've got to be wrong. There must be something else behind it.'

'Convince me. What's *Heart of Glass* about?'

'It's a thriller.'

'About?'

Baz sighed. 'It's a really complicated plot with a lot of psychological suspense that centres around a writer. Every time this guy imagines something, it happens. So he decides to try and see if he can get rid of all the people he hates by writing their deaths into his books. In parallel with that, you've got a surgeon who is a particularly gruesome killer. And their two lives collide via the surgeon's wife, who is the writer's editor. It's "a roller-coaster ride of horror", according to the catalogue copy I wrote six weeks ago. Which reminds me that I have a bloody big hole to fill in next spring's list.' She poked around among the papers on her desk, as if to indicate that she had far more important things to do than talk to Lindsay.

'Sounds like it would have walked straight on to the best-seller lists. What a pity Penny isn't going to be able to finish it,' Lindsay said ironically. 'But that still doesn't answer why someone would want the book suppressed. Was there anything in it that seemed potentially libellous to you?'

Before Baz could answer, there was a tap on the partition behind Lindsay's head. She turned to see a man's face grinning at her. 'Sorry to butt in,' he said in a strong London accent. 'Whenever you like, Baz.'

'Be right there,' Baz said, getting to her feet.

The man moved into the doorway. He looked

to be around forty, with dark wavy hair that needed trimming and creamy white skin that showed no trace of the freakishly sunny summer weather. His smile was cheeky and cheerful, the lines in his face revealing it as a familiar expression. It was his eyes that caught the attention, however; the same blue as the denim shirt he wore, they sparkled like sapphires even in the artificial light of the office. He angled his head to one side, like a bird listening for underground movement, and said,' And you must be the mystery visitor who's come to talk about Penny's tragic death, am I right?'

'Ms Gordon was just leaving,' Baz said repressively, hastily moving across the room to cut off the line of sight between Lindsay and the man. 'And we've got marketing strategies to discuss.' She put a hand on his arm, which he ignored.

'Hell of a thing,' the man said, shaking his head. 'She was the last person you'd expect to die like that. She was lovely, you know? It's hard to imagine how she could drive someone to kill her.'

'I know what you mean,' Lindsay said, pleased to find herself talking to someone who seemed to have valued Penny for the person she was rather than for the profits she could generate. It made a welcome change.

'I loved her work,' he continued. 'Always so sharp, so bright. Just like she was, really.'

'We're keeping everyone waiting,' Baz said, trying to edge him out of the doorway.

'It won't kill them,' the man said negligently. He held out a hand to Lindsay, who was by now also standing. 'Since Baz seems to have lost touch with her manners, I better introduce myself. I'm Danny King. I'm the publisher. And you are?'

'Lindsay Gordon. Meredith Miller's asked me to investigate Penny's murder. To clear her name. She didn't do it, in spite of what the police might think.'

He nodded. 'You're preaching to the converted here, Lindsay. According to Baz, Meredith could never have harmed a hair on Penny's head. And I trust Baz's judgement implicitly. As long as it keeps making me a profit,' he added with another grin. 'So how are your inquiries coming along?'

Lindsay pulled a face. 'Early days. What would really help would be a copy of Penny's manuscript.'

Danny cast his eyes up and tutted. 'You and me both,' he sighed. 'Baz tells me there was enough there for us to craft some kind of an ending. I really want to get this book out there – not just because it'll be a good seller, but because it's a helluva book and it's the only way we've got of paying some kind of tribute to the great writer Penny was. But we haven't got a copy and neither, apparently, does Penny's agent. I don't suppose you know where we could locate one?'

Lindsay shook her head. 'Sorry.'

Danny grinned and gave her arm a quick squeeze. It was clearly a gesture of farewell.

'Maybe I should get you on the payroll too, see if you can come up with the goods? Anyway, nice to meet you, Lindsay. If you need any help from anybody here at Monarch, all you've got to do is tell them Danny sent you.' He winked and ushered Baz ahead of him into the main office.

'I'll see myself out, shall I?' Lindsay said to the empty cubicle. Unfortunately, it was too public to search the desk, so she followed the other two on to the editorial floor. She was in time to see them vanish up a flight of stairs. She sighed. Without knowing who was who, there was no point in trying to screw information about Penny or her book out of Baz's colleagues and minions. Feeling as if she'd wasted a golden opportunity, Lindsay walked back to reception.

As she passed the reception desk, Lauren glanced up. Seeing who it was, she leaned forward and said, 'You got a minute?'

Lindsay stopped. 'Of course.'

'That was really cool, earlier, when you dived in like that with Baz.'

'No sweat. She's obviously got a lot on her mind.'

A sly smile spread across Lauren's face. 'You don't know the half of it.'

'You going to tell me?'

'Might do. You a private eye?'

'Sort of.'

'That means you get expenses, right?'

Lindsay snorted with laughter. 'You watch too

much telly.' Lauren looked disappointed. Lindsay relented. 'I can probably run to a few quid.'

'Okay, you know Riverside Studios?'

Lindsay dredged her memory. 'Other side of the Hammersmith gyratory?'

'That's right. None of this lot can be bothered to walk that far at lunchtime. I'll see you in the café there about quarter to one. Okay?'

'You're not taking the piss?'

Lauren repeated her sly smile. 'Believe me, you won't be wasting your time or your money.'

Before Lindsay could say any more, the phone rang. As she left, she could hear Lauren saying, 'You want to leave a message for Paddy Brown? Yes . . .'

With the best part of two hours to kill, Lindsay consulted her A-Z, then headed down through the artificially bright shopping mall on the traffic island at the heart of Hammersmith towards the river. She turned right under the bridge, where she found a sudden splash of colour against the relentless urban grime. Settling down on a bench in a patch of shade in the lush rose garden, Lindsay took her laptop from her backpack, opened it up and switched it on. With plenty of pauses to contemplate the faded houseboats straggling along the river bank, she typed in all the information she'd gathered so far on Penny Varnavides' murder.

It didn't take long.

* * *

Lauren was right on time. Lindsay bought them both salads and bottles of mineral water and they settled at a table in a quiet, gloomy corner of the café. Lindsay poked at her salad with a fork. 'Pretty bloody dreary,' she muttered. 'Amazing how quickly you forget.'

'Forget what?' Lauren asked, shovelling tuna into her mouth like an apprentice bulimic.

'Forget the sorry mess of tired vegetation that passes for salad in this country. When I rule the world, the person who developed iceberg lettuce will be first up against the wall. No wonder when I come home I live off junk food. No shocks that way. It's the one thing that I actually expect to be as bad as it is.'

'What d'you mean, when you come home? Where else do you go?'

'For some strange reason, I still think of Britain as home, even though I've lived in California for the last six years.'

Lauren's eyes opened wide. 'You live in California? Excellent! How did you manage that?'

'My partner got offered a job over there, so it was go with or split up. I was having a pretty shitty time over here, apart from our relationship, so I went with. Got a job, got a doctorate and stayed.'

'Wow! Cool!'

'Better than Shepherd's Bush,' Lindsay said drily. 'You should give it a whirl if you're that keen.'

Lauren's mouth turned down at the corners. 'I ain't got the skills, have I? Bit of word processing and GCSE Spanish.'

'You never know. Being bilingual in English and Spanish isn't a bad start in southern California. Don't put yourself down.' Lindsay gave Lauren an encouraging grin. 'And they love Brits.'

'Yeah, well. Fantasy Island, that is. Anyway, daydreaming about California's not what I came here for. What's it worth to you, the dirt on Baz and Penny?'

Lindsay shrugged. 'I don't know what it's worth until I know what it is, do I? Look, why don't you tell me what you know and I'll see you right?'

'How do I know I can trust you?' Lauren demanded, scowling.

'You don't. But right now I'm the only show in town, so you might as well skin me for what you can get while you can get it.' Lauren looked unconvinced, so Lindsay tried another tack. 'Look, Lauren, I was Penny Varnavides' friend. Her and Meredith used to come round our house at least once a month. We played beach volley-ball together, we climbed mountains together, we saw the New Year in together. This isn't just a job for me, it's personal.'

'Yeah, okay, you talked me into it,' Lauren said, trying and failing to sound tough and worldly wise. 'I've been working at Monarch for two years, right, so I'd met Penny a few times. I got talking to her one afternoon when she'd come in to see Baz and Baz was late getting back from lunch. I told her how I'd read all the Darkliners books when I was a teenager, and how much I'd loved them. She was great. She laughed her head off and said she didn't think publishers employed anybody that actually *liked* the books they produced. And after that, every time she came into the office, she always brought me some book or other that she'd seen in America and thought I'd like. She's the only author I've ever met who remembered my name without having to read the plaque, never mind what I liked to read. So I always paid attention when she was around.'

So like Penny, Lindsay thought with a pang. She'd always been a woman who paid attention to the seemingly insignificant people. It was why she always got the best table in her regular hang-outs, why her newspaper was never dumped on the step to become a soggy mess, why the local second-hand bookstore always remembered which titles were on her want list. Little touches of consideration that made her life run smoothly. Not that that was why she'd done it, Lindsay reminded herself. Just that she was the kind of person who noticed details. 'Was she like that with other people in the office?' she asked at last, forcing herself back into the present.

'She didn't really have much to do with anybody except Baz and her assistant, Susan. If she had, they might not have got so pissed off with her.'

'Pissed off with her? Who got pissed off with her? Why?' Lindsay asked.

'A bunch of them in editorial. The PC brigade. If that lot went on a march, they wouldn't go, "Right, left, right, left," they'd go, "Right on, right on".' Lauren grinned.

'And what had Penny done to upset them?' Lindsay asked.

'It was about her being gay. I never even knew she was till that lot started going on about it. It turns out they were put out because she'd been in the closet all those years. They kept going on about it being hypocritical not to be out, and how she'd only stayed in the closet for the sake of her sales figures. Which I thought was a bit of a liberty, really. I mean, it's nobody's business who she goes to bed with if she doesn't want it to be, is it?'

Lindsay sighed, lacking the energy for that particular conversation. 'Did anyone make any specific threats, or was it generalised grumbling?'

'Just grumbling, really. People who haven't got anything better to do except indulge in petty jealousy and poison. And nobody had the bottle to front Penny up about it, either.' Lauren frowned. 'Although . . . maybe that's what it was went wrong with her and Baz.'

'Something went wrong? When?'

'This last trip. When I first met Penny, her and Baz got on really well. They were always laughing and joking together, teasing each other, taking the piss, that kind of thing. They'd always go out to lunch or dinner together. More than just duty, like they really enjoyed each other's company. But this time, it was different. They were dead polite to each other, you know?'

'Formal?'

'Yeah, like they hardly knew each other. Awkward. Like it was uncomfortable to be with each other. Penny was in and out a few times, and every time they were dead stiff with each other.'

'As if they'd had a row?'

Lauren frowned. 'Not exactly, no. More like they were sniffing round each other. Like they were trying to avoid a row, almost. Anyway, the upshot was that Penny comes to me and says can I let her into the office last thing at night, once everybody else had gone home. She said she'd make it worth my while. Well, it was no problem for me, was it, on account of I've got a full set of keys so I can get in in the mornings. And nobody notices what time I go home, so long as it doesn't inconvenience them.'

Lindsay stared at Lauren, food forgotten. 'Did Penny say why she wanted to get into the offices?'

Lauren shrugged. 'Not exactly. But she wanted to know if I knew if the computers were on a network and if people like Baz and Danny had their own separate terminals. I said I didn't know what the exact set-up was, but I sussed she was only mentioning Danny as a sort of diversion. It was Baz she was really interested in. I didn't give a toss anyway. I mean, you've seen what a shit that Baz can be. So I said all right, I'd hang on late one night and I'd let her in. We agreed that she'd lock up and drop the keys back round my flat when she'd done.'

'And did it all go off smoothly?'

'Course it did. She made it worth my while, didn't she?' Lauren said pointedly. Lindsay pulled out her wallet and looked inside. Apart from traveller's cheques, she had about fifty pounds in cash. She took out a twenty and slid it across the table. Lauren looked at her pityingly. The second twenty followed, Lauren pointedly staring into the wallet as Lindsay dug it out. She continued to look expectant as she picked up the second twenty.

'Tube fare, Lauren,' Lindsay said. 'I need tube fare. If your information pans out, I'll get you some more money from Meredith, okay?'

Lauren sighed. 'I suppose.'

'What time did Penny bring the keys back?'

'It wasn't that late. About half ten, I suppose.'

'Had she found what she was looking for?' Lindsay asked.

'Don't know. She never said. And I didn't ask, neither. She must've left things the way she found them, though, because nobody said anything about somebody raking through their stuff or buggering up their computer.'

'Did she come in the office after that? I mean, officially.'

Lauren frowned as she gobbled the last of her lunch. 'Yeah, now you come to mention it, she did.

The day before she died. She had a meeting with Baz late morning. But Baz was out. Susan said there wasn't anything in the diary and Penny said Baz must have forgotten to write it down. Penny was a bit put out. She said it had messed up her whole day's writing, so Susan got Danny to take her out to lunch. He had a face like fizz when he came back, so I suppose it screwed up his day too. He gave Baz a right gobful, told her Penny Varnavides was a lot more valuable to Monarch than she was and next time she made an appointment with her, she'd better not forget it unless she wanted to start looking for another job.' Lauren sniggered. 'Baz had a gob on her like a dried prune.'

'And that was the last time Penny was in the office.'

Lauren nodded. 'Far as I know.'

Lindsay drank her water and wondered what to ask about next. Then she remembered the crucial question. 'Do you do the incoming post?'

'Nah. That's Gary in the post room.'

'So you wouldn't know who had access to the manuscripts that Penny sent in?'

Lauren shook her head as she lit a cigarette, leaking smoke from her mouth like a damaged flue. 'No idea. Sorry. Why d'you want to know? I mean, maybe I could find out for you.'

'You know how Penny was murdered the same way one of the victims dies in *Heart of Glass*? Well, I'm just trying to find out who exactly knew what happens in the book.'

Lauren gave a knowing smile. 'You don't need to talk to the post room to find that out. Everybody knew.'

'What? About the beer bottle exploding?'

'Yeah, everybody knew about *that.*' Lauren looked very pleased with herself.

'How?'

'They had a bit of an argy-bargy about it. They were talking to Nigel, who does the covers, about what was going on the front of *Heart of Glass*. Penny told Nigel about the murder method and said the cover should be just the title and her name and a splinter of glass, all on a black background. And Baz said no, she'd been meaning to talk to Penny about that, and the whole thing was just too far-fetched and she didn't believe in it and she wanted her to come up with a different idea. And Penny said no way, José, it was perfectly feasible and she thought it was dramatic and ironic and it was staying.'

'They got heated?' Lindsay asked eagerly.

'Not really. It was like it was part of the whole arm's-length thing. Baz just wasn't prepared to go head to head with Penny. She just backed down and said okay, if it was that important to Penny it could stay. Everybody was gobsmacked, because Baz never backs down with her authors. Like, never. That's why it stuck in my mind. So you see, everybody at Monarch knew about the murder method. And God alone knows who they went home and told.'

10

Lindsay sat in the swaying tube train, her thoughts swirling in confusion. At breakfast, she'd had two suspects – three if she'd been prepared to include Meredith. But thanks to Lauren's revelations, she now had dozens. The publishing world was so riddled with gossip that if anything could be guaranteed, it was that half London would know Penny Varnavides and her editor weren't seeing eye to eye. The disagreement over the bottled beer murder method would have been discussed avidly among publishers, agents and, by now, probably authors too. Rather than narrowing down her list of suspects, Lindsay's visit to Monarch had swelled it a hundredfold.

As if that wasn't bad enough, she didn't have the faintest idea what to do next. But if six years in California had taught her anything, it was that there weren't many problems that couldn't be eased by some judicious retail therapy. For some, that took the form of trawling the department stores and boutiques for designer clothes at charity shop prices. For others, the gourmet food stores were the fount of all comfort. For Lindsay, shopping paradise took the form of second-hand book and CD stores, where she could browse for hours, then emerge with some obscure gem that cost next to nothing. It didn't matter when Sophie pointed out that in the time she had taken to find that single specimen, Lindsay could have written an article that would have earned enough to buy a dozen brand-new CDs or hardback books. The hunt was the fun as much as the purchase, and fun was what Lindsay needed in her present mood.

However, given Sophie's decidedly stiff manner on the phone the previous evening, Lindsay realised a serious peace offering was going to be required at the airport when Sophie arrived the following week. There was nothing more calculated to win her round than some obscure object to add to her collection of historic obstetric instruments. Lindsay could hardly look at them without wincing and crossing her legs, but they fascinated Sophie. And if her memory served her well, one of the antique shops in Camden catered for such perverse tastes. Lindsay could find something for Sophie, then indulge herself in the second-hand stores around Camden Lock. And if she was really lucky, maybe the logical part of her brain, left in peace, would come up with a possible new direction for her investigation.

Just over an hour later, she emerged from the antique shop with an 1860s variant of a Higginson syringe, a fearsome object used by surgeons for aborting the unwanted foetuses of the gentry as well as for routine internal spring-cleaning. Just listening to the shopkeeper describe its function made Lindsay's flesh creep.

As she walked towards the canal, she started to review what she had learned earlier. She'd got as far as rerunning her conversation with Baz when a hand clamped heavily on her shoulder. Her stomach lurched, seized by the same panic she'd felt escaping from Derek Knight's flat. Startled, Lindsay swung round on the balls of her feet, ready to push her assailant away and run for it.

Familiar red curls swirled in front of her. 'What are you doing here?' Helen demanded. 'I thought you were off in darkest Shepherd's Bush making citizen's arrests on publishers.'

Lindsay closed her eyes and let out the breath she hadn't even realised she was holding. 'Don't ever do that again,' she said. 'Jesus, Helen, I've eaten too much cholesterol over the years. Another shock like that and I could drop down dead.'

'You know, sometimes I forget you were a tabloid hack for a million years. Then you go and sound like the front page of the *Sun* and it all comes flooding back to me. Never let the truth get in the way of a good exaggeration, eh? So what are you doing over here?'

'I decided I better arm myself for Sophie's

arrival,' Lindsay said, unwrapping her package and waving it under Helen's nose.

'Yeuuch! That's disgusting. Take it away, you revolting little toerag. And don't tell me what it's for,' she warned.

'It's a peace offering.'

'A peace offering? Bloody hell, Lindsay, I know they do things differently in California, but I didn't realise the sex was that bizarre!'

'It's for Sophie's collection,' Lindsay said, casting her eyes upwards in mock exasperation.

'I know that. So, you finished over at Monarch, then?'

'I'm finished. Don't take it personally, but I really don't want to talk about it just now. This is one of those cases where the more I find out, the less I know. And now I come to think about it, what are you doing walking around the streets instead of looking important in your office?'

Helen scowled like a child caught playing truant. 'I reached the point where if I'd stayed there a minute longer, even you wouldn't have been able to get me off a murder charge. Come on, I'll treat you to something long and cold and you can listen to me moan.' Without waiting for an answer, Helen linked an arm through Lindsay's and dragged her into a nearby pub which promised air conditioning.

'If you called this air conditioned in California, you'd get lynched,' Lindsay remarked as they stood at the bar. The stale air was admittedly a couple of degrees colder than the street outside, but it reeked of smoke and dead beer.

'I'd heard that about the American justice system,' Helen said sweetly, catching the barman's attention and ordering without consultation two bottles of Belgian raspberry beer. Lindsay looked dubiously at the brownish red liquid in her glass, shrugged resignedly and sipped.

'I've tasted worse,' she muttered as she followed Helen to a quiet corner booth.

'I picked up a tasty bit of goss this morning that might interest you,' Helen said, settling herself on the bench and fanning her face ineffectually with a beermat.

'About Penny?'

'Penny's books, actually. I was talking to a mate of mine, Kes, who brokers co-production deals, and I asked her what she was working on and she told me she's putting something together on Penny's books. Some transatlantic deal to do a TV series. Serious players, too. Galaxy Pictures in the States and an independent over here called Primetime, who've got it slotted in with the BBC.'

Lindsay stared. 'The Darkliners novels? Is that what we're talking about?'

Helen nodded. 'Apparently so. We're talking a big deal here. First series will be three books, three thirty-minute episodes per book. If it takes off, they'll do all the books, then they'll do like they did with Morse – use the characters and get other writers to do the storylines.'

Lindsay shook her head. 'There must be some mistake. Penny hated the idea of her books being made into films or TV programmes. Producers were always pitching her and she always turned them down. She said it wasn't like she needed the money, and she didn't want to see her characters trashed on the screen. I remember she used to say, "Any time I'm tempted, I say the magic words 'V. I. Warshawski' and I waken from my enchantment." Are you sure you got it right?'

Helen breathed heavily through her nose. 'I'm sure I'm sure. I didn't realise Penny felt like that. I thought this was some routine agreement they were working out with her. From what Kes was saying, they've just got some final details to iron out, but the deal should be done and dusted within the next few weeks.'

'I just can't believe Penny would agree to this,' Lindsay said. 'She said nothing to me about it, and I'm sure if she'd discussed it with Sophie, I'd have heard. Meredith said nothing about it either. I wonder how they persuaded Penny? It must have taken something really special to get round her objections . . .' Lindsay's voice tailed off and her eyes widened.

'Like murder?' Helen wondered.

'Like murder,' Lindsay echoed. 'If you kill somebody, you don't need their consent any more. Particularly when you're their literary executor.'

There was silence for a moment while they

both considered the implications of what Helen had learned. 'That can't be right,' Helen said eventually. 'This isn't something that's just been cobbled together over the last couple of days. Kes' company must have been in negotiation for months.'

'Would Penny have had to know that?'

Helen pondered. 'Not necessarily, I suppose. Authors tend to get involved in negotiations if they want to write the script themselves or if they want to have a fair bit of input into the end product. But some of them just want to take the money and run, in which case they leave it up to their agents to do the business and they never actually meet the people who are planning to make the film.'

'So what you're saying – let me get this straight – is that Penny's agent could have been working out the terms of this deal without Penny ever having had to meet the other parties? And that's normal?' Lindsay asked, feeling slightly like Alice in Wonderland.

'Penny might not even have known there were negotiations going on. Quite often, agents just don't mention negotiations to their client authors till they're a long way down the road. TV and film companies are always scouting around for stuff. Out of every hundred approaches an agent gets from a film company, they might actually sign five options. And out of every hundred option contracts that get signed, maybe five get made. With those kind of odds, you can see why agents let things move quite a long way down the road before they mention them to authors. Otherwise their phone lines would be permanently clogged with clients demanding to know what the latest was on the deal and how soon they were going to be able to buy the house with the swimming pool. And then nobody would ever get any work done.'

'It also makes the agents look good,' Lindsay said.

'How do you work that one out?'

Lindsay shrugged. 'If the only time you hear from your agent is when she's calling to tell you about the great deal she's got to offer, you don't know how many approaches she's had and fucked up, do you?'

'How did you get this cynical?' Helen demanded, full of mock outrage.

'I hung around with you at a crucial age. What kind of money are we talking about, by the way?'

'For the options, say five grand a book, and there's how many books?'

'Twenty-six, twenty-seven, something like that.'

Helen's eyes swivelled up at an angle as she did the mental arithmetic. 'About £130,000? Then for each one that gets made, say fifty grand. For the first series, we'd be talking options for the lot, plus rights for six – call it £450,000. And these are not high end figures, by the way. For

US and UK rights, you could easily be talking double that.'

Lindsay whistled softly. 'So we could be looking at a million-pound scenario where your mate Kes made Penny's agent an opening offer she couldn't refuse. Catriona Polson – that's the agent – knows how Penny feels about TV and film deals, but she decides that this is too good to miss. She figures that she'll go with it and see if she can talk it up into a deal that's so wonderful that even Penny will abandon all her artistic principles and bite their hands off. How does that sound?'

'So far, so good. I like it. Nothing makes me happier than the sight of one of life's Ms Ten Per Cents getting stitched up,' Helen said enthusiastically.

'Only problem is, Penny throws her hands up in horror and says she'd rather eat razor blades than betray her readers and her masterworks in such a tawdry, money-grubbing way. And bearing in mind that agents usually charge more for TV and film deals, Catriona sees the thick end of 150 grand flying out of the window,' Lindsay theorised.

'Whereas, with Penny dead . . .' Helen interjected.

'The deal is even sweeter. She can probably screw more money on the notoriety basis, plus she's got the added bonus of increased sales on the books that are currently out there. When I saw her, she said that she'd be crazy to kill Penny for a short-term gain when Penny alive would write more books. But if there's TV in the pipeline, that means she'd get long-term benefit anyway, because all the books would be reissued as TV tie-ins. And Catriona Polson's a really big woman. She'd have no trouble grabbing Penny and stabbing her in the neck.' Lindsay finished her beer in a single swallow, suddenly feeling dry-mouthed. 'Same again?'

When she returned with fresh drinks, Helen was looking sheepish. 'Spit it out,' Lindsay sighed.

'You just made out a great case against the agent. It's a good motive. And it's just about credible that the agent would use the murder method in the book as a kind of poetic justice, almost to make herself feel like it wasn't real, just something in a book. Only you can't tell the police about it, can you?'

'I'm not with you. Why not?'

Helen swallowed a gulp of beer and said, 'You told me Meredith is Penny's residuary legatee, yeah? Well, if it plays as a motive for the agent, it works as an even better motive for Meredith. About ten times better, in fact. You need something more solid before you pass this info on to the bizzies.'

Lindsay closed her eyes and cursed silently. Helen was absolutely right. If Catriona had told Penny about the talks, the chances are that Meredith would know it was a possibility. Even if she hadn't, if Helen had heard it on the grapevine it was entirely possible that Meredith had too, Lindsay thought, remembering with a lurch that Meredith's best friend from college worked in Los Angeles, writing machine code to produce computerised special effects for Hollywood. And there would be plenty of special effects in any films of the Darkliners novels. It would be almost impossible for Meredith to establish her ignorance. Proving a negative was always the hardest thing in any investigation, Lindsay knew from her long journalistic experience. 'I can't think about this any more today,' she said. 'I need to sleep on it. Maybe when I wake up tomorrow, my subconscious will have had the chance to work out where I go for proof.'

'You're probably right,' Helen said. 'And I know just how to help you put it right out of your mind.'

Warning bells rang like a smoke alarm in Lindsay's head. 'Oh, yeah?' she said warily.

'Yeah. You can advise me on my little problem.'

Lindsay groaned and raised her hands as if to fend off a blow. 'I already gave you the only advice I know. Dig the dirt, then dish it.'

'Can't you do the digging for me?' Helen asked plaintively. 'I don't have your experience. I'm just a simple TV producer. I don't even know where to start.'

'And you think I do?' Lindsay said, amused in spite of herself by Helen's attempts at pathos. 'I know nothing about this woman. I don't know her surname, her age, what she looks like, where she lives, what she drives or what kind of clothes she wears. I don't know who her friends are, what she does on her days off or anybody she's ever shagged. If anybody's going to get something on Stella, don't you think you're a bit better equipped?'

Helen shook her head. 'Her surname is Piper and she's thirty-two.' She rummaged in her bag and came out with an A3 brochure promoting Watergaw Films. She flicked it open to the back cover. There, beneath Helen and Guy, was a head-and-shoulders shot of Stella Piper. Straight dark hair cut close to her head, liquid brown eyes accentuated with eyeliner and mascara, a pert, upturned nose and a rosebud mouth.

'She looks like Bambi,' Lindsay said.

'Knowing her, it wouldn't have been the hunters who shot her mother,' Helen said darkly. 'She drives a metallic green Fiat Punto and she lives in some trendy warehouse conversion on the canal behind King's Cross station when she's not round Guy's flat in Stoke Newington. She wears that skin-tight fashion that looks great on Kate Moss and would make you and me look like sausages that need to go on a diet. As for friends, I shouldn't think she's got any.'

'Fine, but I still don't know where to start digging,' Lindsay insisted firmly.

'You could start by following her.'

'Helen, I haven't even got a car,' Lindsay protested.

'That's no problem. We use a hire firm just round the corner when we need some extra wheels. I'll take you round there and sort you out with something right now.' She finished her beer in one swallow and looked expectantly at Lindsay.

Lindsay closed her eyes and sighed. In the long years of their friendship, Helen had only ever asked for Lindsay's help once before. It had seemed straightforward that time too, but it had led Lindsay into a confrontation with a murderer that had forced her into the hardest decision she'd ever taken and had altered the course of her life irrevocably. It wasn't an experience she'd willingly repeat. But even putting the most pessimistic of glosses on Helen's present request, it was hard to see how it could get her into the kind of trouble she'd been trying to avoid ever since that bitter tragedy in Glasgow.

She opened her eyes and shook her head with an air of fatalism. 'I have a horrible feeling that I'm going to regret this,' she said, picking up her glass and following Helen's example. 'Let's go and get me a set of wheels.'

11

Lindsay fiddled with the radio tuning buttons again. She'd been parked across the street from the industrial unit that housed Watergaw Films for the best part of an hour. So far, she'd grown irritated with one presenter's attempts at controversiality, bored with a magazine programme that seemed to cater for the prurience of people without a life of their own, and infuriated to discover a play she'd been listening to was the first of three episodes of a serial. Now she'd never know why Prunella had taken the Old English sheepdog to the archbishop's consecration. Giving up on talk radio, she settled for a station that played oldies with minimal chatter between records.

It was at times like this that she missed smoking. It was one of the few pastimes observers could indulge on a stakeout without having to take their eyes off the target. And of course, Lindsay realised with a shock, surveillance was something she had only ever done as a smoker. Since she'd quit, she'd been doing the kind of respectable job that didn't involve spying on complete strangers. It wasn't something she'd missed, especially on a baking afternoon in a car with no air conditioning. Already her whole body felt slick with sweat. Wondering why she'd let herself be talked into this, Lindsay rooted in her backpack for a tissue and wiped the perspiration from her palms again.

Just after four, the metal-sheathed side door opened and a woman appeared wearing a short, sleeveless dress and low-heeled Greek sandals with thongs that criss-crossed half-way up her calves. She was so short that it should have looked absurd, but slender enough for it to seem sexy. She had a boxy leather bag slung across her body and she carried a small holdall that looked virtually empty. As she turned to check that the door had closed behind her, Lindsay caught a momentary glimpse of her face. 'Bambi,' she said aloud, turning the key in the ignition of the anonymous hatchback Helen had hired for her.

Stella crossed the car park, walking more briskly than Lindsay would have cared to in that heat. When she came level with a metallic green car, she slipped into the driver's door. She reversed out of her space and drove straight towards Lindsay. At the gate, Stella turned left and headed towards the tube station. Lindsay was caught facing the wrong direction and had to pull round hastily, amazed at the bus driver who let her out with a courteous wave. Maybe some things in London had changed for the better after all.

At the traffic lights by the station, Lindsay was two cars behind Stella. As they swung across into Greenland Road, one car peeled off towards Kentish Town, leaving only one as a barrier. 'Perfect,' Lindsay muttered as they swung right into Bayham Street. The narrow roads were hot and dusty, choked with cars and delivery vans, motorbike couriers dicing with death as they slalomed through in the canyons between tall houses grimed with a century of metropolitan pollution. Stella clearly knew where she was going, zigzagging through back streets whose bleakness was unrelieved by the afternoon sun, weaving a course that took her behind St Pancras and King's Cross stations, past dozens of struggling small businesses crammed under cheap flats.

A couple of times, it had been touch and go staying close to Stella through traffic that was heavier than Lindsay remembered it being when she had lived in the city. But she'd always managed to keep her in sight at the junctions where crucial decisions were taken. Once they'd cleared the Angel, they picked up speed on City Road, where the traffic was lighter and houses gave way to tall warehouses, old buildings where light industry had lodged since the bricks were first laid, offices nudged in among them down side streets. When they hit the big roundabout by Old Street tube, Lindsay was forced to sit on Stella's back bumper as the van between them peeled off into the middle lane. A quick left and a half right brought Lindsay on to unknown territory. All she knew was that she was heading in the general direction of the City, though she suspected they were going to skirt its eastern edge rather than penetrate the canyons of commerce themselves. Wherever they were headed, it wasn't home.

She wasn't happy with being slap bang in the middle of Stella's rear-view mirror, but she was torn between fear of losing her in unfamiliar streets and fear of being spotted as a tail. The decision was suddenly taken from her when a Porsche shrieked out of a side street, cutting in between her and Stella without even a wave of gratitude. 'Pillock,' Lindsay muttered, but her heart wasn't in it.

They carried on in the same direction, past streets she'd only ever heard of. Whitechapel Road from the Monopoly board. Cable Street, scene of the anti-Fascist riots of the thirties. Just when Lindsay was convinced the next junction must bring them hard up against the Thames, Stella swung left into a wide street. The Porsche roared off to the right, leaving Lindsay a gap to make up. As she turned, she saw the green car a few hundred yards down the road turning right into a narrow street. Swearing, Lindsay shot down to the turning and swung the car across the oncoming traffic in a blare of horns. She was in time to see Stella turn again. When she made it to the junction, Stella was gone, the green car somewhere in a maze of narrow streets. 'Shit, shit, shit!' Lindsay yelled, smacking her hand hard against the steering wheel.

She pulled in to the kerb while she considered. If Stella had spotted her and deliberately shaken her off, there was no chance of catching her now. She'd be back on the main road and miles away within minutes. But she'd shown no signs of trying to shake off pursuit, so the odds were that she'd turned off the arterial road because she was near her destination. Logically, Lindsay decided, if she drove around the nearby streets, she'd come upon the Fiat.

As she drove slowly through the twisting narrow corridors of Wapping, she remembered the one and only time she had been here before. It had been a Saturday night, so cold her breath had puffed in clouds before her. She'd been on foot, one of hundreds of journalists and print workers who had come to demonstrate against the mass sackings of their colleagues by Rupert Murdoch's News International to make way for cheap new technology and the de-skilling of their craft. They'd come to protest but had ended up fleeing through the streets, driven ahead of mounted police gung-ho as Cossacks and with as much concern for those they pursued. The clatter of hoofs, the swish of police batons through the air, the screams of terror and the plumes of steamy breath from the horses' nostrils were still lodged in Lindsay's brain, erupting occasionally as nightmares. Somewhere in the mêlée, Lindsay had become separated from her lover, Cordelia. They hadn't found each other until they'd both arrived home in the middle of the night. Terrified of losing each other in a more permanent way, they'd never gone back on that particular picket line.

Cruising that same patch in broad daylight was a different experience, even though the sun failed to penetrate as far as the pavement in quite a few streets. There was nothing threatening on this warm summer afternoon. Lindsay sighed. It was hard to imagine she was going to get instant access to the skeletons in Stella's cupboard by driving round Wapping in the sun. About to give up, Lindsay made one last turn into a street that was more of an alley, curving like a scimitar and dead-ending by the ornamental canal. Tucked in a vanway between warehouses was the green Punto.

Lindsay felt a mixture of irritation and satisfaction. If she'd lost Stella, she could have gone back to Helen empty-handed but virtuous. Now she was nailed to her tail for another sticky journey, more likely than not. She turned her car round and backed into a space right at the end of the cul-de-sac. It was on double yellows, but she couldn't imagine a traffic warden coming all the way down there on the off chance in heat like this.

She looked across at the building whose vanway held the Fiat. There was nothing to indicate who the tenants were or what they did. It was simply a blank box in dirty red brick with windows that indicated four floors above the ground-floor level, which had no windows at all. Time to take a chance, Lindsay decided. She got out of the car, leaving it unlocked in case she needed to make a quick getaway, and walked purposefully across the street. The building had a side entrance, a pair of heavy wooden doors at the top of three shallow concrete steps. Lindsay tugged the brass handles, relieved when one opened and admitted her into a small foyer. Ahead were more double doors, this time steel and reinforced glass. By an entryphone was a bank of etched metal plaques. *Dessins Domingo* was the tenant of the top floor. Underneath them were Bronzed Bodies – Sculptures, and Media Masters, followed by Heavenly Dolls, Stationary Cycles plc and Gorton Engineering.

Lindsay made a quick note of the names, though she felt fairly sure she wouldn't be far wrong if she looked for Stella Piper at Media Masters. The only question was what Media Masters did, and what Stella was doing there. She walked back to the car and moved it to the street where the cul-de-sac emerged, finding a handy space facing in the direction Stella would logically take to get back to civilisation as Lindsay knew it. She settled down for another wait. This time, she didn't have to hang around long. Within ten minutes, the Punto appeared at the junction and shot off into the Wapping labyrinth.

Once they were back on the main road, the route could not have been more simple. Tower Hill down to the Embankment, round the choked artery of Trafalgar Square and up Charing Cross Road, where the traffic was moving so slowly Lindsay could read the promotional posters in the bookshop windows. There were a couple of times when she thought she'd lost Stella at traffic lights, but the rush-hour traffic was so sluggish, she caught up on the next change. At Cambridge Circus, Stella slipped left into Shaftesbury Avenue, then turned right into the pulsating heart of Soho café society. She dog-legged her way through the streets until they reached a backwater where the flesh trade had not yet been ousted by fashion. Stella had slowed down to a crawl, obviously looking for a parking place. Behind Lindsay, a car pulled out and swung round a corner. Quickly, she reversed into the available space and jumped out in time to see Stella losing patience and bumping her car on to the pavement further down the street. She got out and headed back up the street in Lindsay's direction. Lindsay walked casually towards Stella on the opposite pavement, glad of the weather as an excuse for wraparound sunglasses that let her stare without being spotted.

Before she drew level with Lindsay, Stella turned into a shop. Instantly, Lindsay sprinted across the street and followed her in, realising belatedly she had just walked into a sex shop. Videos for sale covered one wall, magazines another. Two cabinets in the middle of the floor held sex toys. A swift glance revealed dildos of proportions no one but a hard-core masochist could desire. With an inward shudder, Lindsay drifted towards the counter where Stella was standing, lips pursed in impatience, arms folded and one sandalled foot tapping. Behind the counter was a youth so spectacularly lacking in physical charm that it was hardly surprising he'd chosen to work in a place that recognised the importance of fantasy. He had a phone clamped to one scarlet ear. The other stood out at ninety degrees to his shaven head. The tattooed fingers holding the phone read 'shag'. In your dreams, Lindsay thought derisively. Neither of them showed the slightest interest in Lindsay as she pretended to browse the videos.

'He's not answering,' he said in a thickly adenoidal voice.

'I told him I was coming in this afternoon,' Stella said peevishly.

'He never said.'

'He must have told you where he was going.'

'He never. He just said he had some business to sort.' He replaced the phone under the counter. 'D'you wanna come back later?'

'Not especially, no. Did your precious boss say when he'd be back?'

The youth shrugged nervously, one finger creeping reflexively towards a nostril. 'He never tells me nothing. We're open till ten, though.'

'I know you're open till ten,' Stella said through gritted teeth. Lindsay had often read the expression, but she'd never seen anyone perform it before now. It was impressive, she had to admit. Stella hefted the holdall on to the counter. Where it had been almost empty before, it was now bulging, square corners pushing the fabric out in several places. 'Have you got a box?' she demanded.

The youth looked as if gorm had followed couth out of his life a long time ago. 'A box?' he echoed.

'A cardboard box? Big enough to hold the tapes I've got in here? I'll leave them for Keith, but I don't want to leave my bag behind, *capisce*?'

'Yeah, right.' The youth disappeared through a bead curtain. Stella drummed her fingers on the counter top. Lindsay moved casually behind her to the opposite wall and started looking at magazines. Out of the corner of her eye, she could still see Stella. The youth emerged with a box about twice the size of the holdall. 'This do?'

Stella didn't even bother to answer. She simply unzipped the bag and transferred about a dozen video tapes into the box. 'When Keith shows his face, tell him Stella was here as promised. There's twelve samples in there. Six different films, each cut in two versions – one for America, one for Europe. Tell him to call me with his orders before

Monday. Have you got that?' He nodded. 'Repeat it back to me,' she commanded.

'Stella came with the samples. Half a dozen films, American and European versions. Orders before Monday.'

'You forgot the crucial bit,' she snarled. 'Tell him I get seriously pissed off with men who stand me up.' She zipped the bag up again and stormed out. Lindsay couldn't see any point in following Stella any further. There was no need for overkill. Why bother hunting for a rifle when you already had an Exocet missile, Lindsay wondered.

She abandoned her pretence of studying the repulsive magazines and walked out of the shop. She felt like she needed a shower and a change of clothes, least of all because of the heat. But most of all, she needed a drink. Before she could do that, though, she had one more task to perform.

Glancing up and down the street, she saw a pair of telephone boxes on the corner. She walked up there and shut herself into one, seeing to her surprise that, like American pay phones, it took credit cards as well as money. 'Nice one,' she said appreciatively, swiping her card through the slot and calling directory inquiries. A voice worryingly like that of Margaret Thatcher gave her the number of Media Masters and she keyed it in. 'Media Masters, Julie-Anne speaking,' a woman's voice chirruped.

Time to play a hunch. 'Hey,' Lindsay said, going

for Californian. 'My name is Catherine Parvenu and I'm an independent film-maker out of Los Angeles. Now, I'm in town for a few days, and I need some video facilities. Can you tell me, do you have editing suites for hire?'

'Well, yes, we do, but I'm afraid they're fully booked until early next week. I can put you on stand-by, if you like, but I can't make any promises.'

'Gee, that's a pity. I really need something right away. Never mind, I've got a couple other numbers I can call. Tell me, do you also do video copying?'

'We do, madam. Single and multiple copies, US and UK format, overnight express facilities available.'

'And do you have spare capacity this week? I'm looking for fifty copies of a one hour VHS, US format. Can you do that?'

'One moment, madam, let me check the diary . . . Yes, we can accommodate you. When will the master be available?'

'I'll have to get back to you on that. Thanks a lot, Julie-Anne, I'll be back to you tomorrow, okay?'

'We'll look forward to hearing from you.'

'You have a nice day now.' Lindsay intoned the West Coast mantra without obvious irony.

Now she'd confirmed her guess at what Media Masters did, she really needed that drink. Leaving the car where it was, she headed off into the heart of Soho and soon found a café bar where women who were enough like her for it to feel like home sat round a horseshoe-shaped bar drinking beer out of long-necked bottles. She ordered a Rolling Rock and savoured the moment's anticipation before the first swallow. She twirled the bottle, expecting to read through the drops of condensation the legend 'Brewed in the glass-lined tanks of Old Latrobe'. Instead, she discovered it was brewed in the tradition of Old Latrobe somewhere in the south of England. She sighed so hard the woman next to her asked what was wrong.

'You know that saying, "You can never go home any more"?' she asked. The woman nodded, looking a little bemused. 'Well, I think I just found out how true it is.'

12

The memory banks of career waiters never ceased to amaze Lindsay. It must have been at least seven years since she'd eaten in the little family *trattoria* in Camden, but the waiter who had always flirted with her and Cordelia greeted her as if it had been only seven days. '*Bella signorina, come sta*?' he'd asked automatically, sweeping a deep bow in front of her that revealed his hair was starting to thin round the crown.

The exchange continued as it always had. She was fine, how was he? He was so-so, but what was the point of complaining, the government always got in. He ushered her to a familiar table at the back in a corner. The same bad paintings of Sorrento still hung in their identical positions. The walls had acquired some Italia '90 memorabilia, but apart from that everything was the same. Without being asked, the waiter brought Lindsay a Peroni while she studied the menu. It was as if the door to the restaurant was a time slip. When the door opened next, Lindsay half expected to see Cordelia glide in. It was both a relief and a disappointment when Helen swept in instead.

She plonked herself down and mouthed, 'Gin and tonic,' at the waiter. 'God, what a day,' she sighed.

'It's not going to get any better, trust me on that,' Lindsay said. The waiter placed a sweating glass in front of Helen. 'I couldn't believe it when you suggested meeting here. I'd no idea it was still going. I imagined it would have turned into some terrible pizza parlour. I felt really dislocated when you said the name – this was one of the places I always came with Cordelia. It was our private secret. Like we thought we were the only people who knew about it. We never had dinner with anybody else here. So I didn't expect you to know about it. Illogical, I know, but . . .'

Helen snorted. 'You think I could work five minutes' walk away and not know about the best Italian restaurant in north London? Do me a favour! You ready to order? I need the prospect of something solid in me before I can bear to hear any more bad news.'

While they waited for their meal, Lindsay outlined her afternoon discoveries to Helen, who looked more and more glum with every passing sentence. Even the arrival of a lasagne that looked rich enough to have its own Swiss bank account couldn't relieve her gloom. As Lindsay virtuously wolfed her tuna and bean salad, Helen said disconsolately, 'It's a bit of a double-edged sword, isn't it? We've found the skeleton in Stella's cupboard, but if I expose her I'm bound to bring Watergaw's reputation down with her.' She banged the end of her fork angrily on the table, attracting glances from the handful of other diners. 'I can't bear it,' she raged. 'We built this company up from nothing, we've started to get a really good name in the business for delivering what we promise, and now this bitch is using us to make scummy little porno films. How dare she? It's so outrageous that if it had come from anybody except you, I wouldn't have believed a word of it. It's not just that she's exploiting the knickers off me and the company, it's the fact that she's involved in the skin trade. It goes diametrically against everything Watergaw is supposed to stand for.' Her eyes sparkled with anger. 'I don't suppose there's any chance that her nasty little racket doesn't involve the company?' she asked, faint hope in her voice.

Lindsay stretched out her free arm and squeezed Helen's hand. 'It's always a possibility, but I wouldn't hold out too much hope. But I thought the best thing to do was to get as clear a picture of what's gone on as we possibly can. That's why I suggested we got together tonight, so we can map out a plan of campaign.'

'You've got an idea?' Helen said eagerly.

'Nothing specific. We've got to try and uncover how long it's been going on, how involved Guy is, and, if we can, how seedy these films are. We also need to establish what the involvement of Watergaw is in what she's been up to. It might be that there's a way to manipulate the information so you can get her out of the door and out of the business. But we won't know until we've had a good trawl through her computer and her filing cabinets. Which is why I suggested meeting on this side of town.'

'You want to do it tonight?' Helen asked.

'How soon can you finish your lasagne?'

'I want to kill her,' Helen growled. On the TV screen in Stella's office, a slightly built woman was fellating one man while another entered her from the rear. It was the fifth of a couple of dozen video tapes they'd found in the bottom drawer of Stella's filing cabinet. They'd sampled brief sections of each, their disgust and anger mounting with every one. 'I want to kill her with my bare hands,' Helen continued. She'd been delivering variations on the same theme ever since they'd turned their attentions from paperwork and computer files to the videos. 'She's even used the sets from one of Watergaw's drama productions, the cheap bitch. Turn it off, Linds, I'm going to be sick if I watch any more of these.'

Lindsay pressed the 'stop' button with an overwhelming sense of relief. 'We probably should check the others, make sure they're all the same sort of thing.'

'You do it if you feel you have to. I'm going to get some mineral water from my office to try and take the taste away.' Helen walked out and Lindsay slotted the next film into the player. She wound it on a fair way, then hit the 'play' button. The screen filled with a close-up of a woman masturbating. Behind her in the corridor she heard a set of footsteps. 'Did you bring me some?' she asked.

'Who the fuck are you?'

Lindsay whirled round, dropping the remote control, and stared open-mouthed at Stella. She stood in the doorway, a tall man with cropped pepper and salt hair behind her. Stella advanced a step. 'What the fuck are you doing in my office? You're a burglar!'

Regaining her composure, Lindsay shrugged. 'So call the cops. Go on, give them a bell.' She pushed the phone towards Stella. 'You must be Stella. And you, I presume, are Guy.'

Guy pushed past Stella and loomed above Lindsay, so close she could have identified the stone in his nose stud if she'd been interested. 'And who the hell are you?'

From behind them all, Helen's voice came, cold as the ice that clinked in the jug she carried. 'She's with me. She's a friend. It's a concept you won't be familiar with, Guy.'

He flinched at her tone as much as her words. 'Whoever she is, she's got no business in here.'

'He's right,' Stella butted in, finding outrage

from somewhere. 'She's been going through my stuff. Look, there's papers everywhere. And she's been in my filing cabinet. Those tapes were locked in there. She's broken in!'

'No, she hasn't,' Helen said wearily. 'Who do you think has the master keys to all the office furniture, dumbshit? You think I trust my staff not to lose the keys to their desks and storage cupboards? You've never had any idea, have you, Stella?' She managed to make the name sound like an obscenity.

'You're out of order, Helen,' Stella said. 'You've got no right to be doing this. What's the matter with you? Don't you trust your business partners?'

'I don't trust pornographers,' Helen said. 'You do something that exploitative on a routine basis and you forget where the lines get drawn in real life. I wouldn't trust you if your hands were nailed to the wall. Which frankly would be too good for you and I'd resent spending the money on redecoration afterwards. How dare you do what you've been doing?'

Stella looked at Guy, who was hiding his discomfort in the business of lighting a cigarette. 'So what's the charge, Helen? Me and Guy like to watch porn? It's a criminal offence to keep a few horny films for our personal pleasure? I didn't realise you dykes were so puritanical.'

'This isn't about watching blue movies. It's about making them,' Helen said flatly.

Stella laughed. 'What is she on?' she demanded. 'Whatever it is, I don't fucking want any. Helen, where do you get this strange idea that I've been making pornographic films?'

Helen looked as if she was on the point of realising her ambition to kill Stella. 'You were too tight, Stella. You were too keen on making a profit. You used the sets we built for *Home Movies* to make your scummy skin flicks. You didn't even attempt to disguise them.'

Stella's hands clenched into fists and Guy sucked in smoke like it was oxygen. Lindsay decided it was time she butted in to lower the temperature before Helen did something they'd both regret. 'You film on site and do the editing in the suite here,' she said, her voice clinically matter of fact. 'Then you take the edited film over to Media Masters and they make you video versions in US and UK formats. You take the samples to your outlet – *It's Personal* in Robb Street in Soho – and they place their order.'

'That's where I've seen you before,' Stella interrupted angrily. 'You were in the shop. You've been following me!' Her voice climbed in volume and pitch as she made her accusation and she pushed Guy out of the way. 'I'll have you, bitch. Fucking dyke. Just wait, I'll have you.'

'Will that be before you come out of the nick or after?' Lindsay asked sweetly.

Stella laughed in her face. 'I'm not going to jail. That's not on the agenda. You can't hand me over to the cops, because this is all being done under your precious friend Helen's umbrella. I go down and I take my partners with me.'

'Wait a minute,' Guy said nervously.

'It's all right, Guy,' Stella said, reaching out and patting his arm as she would have done a dog. 'I don't think Helen's friend wants to come and visit her in Holloway.'

'I don't think that will be necessary,' Lindsay said, relaxing as she played her trump card. 'We didn't just look in the bottom drawer. We've been right through your filing cabinet and your computer files. Pretty stupid to use Blue as your password when you're making pornography, don't you think?'

Guy looked as if he wanted to be sick. His eyes were everywhere except on Helen and Stella. 'Listen, I'm sure we can sort this out . . .' His voice trailed off as he realised no one cared what he thought.

'Shut up, Guy,' Helen said savagely. 'Listen to some sense for a change.'

Stella cocked her head to one side and put her hands on her hips. 'Okay, smartarse. Tell us what it is you think you know.'

Lindsay perched on the corner of the desk and spoke as dispassionately as she could manage. 'We know all about Shooting Star Investments. We know that since it started with virtually no assets except an interest-free loan of £500,000 from an unspecified source, it has built into a considerable earner. In the space of a mere eight months, it has made profits of around £450,000 from the sale of video films produced by Shooting Star Investments.'

'There's nothing wrong with that,' Stella said, refusing to give an inch. 'There isn't a court in the land that's going to penalise me for being a successful businesswoman. And there isn't a police force in the land that will prosecute Shooting Star for those videos. I'm not a fool. We might have sailed close to the wind, but none of the films we made is anything like hard core enough to interest the Vice Squad.'

'Who said anything about the Vice Squad?' Lindsay asked, a threatening edge slipping past her control and into her voice. 'I'm talking about the Fraud Squad.'

For the first time, Stella's defiance took a dent. She looked momentarily uncertain, glancing at Guy, who was too busy lighting a fresh cigarette off the end of the previous one to notice. 'You're full of shit,' she said, but her eyes told a different story to her words.

'I'm not the bullshitter in this room. As we say where I come from, Stell, the ball's on the slates. The party's over. I've read the paperwork.' Lindsay turned to a neat pile of papers behind her on the desk. As she went through them, she slapped each document down hard on the desk in front of Stella. 'Exhibit number one. Helen's submission to the EU for funding for a three-part drama about asylum seekers. Exhibit number two. A letter from the EU revealing the application has been successful and enclosing a cheque for the cash. Exhibit number three. A forged letter purporting to be from the EU to Helen explaining her application has been unsuccessful in this round of funding awards but it will be reconsidered in the next bidding sequence when it stands a strong chance, and that she need not resubmit her application. Exhibit number four. A bank statement showing the deposit of the identical sum of money in the account of Shooting Star two weeks after the date on the authentic EU letter.'

'A real shit's trick,' Helen said.

Stella closed her eyes and breathed heavily through her nose. 'I'm really fucked off about this,' she said. 'You have no idea how fucked off I am.'

'We were going to put the money back, Helen,' Guy said, moving a couple of steps closer to her and spreading his hands in a supplicatory gesture. 'As soon as we'd generated enough profit, we were going to replace the money with another faked letter saying the money had come from a fresh allocation of funding. It's a licence to print money, Helen. With the profits Shooting Star generates, we can make all the films we want about things that really matter. Like Stella said, it's not as if we're doing hard-core stuff. And if we weren't doing it someone else would be.'

Helen's upper lip twitched in contempt. 'Any minute now you'll be telling me you were only obeying orders. How can you think I'd ever want to make a film with you again? Less than six weeks ago, we were sitting in my office trying to put together a proposal for a film about the evils of sex tourism. Where's your brain gone, Guy?'

'Helen, don't get worked up . . .'

'Don't get worked up!' she yelled. 'Don't get worked up?'

'He's right,' Stella said with an exasperated sigh. 'Look, Helen, you get your EU money, you get to make your films, everything goes on exactly like it did before. There's no reason why not.'

Helen stared at Stella, for once in her life beyond speech. Lindsay jumped in. 'I don't think that's going to be possible, Stella. I don't think Helen would feel comfortable with that.'

'I don't want to be in the same hemisphere as you, never mind the same company,' Helen snarled. 'I'm leaving this partnership and I'm taking my grant money with me and I'm going to set up my own company that is totally vermin-free, even if I have to get Rentokil to vet every member of staff.'

'That's not what we want, Helen,' Stella said calmly. 'Your expertise and your street cred is really important to the company. If you were that dispensable, don't you think we'd have dumped you ages ago? If you go, you go without a penny. The legal battles to dissolve the partnership against our wishes will take years and every penny you've got.'

It was Lindsay's turn to look thunderstruck. 'I don't think you appreciate the position you're in,' she said incredulously. 'We've got you bang to rights. All we have to do to end your career is to call the Fraud Squad and show how you expropriated the money to start Shooting Star with no intention of paying it back.'

Suddenly, Stella jumped forward and grabbed the documents off the desk. Lindsay snatched at them, but Stella danced across to the corner behind Guy, waving the papers. 'No evidence, no case,' she said, grinning crazily. She grabbed Guy's lighter, spun the wheel and let the flame dance along the bottom of the pages. The papers caught and yellow flames started to lick their way up the paper.

With a scream of rage, Helen threw the jug of water she was still carrying across the room at Stella. She raised one arm to fend it off and the jug tipped, then tumbled, cascading down Stella and the papers. The flames died, leaving the papers charred and sodden. Stella laughed. 'You don't stop me that easily,' she said, grasping the soggy paper and tearing it into irregular pieces. 'Get the vids, Guy.'

Showing more *savoir faire* than he'd managed so far, Guy swept the videos off the desk into the wastepaper bin, which he clutched to his chest. Helen leapt at him, clawing his arms with her nails, but he clung on grimly to his burden.

Lindsay stepped up behind Helen and grabbed her, pulling her back.

'Leave it, Helen,' she said.

'But they're destroying the evidence,' she said, her voice teetering on the edge of a sob.

'And we can't stop them. Two on two, nobody with a weapon, it's just going to degenerate into a rammy. She's determined to destroy it, we're not going to stop her, and the cops aren't going to get here in time. Come on, Helen, don't give her the satisfaction.'

All the fight suddenly went from Helen and she subsided into Lindsay's arms. 'Sensible move,' Stella said approvingly. 'By morning, there won't be anything left to tie us to the blue films or to the missing grant. In fact, if you do call in the cops, the only thing they'll be able to investigate is the misappropriation of the EU grant. And let's face it, Helen, the person who could rip that money off easier than anyone else is the person it was intended for. All you had to do was tell me and Guy that the EU had blown you out, and you could have pocketed the readies no trouble. But for me to do that . . . Well, it'd be complicated, wouldn't it?'

'Let's get out of here, Helen,' Lindsay said, steering Helen towards the door. Somehow they made it out of the building without giving way to the fury that bubbled inside them both. Out in the car park, Helen turned back and stared up at the lighted skylight above Stella's office.

'I can't believe we were so stupid,' she said bitterly. 'We let them get away with it.'

'We were scuppered as soon as they found us in there,' Lindsay said, furiously kicking the tyre of Stella's Fiat. 'You'd only ever have nailed her with the element of surprise on your side.'

'I just can't believe Guy was involved with her seedy, scummy little scheme.'

'When sex walks into a relationship, sense walks out,' Lindsay said, squatting down by Stella's car with her Swiss Army knife in hand. She uncapped the valve on the nearest tyre and opened it up with the tip of the blade, taking childish satisfaction in the hiss of escaping air. Methodically she worked round the wheels, letting the air out of each tyre while Helen paced the car park, ranting.

'Let's go,' Lindsay said when she'd finished. 'I'm sorry it didn't work out the way you wanted.'

'It's worse than when we started. At least then I didn't know what her dark secret was. Now I'm implicated.'

'I let you down.'

Helen shook her head. 'No. It's my fault. I underestimated the bitch. Now I'm completely boxed into a corner. I want out and I want revenge, but what can I do?'

'Yeah, well, it's not over till the fat lady sings,' Lindsay said grimly. 'There's got to be a way to screw them like they've screwed you. And I'm the very person to find it.'

13

Lindsay drove back in silence, replaying the confrontation like a tape loop. Somehow, there had to be a way for Helen to get what she wanted out of the mess Lindsay had helped create. She was operating on automatic pilot, her eyes focused on the tail lights of Helen's car in front. At junctions where the car had to come to a halt, her mind seemed to go into free fall, the street and the traffic dissolving into the vile and vivid images she'd absorbed from Stella and Guy's videos. They had only seen short bursts, but it seemed to have saturated her visual cortex, becoming the wallpaper on which everything else was superimposed. Take away the outside world and all that was left were the writhing bodies and her impotent anger.

She was reunited with Helen on the doorstep. 'A stiff gin and a bath, that's what I need,' Helen said wearily as she fumbled her key into the lock.

'A Scotch and a shower for me,' Lindsay said,

following her indoors. 'At least you've got a shoulder to cry on.'

The living room appeared to be empty, though Lindsay wasn't prepared to commit herself. As far as she could tell, there might be a tribe of pygmies living among the detritus. Tonight, though, she was too tired to care. They went through to the kitchen in search of drink and found Kirsten and Meredith either side of a bottle of red wine on the kitchen table. Kirsten looked up expectantly, but seeing their faces contented herself with a quiet, 'Oh dear.'

'"Oh dear" doesn't even scratch the surface,' Helen said wearily. She walked round the table so she could see Meredith. 'We haven't met, have we?'

'This is Meredith,' Kirsten and Lindsay said in ragged chorus.

Meredith smiled. It looked tentative as a first rehearsal. 'You must be Helen,' she said. 'I'm sorry to invade your personal space like this, but I really needed to talk with Lindsay and I didn't want to wait till she checked in tomorrow morning. This has been kind of a difficult week, I guess you know.'

Impulsively, Helen stepped forward and hugged Meredith. 'You're all right here,' she said. 'It must be a complete bastard, what you're going through.' She stood back. 'You're welcome here any time, whether Lindsay's here or not. You need a bit of company, just get yourself round here. Okay?'

Looking slightly stunned, Meredith nodded. 'I thought you English were supposed to be reserved and standoffish?' she asked with a more relaxed smile.

'She's not English, she's from Liverpool,' Kirsten remarked drily.

'A far-off country of which we know little,' Lindsay added.

'Very funny. Come on, K, let's leave Lindsay and Meredith to talk down here. I need the biggest gin in the Home Counties and someone to wash my back while I slag off that scheming cow Stella and gutless Guy the porn king.'

'Porn king?' Kirsten said faintly.

'I'll tell you all about it,' Helen promised, sliding a bottle of eighteen-year-old Macallan towards Lindsay and half-filling a tumbler with gin. She tossed in a couple of lumps of ice, a slice of lemon and a token splash of tonic, then shooed Kirsten out of the door.

'That is one helluva woman,' Meredith said.

Pouring herself a good two fingers of the golden liquid, Lindsay nodded. 'Sophie's ex. You see what I have to live up to? Ebullient. Irrepressible. Generous to a fault. And right now, possessed of a rage that would make the Eumenides look a teeny bit cross.' She took a bottle of still mineral water from the fridge and carefully added about the same again to her glass. Then she swirled the liquid round, watching the sobs of spirit subside down the glass. 'How have you been?' she asked, settling down at the table, taking in Meredith's improved appearance. She looked as if she'd had a decent night's sleep, and her hair was washed and pulled back in a loose pigtail.

Meredith shrugged. 'Up and down. I can go for whole chunks of time on automatic pilot, getting through the day. Then it comes at me out of left field, no warning. It's like I hear her voice, or I half see her out of the corner of my eye. I get a whiff of her perfume. Or some memory ambushes me. I went to the local bakery today to buy some bread, and the baker was coming through with a tray of freshly baked cinnamon Danish and I just burst into tears. Penny loved his Danish, she'd send me down there every morning to pick some up for breakfast whenever we were in London together. I felt so stupid. I mean, how can you get emotional about a tray of Danish?' Even the recollection was enough to make Meredith's voice tremble and her eyes grow damp.

Lindsay swished a mouthful of Scotch round her mouth, making her taste-buds snap into wakefulness and her gums tingle. She swallowed and said, 'The last thing Frances ever gave me was a jar of quails' eggs. I still have them, lurking at the back of the fridge. The oldest quails' eggs in the world. It's not rational, but if Sophie ever threw them away I'd probably take a kitchen knife to her, and she knows it. We're a good pair, you and me. I have a sentimental attachment to quails' eggs and you cry at Danish pastries. We'd better not have a day out in Harrods food hall, eh?'

'I guess.' Meredith gave a watery smile. 'Did I tell you, my employers have shown a novel way of expressing their sympathies?'

'No. What have they done?'

'They fired me. Apparently, I no longer meet their criteria on security. They seem more concerned that I'm a lesbian than they are about me being a suspect in a homicide inquiry.'

'That's terrible,' Lindsay protested. 'They know your partner's been murdered and they phone you up to sack you?'

'Fax, actually. I don't even get to go in and empty my desk and say goodbye to my team.' Meredith sighed. 'I suppose I should look on the bright side. I mean, it kind of ruins my so-called motive for murder, doesn't it? If I'm supposed to have killed her to preserve my in-the-closet status, you'd think I'd have had the sense to realise that I'd be outed by the investigation.'

'It's outrageous,' Lindsay said. 'Can't you sue them?'

Meredith shrugged. 'I don't think so. And why would I want to prolong my connection with them by one single minute? A week ago, it would have been the end of the world to lose my job. Now? It's no big deal. I can get another job. I can't get another Penny.' For a moment, they both sat silent, reflecting. Then Meredith straightened up in her chair. 'Enough moping. How's your investigation going? Have you made any progress?'

'Not as much as I'd have liked,' Lindsay admitted. 'I found out a few interesting things. First, and this is probably the most significant thing from your point of view, there's no closed circle of knowledge about the murder method. Penny and Baz had an animated discussion about it on the editorial floor, overheard by everybody who was close by at the time. Every one of them probably told at least one other person, and chances are it was all over the publishing world by teatime. Second, whoever killed her probably hadn't been a regular visitor to the flat because he or she didn't know the procedures for locking up. Third, did you know about the film and TV deal that Catriona's been working on?'

Meredith frowned. 'A TV deal? With Penny?' She sounded as thunderstruck as Lindsay had felt when she'd heard Helen's news.

'Straight up. Galaxy Pictures in a co-production with the BBC via an independent UK production company. Three Darkliners books in nine episodes planned initially, with more if they get the audience figures. I'm told the deal's near completion.'

Meredith shook her head. 'Somebody's feeding you a line. You know what Penny thought about adaptations. She said it was like hiring cannibals as baby-sitters. They might promise to be good, but you couldn't be sure what they'd get up to as soon as your back was turned.'

'You know that, I know that. But the industry gossip says different. I guess we have to work on the premise that Catriona Polson still hadn't told Penny what was on offer.'

Meredith shook her head in amazement. 'No wonder she wanted to get me out of the way in a police cell,' she said. 'I mean, I know that as literary executor, she can do pretty much what she wants in terms of deal-making, but I'm not going to sit on my hands and let her push this through. Even if it's a *fait accompli*, I can still make sure the world knows that Catriona Polson is taking the grossest advantage of Penny's death.'

Lindsay rolled her glass between her hands and gazed into the amber glow. 'Do you think it's a motive for murder, though?'

Meredith stopped short and stared. 'You think she might have killed Penny?'

Lindsay shrugged. 'She's a strong possibility. A lot depends on her personal and corporate financial situation, which I know absolutely nothing about. But if she's strapped for cash, or if she's just looking to get rich quick, then she's got motive. And she's big enough to have overcome Penny if there had been any struggle.'

Meredith dropped her face into her hands and rubbed the skin round her eyes. 'I suppose so,' she said, her voice muffled. She looked up. 'You know, I can imagine how the passion between lovers leads to killing in the heat of the moment. And I can imagine the casual violence between strangers erupting into murder, because the person you're fighting is a stranger, not a real person with emotions and dreams and a family and a life. What I cannot grasp is what drives a person to kill someone who is a friend or a business associate. It's not a relationship that should contain the kind of passion that leads to murder. But at the same time, it's a killing that means you're involved in the aftermath. I really do not understand it.'

'Me neither, but it happens.' Lindsay swallowed another rich mouthful of whisky and continued. 'Catriona's definitely a contender. She's the only person so far with a known motive.'

'Apart, supposedly, from me,' Meredith said bitterly.

Lindsay ignored the comment and carried on. 'We shouldn't lose sight of Baz, though.'

'Baz, her editor?' Meredith said, looking startled.

'There's another one?'

'No, no, I was just a little surprised, that's all. I hadn't really considered her. I mean, thinking about what you were saying about Catriona, surely Baz is a little on the small side to struggle successfully with Penny?'

'Maybe there wasn't a struggle. Hey, what are you doing?' she demanded, outraged, while

Meredith took a cigarette out of a packet on the table that Lindsay had assumed belonged to Kirsten.

'I'm smoking,' Meredith said out of the side of her mouth as she lit up. 'I know, I know. But I need it right now. I can stop again when all of this is behind me. Don't make me feel any worse than I already do, Lindsay,' she pleaded with a crooked smile.

'I'd probably be doing the same thing in your shoes,' Lindsay said sadly. 'Anyway, as I was saying, if I could only pin down a motive, Baz would be my favourite suspect rather than Catriona.'

'Why so?' Meredith asked, her voice sharp.

'Something happened between her and Penny that changed their relationship. I don't know what it was yet, but it was obviously something pretty important. They went from being easy together, enjoying each other's company, to being stiff and formal on this last trip. There's no evidence of any similar rift with Catriona. Plus Baz is really uncomfortable talking about Penny.'

'Of course she is,' Meredith protested. 'She's in shock. She's grieving. They'd known each other a long time. They were friends.'

'Not any more they weren't. When Penny died, they were awkward and distant with each other. They had a row in the middle of the editorial floor about the very murder method that Penny used in the book.'

'What do you mean, a row?' Meredith demanded.

'Baz said it was a ridiculous, impractical way of killing someone, but Penny was adamant that it should stay in.'

'And you think Penny invited Baz round to give her a demonstration of how well it would work?' Meredith asked sarcastically. 'Use some logic here, Lindsay. That argument says to me that if Baz was going to kill Penny, this is the one method she absolutely wouldn't use because she believed it wouldn't work.'

'Unless it was a double bluff,' Lindsay countered. 'Because she backed down, Baz did, and she never backed down with her authors. Maybe she was thinking ahead and already setting up a defence for herself.'

'She's not like that,' Meredith protested angrily. 'I know this woman. If she was going to kill anyone, that's not the way she'd behave.'

There was a sudden silence. Lindsay looked at Meredith, a strange suspicion growing as she stared at her friend sullenly smoking. She could almost hear crackling inside her head as connections slipped into place. 'It was Baz,' she said slowly. 'Your fling. It was with Baz.'

'You're out of your mind,' Meredith blustered, too quick to convince.

'It was Baz, I'm right. You slept with Baz the last time you were in London. That's why you wouldn't tell Penny who you had your fling with.

Because it was Baz and it would poison their professional relationship.'

'This is bullshit,' Meredith tried. She had more chance of stopping a runaway train with one hand.

'But Baz felt awkward with Penny, knowing why you two had split up. And Penny, who as we both know, was very sensitive to atmosphere, twigged there was something wrong. And she put two and two together, and that's why she wanted to get into Baz's office that night. It was Baz, wasn't it?' Lindsay demanded, slamming her drink on the table. The remaining whisky seemed to rise and fall in a pillar, spilling only a few drops as it settled down.

'You've got no grounds for saying that,' Meredith said.

Seeing she was about to capitulate, Lindsay kept up the pressure, her voice rising inexorably. 'You dragged me over here to sort this mess out for you. I can understand you not levelling with your lawyer, because it looks bad that the prime suspect's last lover was not the victim but one of the other suspects. But you should have levelled with me, Meredith!'

Meredith ground out her cigarette and pushed herself away from the table, the chair legs shrieking a protest as she half turned away from Lindsay. 'It was a one-off, for both of us. Her lover was visiting her family in Ireland. We were both lonely and feeling sorry for ourselves. She was just as keen as I was that nobody should find out we'd slept together. She had a lot to lose, after all – her lover as well as her professional relationship with Penny. And that brought her a lot of kudos there at Monarch. She cares too much about what people think of her professionally to fuck around with that.'

'I think Penny guessed,' Lindsay said flatly. It was neither her place nor her inclination to condemn. Fidelity wasn't hard between her and Sophie. But she had no feelings of self-righteousness on that count. She knew how easy it was to slip out of that habit when a relationship was on a rocky road where reassurance had become a rarity.

'She didn't say anything directly to Baz,' Meredith said.

'Penny wouldn't have. Not without evidence. And that's what she was looking for in Baz's desk and her computer. She bribed one of the staff at Monarch to smuggle her in after everyone had gone home for the day. She was looking for some piece of evidence to confirm her suspicions. I think she found it.'

Meredith swung back to face Lindsay, reaching again for the cigarettes. 'Baz wouldn't have left anything incriminating in her desk.'

'No? What about e-mail?'

Meredith's grey eyes widened in shock. 'Ah, shit,' she said softly. 'Yes, there would be an e-mail trail a yard wide.'

'Still think Penny didn't know?'

Meredith sighed a stream of smoke. 'I guess it's possible she found out. Depends if Baz has her files well protected or not.'

Meredith's words snagged Lindsay's memory. She'd completely forgotten about Penny's missing computer. Clearly, investigating murder and jet lag didn't go together. 'Speaking of computer files, do you know where Penny's laptop is?'

'Her laptop? Isn't it in the flat?'

'No. The power lead is still plugged into the wall, but there's no computer. Do you happen to know if the police took it?'

Meredith shook her head. 'They haven't got it. I know because I got my solicitor to ask if they had taken anything of Penny's from the flat. I wanted to know if they had the answering-machine tape, right? And it turns out that all they took away was the answering-machine tape.' Meredith's expression was wry.

'This is weird. Not only is the computer itself missing, but there isn't a single floppy in the place, not even a box of blanks. And there isn't a single copy of the manuscript lying around either. What was in *Heart of Glass* that's so dynamite?'

'You think someone killed her to prevent the book being finished?' Meredith's tone reflected Lindsay's own incredulity that a novel could provoke such passion.

'I know it's bizarre, but it's looking a lot like it. The only way we're going to know for sure is if we can track down a copy, and I haven't the first clue how we're going to do that.'

They sat in silence until Meredith reached the end of her cigarette. 'She was always paranoid about back-ups. She always backed up on to floppies at the end of the working day. She kept one set in the house and another tucked into the back of her personal organiser. And the third set she took down to Half Moon Bay once a week,' she said slowly.

'What? She never left them with us.'

Meredith shook her head. 'I know. She used to drop them off with her best friend from high school, Carolyn Coogan. She and her husband, John, both teach math up in Pacifica. They live on the other side of the highway from you, about a mile south. She'd drive down one evening a week, or sometimes in the small hours of the morning. If she was late, she'd leave them in the mailbox.'

'Couldn't she just have posted them?'

'By US Mail? Puh-lease! Penny wouldn't trust her disks to them, but she wanted a set somewhere they'd be safe if the house burned down, and where she could have easy access to them if it became necessary. So she'd bring them down herself.'

'That explains why she used to drop in unannounced so often. She always said she'd just come down for a walk by the ocean. She'd borrow the dog and off they'd go, then she'd sit down for a beer afterwards,' Lindsay said. 'Obviously she can't have been doing that while she was over here. Do you think she'd have made alternative arrangements in England? Maybe left the disks with somebody she knew in London?'

Meredith shrugged. 'It's possible. I'd say it's more than likely. But I don't know how we find out.'

'If need be, we go through every single person in her address book,' Lindsay said grimly.

'Oh, great,' Meredith sighed. 'Lindsay, I think you're going to have to handle that one by yourself. I'm not ready to talk to all those people yet.'

'Well, let's hope it doesn't come to that. Oh, one other thing.'

'What?'

'This murder by exploding beer bottle. It's really off the wall. Where did she get the idea for that?'

'You ever notice her scar? On her left forearm, about two inches long? Well, years ago, before she knew me or you guys, she was on holiday in Austria and it was a real hot summer like this one. She had some bottles of this wheat beer sitting on the kitchen table, waiting to go into the fridge once there was room for them. She accidentally knocked against the table, the bottles rocked back and forth, and one of them exploded. She said it was like a bomb going off. Glass everywhere. And one chunk of glass embedded itself in her arm. I guess she should have had the cut stitched, but she didn't want to go to hospital in a strange country, so her girlfriend closed it with surgical tape. That's why she had such a noticeable scar. She always said one day she was going to use it in a book.'

'And when she did, it looks like it killed her.'

Meredith looked at Lindsay while she automatically lit a third cigarette. 'So what are we going to do about it?'

14

Sophie Hartley had just settled her patient on the examining table when the summons came. Rita Hernandez was an illegal immigrant who had escaped from El Salvador in search of the American dream. Instead, she'd ended up working a street corner in the Mission with a pimp who thought wearing a condom was a denial of machismo. Now she was HIV-positive and six months pregnant and she wasn't convinced that the Grafton Clinic was a safe place to be. Sophie had finally persuaded her she wasn't going to turn her in to the authorities, so a nurse telling Sophie she had a transatlantic call was the last thing she needed right then. '*Momento, por favor, señorita,*' she said in her English-accented Spanish, giving Rita a calming pat on the ankle. 'Stay with her, would you?' she asked the nurse, then headed for the reception area.

'Line two,' the receptionist mouthed at her between responding to waiting patients.

Sophie picked up the phone. 'This had better be good,' she said impatiently.

'I love you too,' the familiar voice said. 'Sorry to hit you at work, but it's the time difference. I hoped I could pitch you into doing me a favour this evening when you get off work, then you'd be able to call me back in the morning our time with the results.'

'What kind of a favour?' Sophie said guardedly, running a hand through her hair in the familiar gesture of affectionate frustration that Lindsay tended to produce in her.

'Penny was so paranoid she used to drive down to Half Moon Bay every week with a spare set of back-up disks. She used to leave them with . . .'

'Carolyn Coogan, her best friend from high school,' Sophie finished for her. 'They live on Palisades Drive.'

'How did you know that?' Lindsay demanded.

'There are a lot of miles of shore around the Bay Area. I once asked Penny if she had some sentimental attachment to Half Moon Bay, given how often she used to drop in on us. She said there was nothing sentimental about it, purely practical.'

'You never told me,' Lindsay said.

'Just one of my hundreds of dark secrets,' Sophie teased. 'You want me to go and see Carolyn?'

'Penny's laptop has gone missing. There are no back-up disks anywhere in the flat, and nobody's got a copy of her manuscript. I was thinking maybe she'd stashed another set somewhere, with somebody like Carolyn. And if so, whether she mentioned it to her. I know it's a long shot, but it would save me wasting tomorrow trying to track down everybody Penny knew over here. I'd really appreciate it,' Lindsay added, injecting a dose of pathos into her voice.

'I'll see what I can do,' Sophie said repressively.

'So you won't want to know who Meredith had her fling with,' Lindsay said tantalisingly.

Sophie groaned. 'Make it quick. I have a patient waiting.'

'Baz Burton. Penny's editor.'

'No!'

'Would I lie to you?'

'Not and live. I want chapter and verse on this, Lindsay, but not now. Call me tomorrow, Okay? Love you.'

'Love you too,' Lindsay said to dead air.

Radio stations all smelt the same, Lindsay had realised in recent years. It didn't matter how old or new the studios were. A blind person who had once sampled the ambience would have it indelibly stamped in their olfactory banks for ever. It was an indefinable smell: a history of cigarette smoke now abolished but present like a ghost; a faint whiff of nervous sweat, the decaying molecules of the pheromones still lingering; the unmistakable tang produced by hot coffee in plastic or polystyrene; and dust. The office where Kirsten was working had the radio smell, even though it was in a sixties building behind Broadcasting House which seemed to be occupied almost entirely by teenagers.

Lindsay was sitting on the tiled window-sill, feet on a chair, head tilted back and hanging out of the metal window-frame in a vain attempt to get some air in her lungs that hadn't already been breathed by half the population of London. Kirsten sat at a cluttered desk swigging some designer fruit drink from the bottle while sweat ran down either side of her nose as she talked into the phone. '. . . that's right, you remember! Well, I'm sort of looking at an idea that might make a piece for one of the media magazine programmes . . . Yeah, that's the sort of thing. I was wondering, you know. We still keep hearing about authors getting swag bags of money – Jeffrey Archer getting millions for his backlist, Martin Amis getting half a mill for a two-book deal. Plus, with the end of the Net Book Agreement, what seems to be happening is that bottom of the list authors, the unpromotables, they're getting the bullet, leaving the market-place to the ones who can reasonably claim to be worth half-decent advances, yeah?' Kirsten paused in her flow, obviously listening to the voice on the other end. It was the third call she'd made so far.

At breakfast, Lindsay had moved in for the kill.

She'd tried to talk to Sophie, but she'd only reached their answering machine, which informed her that Sophie had been called in to an emergency and that Lindsay should ring her around six in the morning, California time. Rather than kick her heels until early afternoon, she'd hit on the bright idea of using Kirsten's contacts to dig up background on Catriona Polson. She'd been perfectly prepared to do the research herself, but Kirsten was adamant that she wanted to help out. Lindsay wasn't sure if it was because she'd had the chance to get to know Meredith the previous evening, or because Helen had warned her not to let Lindsay close enough to her contacts to upset them. Either way, it relieved her of the tension of telling lies convincingly to strangers. Looking at Kirsten grafting away there, she wasn't sorry she'd been forced to abdicate the responsibility.

'Yeah, right,' Kirsten resumed, blowing out a cloud of smoke from the forbidden cigarette she'd just lit. 'Anyway, it seemed to me that the people who must really be coining it in off of this are not the authors, who after all, let's face it, have probably spent years in abject penury to write that one special book. And it's not even the publishers, given the balancing act they're all playing at just now with the ending of the Net Book Agreement and getting to grips with electronic publishing. No, the people who must really be raking it in are the agents . . .' Kirsten made a face, casting her eyes upward and holding the phone away from her ear so Lindsay could hear the yakkety-yak coming from the receiver.

'Yeah, yeah, yeah, Clive, but think about it for a minute. All their crap authors get dispublished . . . yeah, I said dispublished, it's the new Americanism for what happens when your publisher tells you to get a life that doesn't include book signings. So you've got these literary agencies, right, with all their dead weight dropping off their client lists, and let's not forget that these are the authors who take up a disproportionate amount of time compared to the actual cash they bring in. So what they're left with . . .' Kirsten leaned back in her chair and mopped her face with a crumpled tissue.

'That's *exactly* what I'm saying. So you get someone like Catriona Polson coming along and not only swallowing up an old, established firm like Paul Firestone but also moving into the kind of naff but flash offices that Saatchi and Saatchi wouldn't sniff at. So I thought we could maybe look at these super-agents, and of course, I thought, Clive's the man. So take somebody like Catriona Polson. How did she go from a three-woman operation in Holborn to head honcho of Polson and Firestone?' Kirsten listened for a moment, then abruptly tipped forward and started scribbling on a scratch pad by the phone, dumping her cigarette in the flower vase on the desk. Now Lindsay knew how the carnations had died. She watched Kirsten take notes, interjecting the occasional, 'Yeah,' or, 'Well, *there's* a surprise.' In spite of the sweat and the pressure, she couldn't help feeling a faint pang of nostalgia for the journalistic trade she'd left behind her. Moments like this, when the adrenalin was pumping and there was the unmistakable sense of a hunch paying off, were simply not available in teaching.

Eventually, Kirsten's writing hand started to slow and she shifted in her seat, reaching into her desk drawer for another cigarette. 'Clive, I owe you one,' she sighed through a cloud of smoke, then replaced the handset. Kirsten grinned up at Lindsay, who found herself wondering just how it was that Helen managed to attract stunning women who also possessed brains and a sense of humour. Sophie and Kirsten were the two who had lasted longest, but they were far from the only ones. 'Bingo,' Kirsten growled happily.

'You going to tell me or do I have to hang you out of the window by the ankles and threaten to drop you?' Lindsay asked, sliding off the window-sill and into the chair.

'Sounds like fun, but I haven't got time for all that sophisticated foreplay,' Kirsten said. 'I'll cut to the chase.'

'I was right, then? There is something dodgy at Polson and Firestone?'

'Well, not dodgy so much as stretched. When she "discovered" Penny, she was literally a one-woman show. It was Penny's success that created her business and brought other writers beating a path to her door. Her business grew and she took on a couple of assistants, but she needed to expand, and the lesson everybody learned in the eighties was that the quickest way to do that was to swallow somebody else, preferably somebody bigger than you.'

'The reverse takeover?'

'Sort of. Only in this case, Catriona Polson was the company that was making the money. The Firestone Agency was struggling, to be honest. They had quite a few talented people on the staff, but Paul Firestone had lost his edge and morale was crap. They lost a couple of their bigger names and soon as they started to slide, Catriona pounced. According to my buddy Clive, who works for *Bookselling News*, Paul Firestone hadn't entirely lost his marbles. He negotiated a deal on the sale of his agency that concluded with a balloon payment after three years, the amount to be dependent on Polson and Firestone's turnover. On a sliding scale that increased geometrically once profits hit a certain target.' Kirsten paused expectantly.

'Wasn't that kind of betting against her own success?' Lindsay asked.

'Yes and no,' Kirsten said. 'Under normal circumstances, no literary agency would hope to generate the kind of profits in a single year that would have caused problems for Polson.'

Lindsay grinned. 'Why do I have the feeling you're about to outline a set of circumstances so far off the normal curve that our instruments have no way of measuring it?'

'Because you're psychic?'

'It's not a phenomenon I'm noted for. So what were these exceptional circumstances?'

Kirsten leaned back in her chair and stared up at the ceiling. 'After Martin Amis got his half-million-pound advance, literary novelists woke up to the fact that they might have a bit of clout. When Milos Petroviĉ won last year's Booker Prize, he decided that he more than deserved what Martin had already achieved, but his current agent couldn't get the deal up above £350,000. Meanwhile, Polson's personal assistant was bonking a chap called Jeremy Dunstan, who's head honcho of a new literary imprint that one of the populist houses is trying to get off the ground. And Polson hears pillow talk that Jeremy is about to go out with a wallet full of dosh to pull in a couple of prime catches so that agents and authors will get their heads round the idea that his list is serious business, not some loss leader to make his company look like they're not dragging their knuckles on the bottom of the cave. With me so far?' she asked, tipping herself forward to extinguish her cigarette.

'Fascinated,' Lindsay said, heavy on the irony. 'I had no idea the world of gentlemen publishers had spun into the orbit of the eighties. So what happened next? As if I couldn't guess.'

'Polson poached Petroviĉ and got him half a million to head up Jeremy's list. His previous agent was chewing the carpet, but there was nothing he could do. Petroviĉ paid him the commission on the £350,000 he'd negotiated already, as per his contract, and Polson got the reputation. And in this business, where reputation goes, authors follow, sure as seagulls follow the sardine boat. The end result being that Polson had to pay Paul Firestone a massive chunk of dosh about three months ago and now her cash flow is plunging through the floor. The business owes money to its landlord, its authors, and Polson's taken out a second mortgage on her house.' Kirsten smiled sweetly. 'Looks like the Darkliners film deal was her lifebelt.'

Lindsay stood up and wiped the sweat from her upper lip. 'Does Helen know about your killer instinct?'

Kirsten grinned like a barracuda. 'What else do you think she sees in me? I'm just glad I could help you out. You're a bit of a legend in our house, you know. Radical feminism's answer to Miss Marple.'

'I wish,' Lindsay said wryly. 'If I was ever radical, it's ancient history now. If I'm the answer, somebody's asking the wrong question.'

The climb to Catriona Polson's office hadn't got any easier since Lindsay had last scaled the heights. Nor had the stairwell become any more appealing. It was hardly surprising, given what she now knew about the agent's finances. If you were looking at losing the roof over your head, paying a cleaner wasn't going to be high on the list of priorities.

The receptionist hadn't become any more welcoming, either. 'You can't see Ms Polson without an appointment,' she announced as soon as recognition sparked in her eyes.

'That what you say to Milos Petroviĉ, is it?' Lindsay said conversationally.

'Anyway, you lied about not being a journalist,' the receptionist continued.

Lindsay shrugged. 'I never said I wasn't a journalist. You assumed I wasn't. However, if you'd looked at that card with half a brain, you'd have seen it was at least eight years out of date. Nation Newspapers moved to Docklands back in '88. And London phone numbers have changed a bit since then, too.'

'She won't see you, you know. There's no point in me even trying.'

Lindsay had always hated gatekeepers who, powerless in their own right, jealously guarded access to the source. If there was one thing she valued about her years as a journalist, it was the selection of methods it had shown her to get past the dragons at the gates. Taking out her notebook, she scribbled, 'Give me one good reason why I shouldn't tell the police about the Darkliners film deal. V. I. Warshawski'. She tore the page off, folded it half and said, 'I think you might find that will change her mind. And don't even think about not showing it to Ms Polson. I can guarantee that that would seriously upset her.' She placed the note on the receptionist's keyboard.

She glowered at Lindsay, then picked up the paper and dialled a number on her switchboard. Picking up the handset as the number rang out, she said, 'Trish, there's a note here for Catriona. Can you come and get it? I can't leave reception right now.' She gave Lindsay a malicious little smirk.

'I'm really not going to steal the art,' Lindsay said, settling into one of the enveloping leather sofas. She leaned back and gazed into the middle distance, affecting not to notice the dumpy gopher who emerged from the tall office door, snatched up the note and disappeared again. Within five minutes, the gopher returned and muttered something to the receptionist, who scowled, gestured with a pen and said, 'That's her.'

The other woman came over and said, 'Catriona will see you now.'

As she followed, Lindsay winked at her antagonist. 'Aren't you glad we didn't take a bet on it?' she asked, enjoying the pink fury of the receptionist's face.

Lindsay was escorted to the same conference room and left to her own devices for the best part of ten minutes. When Catriona Polson finally entered, she found Lindsay sitting staring at the portrait of Penny Varnavides. 'I can't get used to the idea of not seeing her again,' Polson said.

'Really? Don't you worry she might come back to haunt you once Galaxy Pictures have fucked over her books?' Lindsay said, hoping she sounded as offensive as she intended.

'I don't think either of those things is going to happen,' the agent said icily, folding her long body into one of the chairs. 'Look, I really don't want to get into a ruck with you. The only reason I agreed to see you was in the hope that we could strike me off your ridiculous suspect list for good and all. I had no motive for Penny Varnavides' death. Yes, it would have been a blow if she had turned down what is a very attractive TV deal, but it would have been a long way from the end of the world.'

Lindsay snorted with a mockery of laughter. 'Oh, yeah? When your company's so strapped for cash you've had to take out a second mortgage on your home?'

Polson tilted her head on one side. 'You really have done your homework, haven't you? And two weeks ago, you're right, the thought of losing the Darkliners TV deal would have rendered me near suicidal, if not homicidal. And then a deal we thought was dead rose from the grave. A Hollywood producer called to say they'd finally got the green light for a film adaptation of someone else's work. And that means even more in financial terms to this agency than the Varnavides deal.'

Lindsay's stomach seemed to hollow as the agent's words sank in. 'You expect me to believe that?' she tried, knowing it was a last-gasp bluff.

'I've got a file of signed contracts and faxes that demonstrate the truth of what I'm saying,' she said, not unsympathetically. 'I'm not prepared to show you, since I have no conviction that you would treat it confidentially. But I'm perfectly prepared to show it to the police, should you be inclined to make yourself look foolish by involving them.'

Lindsay took a deep breath and stood up. 'I seem to have wasted your time as well as my own,' she said, unable to keep an edge of bitterness out of her voice.

Polson gave her a look of shrewd appraisal. 'I wouldn't beat yourself up too much. I know you blame me for telling the police about Meredith, but I was upset. I don't know Meredith very well, and it seemed to me she had a motive. I applaud what you're trying to do and if I can help, I will. I'm sorry I was so unhelpful before.'

If she'd wanted to make Lindsay feel worse, she couldn't have found a better way to do it. 'Mmm,' she mumbled, looking everywhere but at Penny's picture or her agent. 'Okay.'

'There are more motives than money,' Catriona said. 'There's reputation for a start. Maybe *Heart of Glass* trashed somebody who lives by their name.'

Lindsay found a self-pitying smile from somewhere. 'Like an agent, you mean?'

'It's about an editor.'

15

Back on the street in the suffocating late morning heat, Lindsay walked through the sweating tourist crowds towards Leicester Square, pondering Catriona Polson's final suggestion. Whatever Meredith felt about Baz, she was going to have to have another confrontation with the editor. But Lindsay needed all the ammunition she could lay her hands on before then, and since *Heart of Glass* might contain some of the answers, it seemed sensible to wait until she'd spoken to Sophie and discovered whether there were any extant copies that the killer hadn't taken.

Sensible had never been her strong suit, but for once she was able to possess her soul in patience, since she had something else on her mind that was sufficiently interesting to occupy her. She emerged into Leicester Square and waited for an empty phone box. The one she ended up in smelt of sour milk and strong after-shave, its windows papered with postcards advertising the services of an assortment of prostitutes. Lindsay found it as sexually alluring as the inspection pit of a garage. Trying to ignore the pathetic faces whose photographs stared down at her in a parody of desire from several of the cards, she called Helen. 'I've got an idea,' she said. 'Can you meet me for lunch?'

'I can't really go out, I've got a million and six things to do and I'm expecting a phone call from New York that I don't want to miss. Why don't you come here?' Helen said. 'Those two gobshites are out filming today, so you won't have any embarrassing encounters. I'll order in some sandwiches and we can have a picnic in my office, okay?'

'Perfect,' Lindsay said. 'See you around one.'

Her next call was to Eleanor Purdey, a fellow alumna of her Oxford college. Although they'd both read English, Ellie had abandoned literature for the law, joining a large commercial firm just as the eighties had started to boom. Now she was a full equity partner, a profitable role since her company had avoided the worst excesses of the recession by moving neatly into rescue packages for companies facing financial and fiscal disaster. They'd never been close at university, but when they'd met a few years later at a party Lindsay had attended with her barrister lover, they'd discovered they were both gay. Coupled with their St Mary's connection, it had been enough to forge a bond. In spite of their widely differing political perspectives, Lindsay and Ellie had always stayed in touch. In Lindsay's journalist days, Ellie had been a valuable insider contact. For Ellie, Lindsay suspected, she had provided a tad of street cred in a lesbian scene where establishment professionals like Ellie were mistrusted and often excluded.

Once she'd made it past Ellie's secretary and they'd exchanged greetings and agreed to meet for a drink in a day or two, Lindsay got straight to the point. She outlined an idea that had dawned on her as a possible answer to Helen's problems and was gratified to hear Ellie confirm what she'd thought to be the case. Not only that, but after a couple of minutes during which Lindsay could hear the tapping of her computer keys, Ellie was able to cite cases that would give Lindsay details of how to set up her little sting. 'A couple of these cases got quite extensive coverage in the press,' she added. 'Not the tabloids, but the *Telegraph* and the *Financial Times*. The *Economist* ran something as well, I seem to remember. If you can get Internet access, you can look it all up for yourself.' She gave Lindsay the necessary details, which she scribbled down in her notebook.

'I owe you one,' Lindsay said, after she'd double-checked she'd got all the dots and slashes in the right places on the Internet addresses Ellie had provided.

'And not for the first time. Give my love to Sophie when you speak to her.'

'Will do. Oh, and Ellie? Will you be at home this evening?'

Ellie made no attempt to hide her sigh. 'Exploit-a-friend not done enough for one day?'

'Sorry, but no. I might need some practical assistance if what I'm planning comes off. Just by phone . . .'

'I'll be here till around eight, then I'm going straight home to sit on my balcony with a very sexy futures trader and an ice-cold bottle of Chardonnay. So you can take your chances,' Ellie said, sounding amused.

Armed with the information from Ellie, Lindsay headed back across the square towards Charing Cross Road, stopping at a computer supplies shop to buy a few blank floppies. She cut through side streets until she found Cyberia, the Internet café she had read about but never visited before. A few pounds bought her an hour's access to cyberspace and an icy Diet Coke, and she settled down at one of the table-top terminals to check out the sources Ellie had suggested to her.

It didn't take long to unravel the web that took her to the heart of the information she needed, since America was still only waking up and there wasn't too much traffic on the Net. Her initial idea had come from a distant memory she'd dredged up of a court case she'd heard referred to on the BBC World Service. With Ellie's guidance and a little manipulation, she could see how it might be possible to use the bare bones of the case to construct a sting that would cut the feet from under Stella and Guy far more effectively than the Obscene Publications Squad could ever have managed.

She downloaded the relevant files on to her blank disks and closed down her terminal with twenty minutes to spare, which she passed on to a grateful youth who'd been hanging around looking wistfully at her and her fellow netheads. A quick glance at her watch told her she'd better get a move on, so she walked back to Leicester Square tube and endured the stifling and stale wind of the Northern Line tunnels until a train groaned into the station to jolt her to Camden Town.

Helen closed the door of her office behind Lindsay, who caught the look of surprise on her secretary's face. 'It's not that I don't trust her,' Helen said defensively, seeing Lindsay's raised eyebrows. 'It's just that I don't actually trust anybody in here as of last night. Isn't that the pits? As if it's not bad enough that they've done what they've done, they've got me so paranoid I think everybody's in it with them. Toerags.' As she spoke, she unwrapped a series of soft ciabatta rolls with a variety of fillings. They looked like a row of mismatched children's slippers arranged on a plate.

'Serious sandwiches,' Lindsay commented, settling herself in the canvas director's chair facing Helen.

'They probably go through the books as stationery supplies,' Helen said sourly, opening a small executive fridge and taking out a couple of bottles of alcoholic lemonade and uncapping them. 'So what's new?'

'I had this idea of how we can screw Stella and Guy,' Lindsay said simply. A wide grin split Helen's face. 'Now I remember why I like you so much,' she said.

'What you do here at Watergaw, you work quite closely with ethnic minority groups, am I right?'

'That's supposed to be our brief, yeah. Couldn't you tell from the women in those delightful films we saw last night?' Helen asked savagely, grabbing a sandwich and biting into it as if it were Stella's head she was snapping off.

'So would I be right in thinking that means you film abroad from time to time?'

Helen nodded, managing to look puzzled even with a mouthful of sandwich.

'Is there anywhere that Guy and Stella have been on a joint project, relatively recently?'

Helen swallowed, her brow furrowing. 'The most recent trip they did was for a series of Channel Four documentaries. We had this idea of going back with immigrants from the subcontinent to the villages they left thirty years ago. We wanted to see how the villages had changed, and we thought it would be interesting to do it through the eyes of the villagers who had stayed and those who had left. *Thirty/Three,* I called it. It was my idea, but I couldn't fit the filming timetable in with other stuff I already had booked in. It's always the same in this game, feast or famine. I've either got three projects all demanding my attention or else I'm running around like a headless chicken doing a rain dance, trying to raise funding from anywhere to make the next film.'

'So Guy and Stella had to make the films for *Thirty/Three* without you?'

'That's right. Why d'you want to know? Are you on to something?'

'In a minute. Which country were they in?' Lindsay asked through a mouthful of cream cheese and sun-dried tomatoes.

'India, Pakistan and Bangladesh. We made one film in each of the three of them,' Helen explained. 'We took three families back, original immigrants and their kids, so that we could compare and contrast the achievements and expectations of both groups, as well as the straightforward lifestyle stuff. It wasn't a particularly cheap or easy set of films to make. It's never simple when you're juggling that many people with their own separate agendas, but they got some good stuff.'

'Were you involved in the project at all after the early stages?' Lindsay asked.

'Are you kidding? I was in the middle of making a six-half-hour drama series for children's

TV about racist bullying. I hardly had enough brain cells to spare for going to the toilet. I just told them to bugger off and come back with enough film for three forty-minute slots.'

'Perfect,' Lindsay breathed.

'Linds, I know I can be a bit slow sometimes, but I'm obviously missing something here. Why does it matter where Stella and Guy were filming and whether I was there or not?'

'Kickbacks,' Lindsay said.

Helen managed to look both worried and suspicious. 'What about kickbacks?'

'You know and I know that to operate any kind of business in certain developing countries, you need to pay nearly as much in backhanders as you do in legitimate fees.'

'More sometimes,' Helen interrupted gloomily. 'If I live to be a hundred, I will never ever film in Sierra Leone again. But I don't see what that's got to do with stitching up that pair of gobshites.'

'You will, Oscar, you will. Okay, so we've got a scenario where Guy and Stella are off on their Asian tour, handing out kickbacks right, left and centre. Which, of course, is against the law over here and therefore not a legitimate company expense.'

'Yeah, but hang on a minute,' Helen protested. 'Every company that works in places like that has to pay kickbacks and bribes. You disguise it in the books. You make it look like something else. Guy told me once the accounts were done on the Asian trip, it would all look kosher. Just like everything we've ever done abroad in the past. You're not going to get him for paying kickbacks.'

'I know that,' Lindsay said, calmly finishing her sandwich and mopping her lips with a paper napkin. Then she beamed at Helen. 'What we *are* going to nail them for is defrauding the VAT and the Inland Revenue.'

For a moment, Helen was speechless. But only for a moment. 'Do what?' she said weakly.

'Defrauding the VAT and the tax. If you disguise the kickbacks and bribes as something else in the books, you're acting fraudulently. Inevitably, you're making false declarations to the Inland Revenue and to Customs and Excise. It doesn't matter that everybody does it – when it's reported to them, they take action all the same. Guy and Stella are not going to know what hit them. You can mess with the law, but you never mess with the VATman and the taxman. Or woman. When I was a freelance, I remember one of the first things my accountant ever told me was never get clever with the VAT. "Take out a second mortgage if you have to," he told me, "but always pay the VATman."'

'You're out of your mind,' Helen said weakly.

'No, I'm not. Customs and Excise have more powers than the police. They can kick your door down in the middle of the night without a warrant. They can kick your mother's door down in the middle of the night without a warrant if they have reasonable grounds for suspecting you've hidden your second set of books in her linen cupboard. They can freeze your bank accounts and make you a social leper faster than appearing on a daytime game show can.'

'I know all that,' Helen interrupted. 'But you seem to be forgetting something here. I'm one of the partners in this company. They go down, I go down.'

Lindsay shook her head. 'That's the beauty of it.' She smiled. 'Trust me. What time is this place empty tonight?'

Helen shook her head. 'I've no idea. Stella and Guy'll be coming back here after they've done their filming and they'll probably hang around to take a look at what they've got. There's no knowing how late they'll be working. Whatever dirty deeds you've got up your sleeve, do they have to be done at night?'

Lindsay grimaced. 'It'd be easier if I can get a straight run of a few hours when I can be sure there won't be anyone else around.'

'Will it wait until tomorrow? Only, they've got a night shoot and there's no way they'll be back here before two or three in the morning. There'll only be me here after about half past six.'

Lindsay winked. 'Let's make it seven tomorrow, then.'

'But . . .' Helen said.

'Like I said, trust me. By this time the day after

tomorrow, they'll be done up like a pair of kippers and you'll be smelling of roses.'

'Oh, yeah?' Helen said dubiously.

'Yeah. One thing I will need is superuser clearance for your computer network. Can you get that for me? Your systems manager should be able to give you the codes, no trouble.'

'Superuser?'

'The systems manager will know what you mean, honestly. Now, can I use your phone? I have to speak to my stitching-up consultant. Oh, yeah, and then I need to speak to Sophie. If your phone bill will stand it.'

'She was a creature of habit,' Sophie said. 'Just because she couldn't get round to Half Moon Bay didn't mean she felt she had to change her usual routine.'

Lindsay leaned back in Stella's executive leather desk chair, a sharp contrast with Helen's rather battered cloth seat. Helen had shunted her down the corridor because her New York call had come through just as Lindsay had finished making arrangements with Ellie to postpone her consultation till the following evening. Now Lindsay had privacy for her call to Sophie. 'I can't believe she trusted the post,' Lindsay said. 'She wouldn't even trust them to deliver a package from San Francisco. That's why she used to bring the back-ups down to Half Moon Bay in person, according to Meredith.'

'She didn't. But she did trust courier service,' Sophie said.

Lindsay gave a low whistle. 'She wasn't afraid to spend her money, was she? Transatlantic courier, eh?'

'In fairness, she didn't go for the expensive overnight service. She just sent them by regular courier, five or six days, especially if the weekend got in the way.'

'So when did the last lot arrive?' Lindsay asked eagerly.

'Six days ago.'

'Have you got them?' Lindsay demanded.

'I managed to persuade Carolyn to let me make copies of them,' Sophie told her. 'I also took copies of the previous disks Penny had sent since she arrived in England. The first disk has *Heart of Glass* from the beginning to Chapter 12, the second from the beginning to Chapter 15 and the last one goes up to Chapter 18. There seem to be about twelve pages to a chapter. But bear in mind, these chapters must have been completed about a week before Penny died. They may not be current enough to be any help to your investigation,' Sophie cautioned.

'Have you looked at them?'

'I spent most of the night with a very awkward delivery,' Sophie protested.

'I'm sorry, I'm sorry, I'm just a bit keyed up over this,' Lindsay apologised. 'What's the best way for you to get them to me? Express courier?'

Sophie chuckled. 'You're still a Luddite at heart,

aren't you? I thought you were supposed to have embraced the new technology now?'

'Eh?'

'If you pick up your e-mail, you'll find them all there. In the few odd moments of calm during the night, I put the files into a format I could transmit, and sent you a bunch of massive e-mails.'

'Hellfire!' Lindsay exclaimed. 'You are a fucking genius, Doc! Oh, God, now I've got to get right across town to Helen's, I don't have my laptop with me and she's got a different network provider for her Internet connection and I don't know how to use the software and I've got to read up on all the stuff Ellie pointed me at . . .' She stopped gibbering and subsided into thought.

'Carolyn reckoned there could be another delivery in the pipeline, if Penny was sticking to her usual weekly cycle. She was due to have sent another disk off the day she was killed,' Sophie said.

'Yeah, yeah,' Lindsay said, too distracted to take in what Sophie was saying. 'That's terrific. Soph, you're the berries. The absolute berries. Listen, I'm going to have to run. I've got to pick up my laptop and start ploughing through this stuff, plus Helen's got a hell of a situation going on here that I'm trying to help her out with, so I'm going to have to steam off. I'll call you, okay? I love you.'

'I love you too. Take care,' Sophie said. But she was already speaking to herself.

16

Lindsay rubbed her eyes and drew the curtain a few inches further across her bedroom window to keep the sun at a distance. In vain she'd searched for a lead that would connect her computer to Helen's printer, so instead of printing out the long files of text that Sophie had sent her so she could read them on paper, she was forced to struggle with a laptop screen that was perfectly adequate for normal use, but never meant for long hours of close scrutiny.

It wasn't just having to read the novel on screen that was causing her problems. If she'd been able to print out the three versions of the book she would have been able to lay them alongside each other and make a page-by-page comparison. But even with the split-screen facility her word-processing software allowed, she could only compare two versions at a time. She had decided to work through it chapter by chapter, first comparing the original version with the second, then the second with the third.

It was heavy going, even with the work of a writer as talented as Penny Varnavides had undoubtedly been. Lindsay, who had read most of the Darkliners series, at first out of loyalty and later pleasure, was astonished by the maturity and depth of the writing. If Penny had had work of this calibre in her, it was no wonder she was frustrated by the scope of teenage fantasy. The only marvel was that it had taken her so long to develop the confidence to break out of the comfort zone and stretch herself.

Lindsay wriggled around, trying to find a more comfortable position on the bed. She knew she was welcome to set herself up either at the kitchen table or in Helen and Kirsten's home office, but she wanted neither to be in their way when they got home nor to have the distraction of their inevitable interest. So she had holed up in her room with a bunch of grapes from a stall by the tube station and a six-pack of Rolling Rock. The beers were cooling in a basin filled with the bag of ice she'd bought at the small supermarket at the corner of Helen's road. After five hours of staring into the screen, she was starting to wonder if she should be applying the ice to her gritty eyes.

It wasn't as if she was coming up with anything that pointed the finger of suspicion at anyone she knew about. *Heart of Glass* was the terrifying story of two serial killers, one deliberate, the other accidental. The central character was a mystery novelist who realised that every time he created a particular murderous scenario, it was reflected almost immediately in real life. As an experiment, he deliberately wrote a book where his despised older brother, thinly disguised, died in a murder made to look like a freak accident with an exploding beer bottle. Just as Penny herself had died. Within weeks, his brother was dead, by almost identical means.

With this gruesome proof of his gift, the writer set about killing off everyone he had ever disliked. Judging from Penny's novel, he'd devoted a lot of energy over the years to hatred. In parallel with his remote-controlled homicidal spree ran the story of a surgeon who had developed his surgical skills in the bedrooms of his victims as efficiently as he had in the operating theatre. He had been killing successfully for years, escaping detection by never murdering in the same city twice. An international serial killer, he'd earned frequent flyer miles for murder.

The connection between the two men was the surgeon's wife, who was also the writer's editor. The final ingredient in the heady stew was the wife's lover, a charismatic congressman about to mount a presidential campaign.

Knowing that Penny used elements of her friends, acquaintances and professional contacts in the construction of her characters, Lindsay tried to match the characters in the book to people she knew in Penny's life, to see if any clues lay there.

But Penny was too skilled in her craft to have left an obvious trail leading back to her immediate circle. Even where parallels seemed possible, there were no correlations that struck Lindsay. The editor was nothing like Baz, being a weak character swept along by events, unable to control her life. Nothing like the woman Meredith had described, a woman capable of seizing the opportunity for infidelity, then taking steps to make certain it didn't disrupt the relationship at the heart of her professional life.

There didn't even seem to be any signposts in the changes Penny had made between the drafts. There was a certain amount of linguistic tinkering, some reorganisation of material, rearranging the order in which certain sections appeared. But there was no structural rewriting that went to the heart of the book. However Penny had fiddled superficially, her central storyline had driven forward with the impetus of an arrow flying from a bow.

By the time she had reached the end of the final chapter, it was after midnight and Lindsay was no nearer an answer. Whatever Penny's killer had feared from the pages of *Heart of Glass*, it was far too subtle to strike her.

'You're never going to believe this,' Sophie said, the excitement in her voice travelling easily across ocean and continent.

'Mmm,' Lindsay grunted, forcing her eyebrows

upwards in a vain attempt to get her eyes to stay open. It was quarter past seven in the morning, but it felt like the middle of the night. Seeing her plight, Kirsten thrust a mug of pitch-coloured coffee in front of her. Lindsay took a scalding sip and felt synapses snap to attention all through her brain. 'Believe what?' she asked, sounding like a reasonable approximation of a human being.

'Penny's latest draft. *Heart of Glass*. The package arrived by courier today and Carolyn called me right away, at work. She knew you'd want to see it. Penny actually sent it the day she died. Three new chapters plus the very last revisions she ever made to the text.' There seemed to be an exclamation mark hanging in the air at the end of each of Sophie's sentences.

'And?'

'I skimmed it. I knew you'd want chapter and verse on any substantial changes as soon as possible.'

'I didn't realise you'd read the earlier drafts,' Lindsay muttered.

'I dipped in and out of it whenever I could get a spare moment,' Sophie said. 'Darling, she'd made a lot of changes in this draft. The surgeon's wife – the editor? She's had a complete personality change. You know how she was passive and weak in the first drafts? Well, she's not any more. She's been turned into a strong, scheming bitch. A real sexual adventurer. Now it's her who seduces the politician, not the other way round. And it's clear she's not a victim any more. In fact, it looks like Penny was shaping up to turning her into a killer – I think the twist she was aiming for is that the novelist isn't really capable of causing death by remote control, but his editor goes out and makes his books come true, partly as a publicity stunt and partly because she enjoys it.'

By now thoroughly awake, Lindsay drew her breath in sharply. 'Now that's what I call a significant change. Tell me, Soph. Has Penny changed the physical description of the wife at all?'

'Funny you should say that,' Sophie said. 'In the first draft, she's described as slightly built with mousy blonde hair, pale skin.'

'Human wallpaper,' Lindsay interjected. The coffee was starting to do its stuff.

'Right. But the description this time is quite different. Hang on, I printed it out . . . "Her hair was hennaed a dark, glossy auburn, cut like Mia Farrow's in her waif period. It contrasted with dark eyebrows and eyes the colour of Hershey kisses, and served to emphasise chubby cheeks that reminded Carradine of a squirrel storing a lucky find of nuts for later. Somehow, he wouldn't have been surprised to discover her body pierced in places that would make most women wince."'

'King hell,' Lindsay said.

'I take it that means something to you?' Sophie asked.

'With a description like that, you could pick

Baz Burton out of any line-up,' Lindsay said. 'You think there's any doubt that Penny knew about Baz and Meredith's night of passion?'

Sophie chuckled at Lindsay's ironic tone. 'Is the Pope a Catholic? Remind me never to cross a writer. If what you're saying is right, the character would have been instantly recognisable to everybody at Monarch as Baz.'

'Not to mention the rest of the publishing world. And not just in London. What do you think they'd be gossiping about at the Frankfurt Book Fair, if not the way that Penny Varnavides had extracted her revenge against her former editor? Make no mistake, sending a message like that to Baz is the longest sacking note in history,' Lindsay pointed out as Helen barged into the kitchen.

'What is this, Pinkerton's Detectives, we never sleep?' she demanded loudly enough for Sophie to hear her in California.

'Tell Helen to shut up, we're talking serious murder motives,' Sophie said.

Lindsay relayed the message and Helen poked her tongue out at the phone. Kirsten shook her head in amusement and gestured at the oven with her thumb. 'Get on with your call then, Sherlock,' Helen mock-grumbled, taking warm pastries out of the oven.

'It is a motive,' Lindsay said. 'No two ways about it.'

'It's horrible to think of Penny dying for something so petty,' Sophie said soberly.

There was a long silence as they both recalled what lay behind the excitement of the hunt. Then Lindsay said, 'I need to see this stuff soon as.'

'I know,' Sophie acknowledged. 'But I'm up to my eyes. I've had to come back into the clinic.'

'The joys of high-risk deliveries?'

'Yeah. I had to come back into the city after I'd picked up the disk from Carolyn. I don't know how soon I'll have the chance to reformat these text files and e-mail them to you.'

Lindsay groaned. 'Oh, God.' Both Helen and Kirsten looked up momentarily from their morning paper and Danish, decided it was nothing serious and carried on, ignoring Lindsay's histrionics.

'I'm doing my best, Lindsay,' Sophie said, sounding hurt.

'I know, I know, I wasn't having a go,' Lindsay said apologetically. 'It's just so frustrating.'

'I promise you'll have them by the end of the day,' Sophie said.

'That's terrific, honestly. That's fine,' Lindsay reassured her. Then she sighed. 'I really miss you, you know. Helen and Kirsten have been great, but it's not like having you around.'

'It won't be long till I'm back in Britain too. Don't forget, we already had our flights booked for next week.'

'I know. I just wish I didn't have to do without you that long. You're always telling me I'm not fit to be let out on my own.'

'You need some back-up, huh?'

Lindsay grinned. 'That's right. I need someone to cover my back when I'm dealing with these heavy people. Violent types like publishers.'

'Joking apart, you be careful. At the risk of sounding like the last line before the commercial break in *Murder, She Wrote,* there's a killer out there, and I don't want you to be the next victim.'

'Don't worry,' Lindsay said. 'With what you've told me this morning, I think I've got a pretty good idea who killed Penny. And I'm not about to confront her up a dark alley. I don't think that even Baz Burton has the bottle to jump me in an open-plan office in front of the entire office staff of Monarch Press.'

'I don't suppose there's any point in me suggesting you hold off on this confrontation till you've had the chance to read the revised text for yourself? So you can quote chapter and verse at Baz?'

'Absolutely correct. What would be the point in that, unless you're winding me up and telling me stories?'

Sophie sighed. 'Promise me you'll be careful?'

'I promise I'll still be in one piece when you get here,' Lindsay said.

'So let me speak to Helen now,' Sophie said. 'I love you.'

'Love you too,' Lindsay said, waving the phone at Helen, who grabbed it and had a short conversation with Sophie which was remarkable for its monosyllabic quality. Lindsay had never seen anyone but Sophie reduce Helen's dialogue so drastically, and it appeared the old gift hadn't left her. After a series of grunts, yeahs and 'no problems', Helen hung up.

'So,' she said to Lindsay. 'Are we on for tonight? The big sting? Or are you going to be too busy catching murderers?'

'Trust me, I'm a doctor,' Lindsay said.

Helen snorted. 'It'd take more than an American PhD to make me trust you, kiddo.'

Lindsay stood up, pretending to be on her dignity. 'It'll all be done and dusted by seven. Then you and I will be ready to roll.'

Impatiently, Lindsay drummed her fingers on the arm of the chair she was reluctantly occupying at Monarch Press. Seeing her scowl, Lauren leaned forward across the reception desk and said confidentially, 'She won't be long now. The editorial meeting never lasts past eleven. Danny's always got too much on to waste time letting them rabbit. He only allows the editors five minutes max to pitch any of their titles.'

Lindsay pursed her lips and glared at her watch again, as if that would make the time pass more quickly. She couldn't even use the minutes constructively to see if Lauren's brain contained anything else worth picking since the reception area was never empty for more than a minute at a time. The longer she had to wait, the more her conviction of Baz's guilt grew. No matter that the meeting Baz was in was a routine weekly session, Lindsay couldn't prevent herself feeling Baz had made herself deliberately unavailable to spite her. Illogical and paranoid, she knew, but the feeling still wouldn't depart. She flipped open the front pocket of her backpack again and checked that her microcassette recorder was in voice-activated mode. She wasn't taking the risk that Baz would confess something she'd later try to deny.

Finally, as the minute hand crawled towards the hour, a young woman appeared, looking harassed. 'You're waiting to see Baz, right?' she greeted Lindsay. Without waiting for an answer, she gestured impatiently to the door. Lindsay got to her feet and forced herself to follow the woman through the editorial floor at a measured pace rather than the trot that would have matched her mood.

Baz was sitting behind her desk shuffling papers when Lindsay walked in. She glanced up. 'Hi. Siddown, yeah?' she said as she finished reading the top sheet and scribbled what might have been a signature across the bottom of it. Then she looked up, her face still a painful scarlet from too much sun. 'I've spoken to Meredith,' she said bluntly.

'Good. That's one less awkward conversation for us to have,' Lindsay said, her voice the only chilly thing in the partitioned space.

'So what brings you back here?'

'Your boss asked if I could track down a copy of *Heart of Glass,*' Lindsay said, avoiding the guest's chair and perching on the edge of a credenza stacked with manuscripts that ran along one wall, forcing Baz to turn awkwardly in her chair to maintain eye contact.

'You've managed to find it?' Baz asked cautiously. 'Where was it?'

'Penny always deposited a set of back-up disks with friends for safekeeping. It wasn't hard to find out where they were and to get a copy. You don't seem as excited as I expected.' Lindsay crossed her legs at the ankles and leaned back on her arms.

'I'm just relieved,' Baz said, a note of defensiveness creeping in. 'I've got a lot riding on this book.'

'Oh, I know you have. A damn sight more than a bloody big hole in your catalogue.'

Baz shifted in her chair, almost imperceptibly altering her position to close herself off from Lindsay's probing stare. 'You're going to have to explain that. I'm not quite sure what you're getting at.'

Lindsay snorted with sardonic laughter. 'Was that meant to be a subtle attempt to find out which draft I've got? If so, there was no need for the subtlety. I'll happily tell you, Baz. I've got the lot. I've got three early drafts, going as far as Chapter 18.' Lindsay paused, gauging Baz's watchful stare. She thought she saw relief there, but couldn't be sure.

'How soon can you let us have a copy?' Baz asked, fiddling obsessively with the pen she'd used to sign the document.

'That's going to be up to Meredith and Catriona Polson,' Lindsay replied. 'Oh, and probably the police as well.'

'Why should it have anything to do with the police?' Baz asked, her busy fingers freezing, the pen stationary in mid-turn.

'I've also got the final draft.' Lindsay stared steadily at Baz. 'The one I wouldn't want anyone to see if I was in your shoes. The one that gives you a motive for wanting Penny Varnavides dead.' Her words cut through the humid air like the hiss of a thrown knife.

Baz's mouth twisted into the kind of smile that's normally only seen in distorting fairground mirrors. 'Come on,' she said in an attempt at jokey contempt. 'You can't be seriously suggesting that a rewrite Penny did in the heat of anger would give me a motive for *murder*?'

Lindsay's grim smile would have worried a shark. 'One,' she said, ticking off her points on her fingers, '*Heart of Glass* as rewritten represents total humiliation for you, personally and professionally. Two, Penny and you could never have worked together again, which scuppers your brilliant career. Three, your girlfriend's going to be more than a little baffled as to why your formerly fabulous relationship with your most successful author has turned so sour, and I'm sure Penny would have been more than happy to enlighten her. Will that do for starters?'

Baz's eyes narrowed perceptibly, but when she spoke her voice struggled for lightness. 'This is madness. Look, whatever Penny may or may not have done in some intermediate draft, I was her editor and the final shape of the book depends on me as much as on her. I have the authority to demand that she change back to what was, after all, the book outlined in her synopsis, the book I had commissioned.'

'Oh, sure! If it came to a showdown between what Penny wanted and what you wanted, obviously Danny King's going to side with you,' Lindsay said sarcastically. 'Come on, Baz. Let's get real here. Penny wasn't exactly Ms Nobody submitting her first novel. If it was a case of losing Penny or losing you, I can't imagine Danny having to agonise for more than ten seconds.'

Lindsay didn't think it was possible for anyone to have a higher colour than the editor had already, but she was proved wrong as Baz darkened almost to purple. 'It wouldn't ever have come to that. Penny reacted the way she did because she was hurt and angry and that was the easiest way to get back at me. But she wasn't a fool. She was planning on coming out when this book was published. If she'd gone with the draft you're talking about, then someone would have sussed that we'd fallen out and, eventually, why. The last thing she would have wanted was that kind of tabloid notoriety. If you knew her half as well as you claim to, you'd know what I'm saying is the truth,' she added defiantly.

Rather than give Lindsay pause for thought, Baz's words served only to add fuel to the flames of her conviction. 'Maybe so. But it doesn't alter the fact that enough people would have seen that draft to humiliate you in the business, and jeopardise your relationship with your lover. And you can't tell me Penny Varnavides would ever have worked with you again after the way you wrecked her relationship with Meredith!'

'What the hell is going on in here?' a male voice interjected.

Lindsay turned to see Danny King in the doorway looking baffled. Baz wiped her sweating upper lip with the back of her hand and said bitterly, 'Glasgow's answer to Emma Victor here is accusing me of murdering Penny.'

Danny King threw back his handsome head in a guffaw of laughter. 'You mean you haven't told her about your alibi?' he gasped.

17

Thunderstruck, Lindsay's head swung from Danny to Baz and back to Danny again like a nodding dog on a car parcel shelf. 'Alibi?' she said faintly, clinging to the hope that life would imitate crime fiction, where alibis, like rules, were made to be broken.

'Obviously not,' Danny chuckled. 'Go on, Baz, put her out of her misery.'

Baz's tight-lipped smile was closer to a sneer. 'I was taking part in a panel of agents and publishers at a literary festival in Colchester at the time Penny died,' she said smugly. 'I travelled down by car with Elizabeth Root. She's an agent, her office is a few minutes' walk from here. We had a drink together, then did the panel – which, incidentally, was broadcast live by Oyster FM. All four of us on the panel went for a meal afterwards, and I didn't get back to London until nearly midnight. As I explained to the police the following day,' she added with a vicious little smirk.

Danny moved into the office and laid a friendly arm across Lindsay's shoulder. 'So you see, I'm afraid you're barking up the wrong tree with Baz. Whoever killed Penny, it was nothing to do with Monarch Press.'

Lindsay edged away from Danny's arm, making the excuse of standing up and moving towards the door. 'Just because Baz seems to be off the hook, it doesn't mean Monarch is in the clear,' she said in an attempt at a defiant face-saver.

Danny opened his mouth but before he could say anything, Baz butted in. 'She's got the book,' she said urgently.

He looked astonished. 'You managed to track it down?' he said. 'But that's . . . that's amazing. Wonderful. How soon can you let us have it?'

'It's not up to me to let you have anything,' Lindsay said stubbornly. 'It's up to Meredith. She inherits everything from Penny. She might not want you to have it.'

'She's got to, I'm afraid,' Danny King said, his patronising tone setting Lindsay's hackles on full-scale bullshit alert. 'Penny signed a contract. She'd been paid the first chunk of a very substantial advance. The biggest we've ever paid, as a matter of fact. That manuscript belongs to us.'

Lindsay shook her head. 'Not if Meredith decides to repay the advance,' she pointed out as she sailed out of the office, head held high.

The satisfaction of her parting shot lasted for as long as it took her to cross the rapt editorial floor and reach the street. Never had she been more grateful to breathe the fumid air of a steamy London morning. Without hesitating or allowing herself to think about what she'd just experienced, Lindsay strode across the supermarket car park and into their blissfully air-conditioned cafeteria, where she found a quiet corner to drink her mineral water and regroup.

She had been so certain that Baz had killed Penny. Ever since Sophie had passed on the information about the changes to the latest draft, she'd been running the film in her head of Penny inviting Baz to her flat, maybe even for a showdown over Meredith; of Baz arriving with her bottles of wheat beer; then of the murderous attack that had left Penny bleeding to death somewhere as prosaic as an Islington kitchen.

But she'd been wrong. Completely, utterly wrong. Her first serious suspect, Catriona Polson, had been stripped of motive. Now Baz Burton had been revealed as devoid of opportunity. Of the limited group of suspects she'd started with, only Meredith remained. And since she'd known from the start that while Meredith might have killed Penny in a moment of passion, so carefully staged a crime was beyond her, Lindsay was left with no one in the frame.

There was nothing for her to do now except admit to Meredith that she was utterly defeated by the mystery of Penny's death. With a sigh that turned heads at nearby tables, Lindsay acknowledged to herself that she had failed not only Meredith but also Penny. Although her mind knew it for an over-reaction, her heart comprehended it as a betrayal of a friendship that had often sustained Lindsay when she needed it most. To admit that failure to Meredith of all people would be one of the hardest things she had ever faced. Leaving most of her drink untouched, Lindsay walked out into the sunshine and headed for the tube station.

She caught Meredith coming back from buying the newspapers. 'At least they've lost interest in me right now. Kinda late, though,' Meredith had said as they went up in the lift. She had visibly lost weight even in the short time since Lindsay had last seen her. Her eyes lurked at the bottom of darkly shadowed sockets and her cheekbones seemed on the point of bursting through her taut skin.

'When did you eat last?' Lindsay had asked while she watched Meredith make them coffee.

'I went out for a pizza last night,' Meredith said. 'I managed to get some down. But it's hard to eat. I feel like I've got a rock lodged in my throat.' Lindsay's heart went out to her, and she reached out impulsively to hug her friend. But this time, Meredith's grief didn't burst forth like an undammed stream. She sighed deeply, but her hand mirrored Lindsay's, each stroking the other's back in mutual sympathy. 'When you love somebody and you commit yourself to sharing her life, you can't help imagining what it would be like if she died,' she said softly. 'Only nothing you imagine ever prepares you for the reality.'

'I know,' was all Lindsay could manage. They held on to each other until the urgent spluttering of the coffee pot forced them apart. Then, sitting with Meredith in the stuffy gloom of the flat, Lindsay reviewed what she had done in the previous couple of days. 'I've hit a dead end,' Lindsay confessed finally. 'I really don't have any idea what to pursue.'

Meredith nodded sadly. 'I guess it was a long shot, bringing you over here. But don't think I don't appreciate it. There is one other thing you could do for me, though,' she added, almost as an afterthought.

'Sure, if I can.'

'Leave me a copy of *Heart of Glass*. I think it would be good for me to see the last thing she was working on. I also need to decide if it's possible for another person to finish what she'd started.'

Lindsay rooted in her backpack and came up with the floppy disks on which she'd made back-up copies of the files Sophie had e-mailed to her. 'There you go,' she said, passing them across. 'I've not got the final draft yet, but I should have it some time this evening. Are you on-line here?'

Meredith gestured with her thumb towards a

repro Regency table where a laptop sat incongruously. 'Sure. Did you want to e-mail it to me? You've got my address, yeah?'

'Soon as I've got it, I'll shunt it on to you.'

'Who knows?' Meredith said wistfully. 'There might be something there that'll give us a clue. Maybe even point you in a fresh direction.'

Lindsay shrugged. 'I wouldn't hold out too much hope. But if there is anything there, you can rest assured I'll be on to it like a rat up a drain.' She finished her coffee and got to her feet. 'I've got to go now, Meredith. I've got a bit of business to sort out for Helen. But I'll be in touch.'

Out in the sunshine again, Lindsay sought out the shade of the plane trees that lined the street. She could escape the merciless heat, but there was no escaping the overwhelming guilt she felt at her failure to exonerate Meredith. She'd blown any attempt to place the blame for Penny's death at someone else's door; she hadn't even managed to come up with any concrete evidence that would clear her friend. And her ridiculous antics with Derek Knight meant she didn't dare to return to Islington to question the neighbours on the off chance that someone had seen something that would cast doubt on the police's seeming conviction that in Meredith they had found the killer.

No matter how she cut it, she couldn't see any way forward. To someone as stubborn as Lindsay, it was a bitter blow. But she was no quitter. If she couldn't go forward, maybe she could go backwards. As soon as Sophie managed to snatch a moment to send her Penny's final draft, Lindsay decided, it was time to start working in a completely different direction.

Just after seven, Lindsay faced Helen across Stella's desk, the terminal in front of her switched on, with Lindsay logged in as a superuser. 'Okay,' she said. 'This is how it goes. Companies like Watergaw need to pay kickbacks and bribes if they're going to operate in certain countries. Traditionally, the Inland Revenue have taken the view that, while payments like these aren't strictly tax-deductible, if they go through the balance sheet as commissions paid to third parties, they'll turn a blind eye and allow the company to offset them against their profits. However, a couple of years ago they announced they weren't going to allow that any more. In practice, nothing has changed, it's just that the Revenue have taken a position that means they keep their hands clean. And every now and again, they'll do somebody, just to keep everybody else on their toes.'

'Yeah, yeah, I know all that,' Helen said impatiently. 'I still don't see how you're going to use it to nail Guy and Stella. We're a minnow compared to the multinationals that get away with it every day of the week.'

'Bear with me,' Lindsay said. 'This is where it starts to get interesting. There are two separate issues that make it possible to create a scenario that looks very unpleasant for Guy and Stella. First, you have to consider why the tax authorities have been prepared to look the other way. Why do you think that might be?'

Helen shrugged. 'Because the companies involved go out there to make a tasty profit? And if the taxman stopped them paying bribes, their nice healthy profits wouldn't be there to be taxed in the first place?'

'More or less. Traditionally, it's been the manufacturing and service sectors that have benefited from this selective blindness. That's because the Revenue are perfectly well aware that if our companies don't win contracts, they go to our competitors in Europe and America and, increasingly, on the Pacific rim. So not only do we lose taxable profits, we ultimately lose more jobs. Which is not something this government can afford.'

Helen nodded, on familiar ground. 'Even if it means turning us into the Taiwan of Europe, outside the Social Chapter and without a single employment right among us.'

'So in those terms, technically what you've been doing at Watergaw falls into a grey area. It's not the kind of fraud that gets the taxman too excited. It's not like some companies, where they set up a dummy outfit in a tax haven and pay the commissions through that,' Lindsay added.

'What's wrong with that?'

'In itself, nothing. But in practice, what usually

happens is that for every ten dollars that goes out in bribes, a couple go into a separate numbered bank account for the company's directors. So they can pay themselves a tasty tax-free bonus for being clever enough to bribe their clients.'

Helen shook her head. 'You know, the sheer deviousness of financial crooks never ceases to amaze me. But this still doesn't explain how you're going to drop Guy and Stella in it.'

Lindsay sighed. It wasn't as if she really understood all the ins and outs herself, only the bare bones on which Ellie had put sufficient flesh for her to understand what she had to do. Explaining it to Helen was turning out to be more difficult than she had anticipated. Still, it was good experience for getting it straight in her own mind before she tried to put the theory into practice. 'Watergaw isn't a manufacturer, in the sense of making something for export. It's not a service company in the sense of earning money for Britain by selling insurance or financial services abroad. The bribes you've paid have been handed over to make your filming run smoothly, yeah?'

'Of course. You'd never believe some of the things you have to hand out the readies for. I've paid people to muzzle their goats so they wouldn't bleat at a crucial moment, I've paid yobs to let actors walk down their street without them mooning in the background, I've paid traffic cops not to give parking tickets to film units. I once bought fried-chicken dinners for an entire African village and laid on the coaches to take them to and from the fast-food stall.' Helen leaned back in her chair with the air of a woman who has only just opened the doors on her stock of anecdotes.

'Exactly,' Lindsay said hastily. 'And what would happen if you hadn't paid those bribes?'

Helen frowned. 'We wouldn't have got the films made.'

'And would people have lost their jobs if you hadn't been able to make those films?'

'Well, probably, if we'd gone out there and then not been in a position to film.'

'But if you'd known in advance that you'd be penalised for paying kickbacks, you'd have been crazy to contemplate making those films, right?'

Helen frowned, unable to see where Lindsay was heading. 'Right. So we'd have made other films instead. Films set over here. Or in developed countries where the bribe culture is more or less dead.'

'My point exactly,' Lindsay said triumphantly. 'For manufacturers, the paying of bribes is a *necessary* business expense or else they go to the wall. For you, it's a luxury. You could conceivably make other films that would equally ensure your continued success. So if someone grassed you up to the taxman, you'd be a perfect case to use to trumpet to the world that this government is encouraging the Inland Revenue to clamp down on corruption.'

Helen looked gobsmacked. 'You are fucking wicked,' she said admiringly.

'You've only heard the half of it. Customs and Excise have never really gone along with the Revenue on this one. Their view has always been that if there's anything in the VAT accounts that looks dodgy, they'll come down like a ton of bricks. Mostly, foreign kickbacks don't have any impact on the amount of VAT a company's due to pay. But there are circumstances where they do – like if you've disguised a bribe as a payment for goods or services and you've paid it to a company with a UK subsidiary. Would there be anything like that in these accounts?'

'Oh, yeah,' Helen said eagerly. 'I can show you, if you like.' She pulled the monitor towards her so she could see the screen. Lindsay passed the keyboard across and Helen moved expertly through a set of accounts till she found what she was looking for. 'We keep the accounts for each project totally separate,' she said as she moved the cursor down a list of payments. 'This is *Thirty/Three*, Guy and Stella's little honeymoon on the subcontinent. There, that's what I'm looking for. Canopus Islamabad.' She double clicked on the file. A window popped open detailing dates and amounts of payments. 'We hire our lighting from them. We pay them in the UK, with a hefty slice on top of the actual hiring charge.'

'Perfect,' Lindsay said softly. 'Now I need you

to show me the way round your accounts software.'

'You're not going to alter them, are you?' Helen asked, looking aghast.

'Nothing that crude,' Lindsay said. 'I just want to get familiar with the ins and outs of what was paid, when it was paid and who got the cash. Then I can get to work.'

'So what are you going to do?' Helen nagged.

'I'm going to plant some files in Stella's personal desk. And some in Guy's. I can't tell you the details, because I don't know what they are yet.'

'Are you sure you know what you're doing?' Helen asked, worry replacing fury for the first time since Lindsay had revealed Stella and Guy's racket to her.

'Sort of. Where I don't, I know a woman who does. And she's only a phone call away. Helen, you've got to trust me on this. Unless you've got any better ideas, I'm your best chance of getting that pair out of your life for good.'

Helen fiddled with a strand of hair, a strangely coy gesture from a woman normally so upfront she made Roseanne look demure. 'I just don't want you getting in too deep,' she said.

'I think I can look after myself,' Lindsay said gruffly. 'Now, are you going to show me how this bloody software works, or do I have to work it out for myself?'

An hour later, Helen reluctantly left. She had given Lindsay a swift tutorial in both the accounts and the word-processing packages that Watergaw used as standard on their network of computers. Then Lindsay had insisted she go home. 'It's better you don't see how I do this,' she said. 'That way you can't let anything slip.'

Left to her own devices, Lindsay spent a couple of hours gaining a thorough grasp of the payments that had been made as part of the production budget of *Thirty/Three*, taking notes as she went. Then, exploiting her superuser status, she changed the computer's internal date stamp so that it read a few days after Stella had joined the company. Next she entered Guy's private directory and created a memo, dated to correspond with the new internal date on the computer. The long document outlined for Stella's benefit a series of fraudulent practices which 'Guy' explained were standard. It also contained a caveat warning Stella not to discuss these procedures with Helen. '*Our partner*,' Lindsay typed, '*has rather old-fashioned views on fiscal matters. I have tried in the past to explain to her how the real world works, but her response hasn't encouraged me. However, she doesn't have enough experience of commercial matters to unravel the accounts I prepare for her. When we set up the company, I promised her faithfully I would be fiscally prudent, and she took that to mean I'd stick to the letter of the law. You've no idea how liberating it is to be working with someone like you, who understands the realities. It's a jungle out there, and we need to use whatever weapons come to hand so we can survive. Besides, everybody rips off the taxman and the VATman. It's the national sport.'*

Then, changing the internal date to the following day, she moved to Stella's personal desk and produced a second memo, acknowledging Guy's to her and suggesting a couple of dodgy wrinkles of her own. Next, she changed the computer's date to that of a couple of weeks after the end of filming on *Thirty/Three*. With constant reference to her notes, she constructed a long memo purporting to come from Stella to Guy, explaining in detail the subterfuges she had employed to disguise the crooked payments. It finished with a contemptuous reference to Helen, looking forward to a time when she and Guy could dump her from the partnership. Finally, after changing the internal date on the computer to the correct one, she printed out all three memos.

It took a little longer to make them look appropriately aged. A coffee mug ring here, a smudge of cigarette ash there. Here a curl at the corner, there a crease. Her *pièce de résistance*, Lindsay felt, was to copy a doodle she saw replicated a dozen times on Stella's scratch pad, a five-pointed star with the central pentagon inked in. Then she put Guy's into Stella's desk drawer, towards the bottom of the pile of papers in there. She walked down the dim corridor to Guy's office, where she deposited the fake memos from Stella among a stack of papers in a deep tray marked 'To be filed when hell freezes over'.

Back at the computer, she used the system's in-built retrieval system to recapture the forged EU letter about Helen's grant which Stella had deleted the previous evening in her and Guy's attempts to cover their tracks. Like most people, she had once thought deleting something was enough to erase it from the system for ever. Thanks to Meredith's teaching, Lindsay now knew different.

Finally, she made a lengthy call. Just after midnight, Lindsay put the phone down. She had run the final details past Ellie, and been assured that what she had put in place was the perfect frame that would cheerfully convince any investigator from Customs and Excise or the Inland Revenue. One of the knock-on effects of new technology that usually worried her was how easy it had become to frame the innocent. It made a pleasant change to exploit it against the guilty. She stretched her back, thrusting her arms into the air and yawning like a basking lioness. The sooner she got back to a routine where she could run and work out, the better she'd feel.

She switched off the computer and gathered her papers together, making sure she had left only the materials she wanted the investigators to unearth all by themselves. Then she let herself out of Stella's office and headed for the exit. There, she consulted the note Helen had given her and set the alarm as she opened the door to the car park. As Watergaw's door closed behind her with a sharp click, Lindsay was uneasily aware of how dark the car park was. She could have sworn she'd previously noticed security lights mounted on the side of the building, angled to shine across the car park, but now the only light came from the distant streetlights, reduced even further by the bulk of the Watergaw building.

Swallowing her apprehension, Lindsay walked boldly along the side of the building to the place where she'd left her car. Suddenly she was aware of glass crunching under her feet and she stooped to look more closely. As she registered the broken glass of the security lights, she heard the soft footfall of running trainers on asphalt. Startled, Lindsay jumped up and swung round to face the direction of the sound. As she turned, she saw outlined against the pale orange of the sodium streetlights the unmistakable shape of a baseball bat. It was heading straight towards her as if she was the pitcher's finest curve ball.

18

Using the momentum she'd gained straightening up from her crouch, Lindsay pushed off from the ground and veered out of the way of the bat, stumbling backwards as her assailant continued towards her, drawn forwards by the follow-through of that first vicious swipe. Her feet scrabbled against the asphalt of the car park, the grip of leather sandals puny in comparison with her attacker's trainers. She could make out only the vague outline of a medium-sized frame with a head sleek as a seal, but that was enough to see that already the shoulders were tensing to lift the bat in a second backswing, aimed straight at her head.

With no time even to think, Lindsay acted on pure instinct. As he swung the bat from above his left shoulder, she leapt forwards and to the side, so that she undercut the arc of the blow. Then, hitting the ground running, suddenly she was past him, sprinting for the street with a turn of speed she had no idea she possessed. Faster than she'd ever run along the beach at Half Moon Bay, she headed across the car park at the angle that would bring her to the street most quickly.

Her blood thudding in her ears and her own breathing sounding loud as a steam engine to her heightened senses, Lindsay pounded the asphalt, aiming for the light. So obsessed was she with reaching the relative safety of a street with traffic and other human beings that she completely failed to register the low wall that bordered Watergaw's unit until it was too late. Like a badly prepared showjumper, she tried to adjust her stride to take the wall, but mistimed it completely.

The sandal on her trailing leg caught the top of the foot-high wall, catapulting Lindsay into a scrappy somersault. She flew over the pavement, landing in an awkward sprawl a yard into the road. White light bathed her as a taxi's brakes screeched in a screaming swerve, bringing it to a juddering halt in a stutter of diesel engine mere inches from where she lay groaning in the road.

The taxi driver jumped out and ran round to the front of the cab, his 'What the fuck?' strangled at birth when Lindsay lifted a face that was a Janus mask half blood, half green-tinged flesh. 'Jesus Christ,' he gasped instead.

Lindsay pushed herself on to her knees, then, using the cab's radiator as a prop, to her feet. Casting a desperate glance behind her that seemed surprisingly agonising, she stuttered, 'A bloke. With a baseball bat. Chasing me.'

'I can't see nobody, love,' the cabbie said. 'Whoever he was, he must have legged it when he saw you flying through the air with the greatest of ease. He's gone, love. You're all right.' He reached out a hand. 'Well, when I say all right . . . maybe we should get you to hospital.'

Lindsay shook her head. Again pain shot along her jaw. But she couldn't work out why. She must have scraped her face on the asphalt when she hit the ground. Bruises and a nasty graze, that's what it would be. 'I'm just a bit bruised. Nothing broken. I'll be fine,' she said, her voice clear with the disengaged calm of deep shock.

The cabbie put a firm arm round her shoulder. 'Hospital, love. You can't see what I can see. You must have hit a bit of broken glass in the road. Look, you can see it shining there. A broken milk bottle, it looks like. Whatever, that face of yours is gonna need more than an Elastoplast, believe me.'

Lindsay frowned, bewildered. What was he talking about? She put her hand up to the side of her neck that seemed to be causing her most pain. There was something warm and wet all over her jawline. Along the bone, it didn't feel like skin. It felt like raw meat. And it hurt. As she took her hand away and saw it was covered in blood, she started to shake. It began as a slight quiver, but by the time the cabbie had virtually carried her into the back of his taxi, she was shaking from top to toe like someone on the edge of hypothermia, her teeth chattering and her hands twitching.

All the way to the Royal Free's casualty department, the cabbie talked reassuringly to her. He talked about his wife and his two teenage daughters, about their forthcoming holiday in Turkey, about his hobby, angling, and how it wasn't a hardship to work nights on account of the rubbish they put on the telly. And all Lindsay could think about was how near she'd come to something far worse than whatever it was that had happened to her.

By the time they reached the hospital, the worst of the shakes were behind her and she could just about manage to climb out of the taxi unaided. The cabbie took a clean, soft handkerchief out of a satchel on the floor by the driver's seat and folded it into a long pad. 'You just hold that against it,' he said, sounding nervous as he demonstrated what he meant. 'It'll stop the flow of blood.' Numb now, she did as she was told. He helped her out and led her into the reception area, where a man who looked less healthy than she felt started to take her details. When she turned to thank her rescuer, he was gone.

'I didn't even pay the fare,' she said vaguely to the receptionist, who looked blankly at her and said, 'GP?'

Unable to bear the complication of explaining that she lived in America, Lindsay gave the name of the woman who had been her doctor seven years before, when she'd lived with Cordelia in Highbury. It seemed to satisfy the receptionist. It clearly wasn't his job to care why she was giving an address in west London and a GP in north London. Telling her to take a seat, the receptionist turned back to stare at his computer screen.

Feeling more disorientated than jet lag had ever left her, Lindsay walked slowly towards a bank of pay phones on the far wall. Her legs felt out of her control, as if her knees had been replaced with some flexible rubbery solid which left her out of touch with her feet. Every step was tentative, in case the place where her knees used to be suddenly rebelled and deposited her in a crumpled, helpless heap on the floor. But she made it to the phone without incident.

By some miracle, she still had her backpack. Awkward fingers fumbled some change out of her wallet and she punched in Helen's number. It rang five or six times without reply, then the answering machine clicked in. Lindsay leaned against the wall and waited for Helen to stop giving her instructions. She couldn't understand why no one was picking up the phone. She knew it was late, but there was an extension in the bedroom, right next to Helen's bed. They couldn't sleep through this, could they?

The machine beeped and Lindsay said, 'Helen? Kirsten? Is anybody there? Can you pick up? It's Lindsay? Hello? . . .' She waited for a moment, but no one answered. She sighed. 'Bit of a problem. Um . . . I'm at the Royal Free. In casualty. Had a bit of an accident. Nothing to worry about, but if you get this message, can you come? I'll . . . I'll speak to you later,' she ended up, unable to think straight.

She replaced the receiver and wobbled over to the nearest vacant chair. She slumped into it and looked around vaguely. There seemed to be a lot of people here, considering it was nearly one in the morning. They mostly looked stunned with pain or indifference, especially those who were only accompanying someone more obviously damaged. Lindsay closed her eyes and sighed. Where could Helen and Kirsten be? Helen hadn't said anything about plans for the evening, and she'd have been too desperate to hear Lindsay's report on her mission to consider going out on the spur of the moment. She couldn't believe they'd turned off the phones and gone to bed either. Helen's eagerness to hear that Stella and Guy had been stitched up would never have allowed her to go to sleep. Besides, Helen would be conscious of the possibility that things might go wrong. She wouldn't leave Lindsay hanging on the telephone needing help.

It was a mystery, but right then it seemed to Lindsay about as intractable as Penny Varnavides' murder. Before she could worry about it too much, she felt a hand on her shoulder. She opened her eyes to see a nurse's uniform containing a stocky redhead who looked about twelve years old. 'I'm the triage nurse,' she chirped cheerily in a harsh Belfast brogue. 'If you'd like to come through to a cubicle, I can assess your injuries there.'

Lindsay got to her feet and followed the nurse past the reception desk and into a curtained cubicle. 'Up we get,' the nurse said, helping her on to an examination table and gently removing hand and handkerchief pad from Lindsay's now throbbing jaw. 'My, we have been in the wars, haven't we? That's some mess you've got yourself into there. Never mind, we'll soon have you cleaned up and good as new.' Lindsay could see why the woman had become a nurse; with that degree of insensitive exuberance, she wouldn't dare work with the able-bodied and expect to live.

The next hour was a blur. No, she hadn't lost consciousness. No, her shoulder and knee didn't hurt any more than she'd expect from grazed skin. Yes, she could see how many fingers the doctor was holding up. No, she wasn't allergic to penicillin. Eventually, a soft-voiced Asian man with cool, gentle hands cleaned up her face, stitched the long cut that sliced up the line of her jaw, reassured her that the scar would be virtually invisible and fetched her a cup of tea. As she struggled to swallow it without losing half out of the side of her mouth that felt numb, Lindsay heard a familiar voice.

'I told you, soft lad, we're the nearest she's got to family, that's why she phoned us to come and get her. How else do you think we knew to come here?' Helen announced. A man's voice mumbled something in response. 'Cubicle three? Right, come on, girls.'

'Girls?' thought Lindsay, vaguely wondering who else Helen had in tow. She didn't have to wonder for long. The curtain parted and Lindsay had her second shock in the space of a couple of hours. 'Sophie?' she said, not entirely certain whether she was hallucinating. 'Is it really you?'

Sophie crossed the cubicle in two strides and gripped Lindsay's shoulders, her expression a mixture of relief and affectionate exasperation. 'What am I going to do with you? I turn my back for five minutes, and look at you!'

Lindsay felt her eyes film over with tears. 'This is a nice surprise,' she said, her voice shaky. 'You'll have to forgive me if I don't kiss you just yet.'

Sophie crouched down and stared intently at her lover's battered face. 'Whoever stitched you did a good job. You'll not have much of a scar.'

Lindsay dropped her head so it rested on Sophie's shoulder. 'I'm so pleased to see you,' she said. 'How come you're here?'

'I managed to get away from work a few days early. The housesitter was delirious to swap her parents for Mutton this soon. Changing the flights was slightly more difficult. But I missed you, and besides, I didn't like the idea of you chasing a killer on your own. Looks as if I was right to be worried, doesn't it?'

'I don't think it was anything to do with Penny,' Lindsay sighed. 'Can we get out of here now? You know how much I like hospitals.'

'Sure,' Sophie said, gently stroking Lindsay's head.

'Oh, my God, look at the state of you. This is all my fault! What happened? Was it Guy or was it Stella?' Helen demanded, unable to contain herself a moment longer.

'Later, Helen,' Sophie said. She kissed the top of Lindsay's head and tenderly extricated herself from her lover's embrace. 'Go and find someone in authority, tell them we're taking her home.'

Before Helen could leave, a white-coated doctor whom Lindsay had a dim recollection of seeing earlier appeared at Kirsten's shoulder. 'What's going on here?' he demanded. 'This patient has had a head injury. The last thing she needs is crowds of people around her. I could hear the shouting half-way down the corridor.' Helen had the grace to look embarrassed.

'Doctor,' Sophie said. 'The very person I wanted to see. We're taking Ms Gordon home now.'

'Oh, no, you're not,' he said obstinately. 'Ms Gordon is my patient and we're keeping her in overnight for observation. It's standard procedure in cases of head trauma.'

Sophie ran a hand through her silver curls. 'I'm a doctor myself. I know what the symptoms of concussion look like, I know the procedures. I'm prepared to take responsibility for her.' She pulled her wallet out of the back pocket of her jeans and gave him a card that announced she was Dr Sophie Hartley, consultant obstetrician and gynaecologist of the Grafton Clinic, San Francisco. He looked slightly dazed as he read it, then looked at this tall woman wearing a T-shirt that read 'Netheads do IT better'. Sophie grinned disarmingly. 'So, we'll be leaving shortly,' she said with all the authority of half a dozen years as a consultant.

'But I've managed to get her a bed,' the hospital doctor protested. 'Have you any idea how hard that is these days?'

'Looking at the patient, I'm sure you've done a really good job,' Sophie said, reassuring without patronising. 'Look at it this way – now you know there's a bed available for one of your other patients.'

He muttered something under his breath, then said, 'On your head be it.'

Within ten minutes, Lindsay and Sophie were settled in the back of Helen's car, with Kirsten driving so Helen could turn round in her seat and demand information. 'So what happened?' she asked again.

'Helen,' Sophie, warned. 'Not now.'

'No, it's okay,' Lindsay said. Either Sophie's arrival or the hospital tea seemed to have revived her. Apart from the ache in her shoulder and leg and twinges penetrating the local anaesthetic in her face, she felt almost alert. 'My brain seems to have reconnected with the rest of me.'

'See?' Helen said triumphantly. 'Call yourself a doctor, Hartley?'

Sophie smiled. 'You have your medical adviser's permission to tell her to shut up any time you want,' she told Lindsay, pulling her closer. 'To be honest, I'm curious myself. Helen met me at Heathrow and told me you were working alone at her office, where nothing bad could possibly happen. The next thing I know is you look like Mike Tyson's speed bag.'

'Watch who you're calling a bag,' Lindsay said. 'The short answer is that I don't really know what happened. I'd done everything I had to do at Watergaw, so I set the alarm and locked up. The security lights weren't on, so it was really dark. I was walking to my car and I stood on some glass. I bent down to see if I could see what it was, then I heard these footsteps running behind me. I jumped up and turned round just in time to get out of the way of some maniac with a baseball bat. I managed to dodge him, but I was concentrating so hard on getting away that I didn't see the wall until it was too late.' For Sophie's benefit, she added, "There's this little wall runs along the frontage of Watergaw, and I took a header over it. Unfortunately, I came down on a bit of broken glass. Hence the duelling scar.'

'It sounds like you would have come off a lot worse if you'd stuck around,' Kirsten commented.

'Trust a journalist to look on the bright side,' Helen said. 'So, did you see who it was doing the

Joe DiMaggio impersonation? Was it Guy? Or even Stella?'

Lindsay sighed. 'I don't think it was Stella. I couldn't see much except a silhouette, and it looked like a male body shape. I don't think he was as tall as Guy, but I couldn't swear to it. I think he was wearing a stocking over his head as well. I was giving it some thought back in the hospital. At first I couldn't work out why his head was such a neat shape, then I realised what he must have done.'

'It must have been Guy,' Helen said. 'He knows me well enough to realise I wouldn't just lie down and die after what he's done to me. He'll have left that bitch Stella in charge of the night shoot, and he'll have come back to stake out the offices. The bastard!'

'It certainly sounds a possibility,' Sophie said. 'But what about your murder investigation? Isn't it possible that someone connected with that has been tailing you, waiting for an opportunity to strike?'

Lindsay sighed. 'It's not very likely, given that I seem to have hit a brick wall. Unless there's something in Penny's last draft to point me in a different direction, I'm stuck. I can no more prove Meredith innocent than I can show someone else is guilty. Helen's probably right. Most likely it was Guy.'

'You've got to go to the police,' Helen said firmly.

'No way. That's the very last thing I should do,' Lindsay said wearily.

'You can't let him away with this,' Kirsten chipped in as she braked for a pedestrian crossing. 'He could try again, and next time he might really hurt somebody.'

'It's not worth it. He didn't actually hit me. All this,' she said, fluttering her fingers in the direction of her face, 'was incidental. I doubt he'd even get a custodial sentence. No, the revenge I've got lined up for Guy and Stella is going to hurt them a lot more than a something or nothing charge in a magistrates' court. And to make it work, the last thing we want to be doing is explaining why I was in Watergaw's car park the wrong side of midnight.'

'This sounds devious,' Sophie commented.

'You haven't heard the half of it,' Helen said ominously.

'And you don't want to, either,' Kirsten chipped in. 'I had it over dinner and then all the way to Heathrow. Believe me, Sophie, this is one case where ignorance is bliss.'

'I'll tell you later, Soph. Suffice it to say, Guy turned out to be a real shyster, so I've been fitting him up good style,' Lindsay said. 'But I need to brief you now, Helen. If you go into my backpack, you'll find a document wallet with three printed memos in it.' As Sophie passed the bag over and Helen unzipped it, Lindsay continued. 'First thing in the morning, you go to your local

VAT office and request an interview with an investigator. Failing that, you want the inspector who deals with Watergaw. You tell him you had been told that one of your staff had been using your computer to run their own business on the side, so you were doing a file audit. While you were in there, you found these memos in the private desks of your business partners.'

Helen was skimming the documents as she listened. 'Jesus!' she exploded. 'This is dynamite. You don't take prisoners, do you?'

'And that was presumably written before your colleague tried to cave her head in,' Sophie said drily. 'Probably just as well. If she was framing him now, she'd not be satisfied with anything less than serial murder.'

'Never mind all that,' Lindsay said. 'The important thing is that you stress that you knew nothing about all of this, and you want them hammered because you don't want your company destroyed. I know it's casting against type, but for once play the dumb broad,' she added wryly.

'Oh, God,' Helen groaned. 'I should have known better.'

'That,' said Sophie, 'is what they all say.'

19

At first when she woke, Lindsay couldn't figure out where she was. She knew she wasn't at home, remembered she was staying with Helen, but the silence disorientated her. She couldn't recall ever waking into quiet in Helen's home. If it wasn't the radio, it was music, the volume pumped up till it threatened to explode. But there was nothing. Just the distant hum of traffic on Fulham Palace Road and the chatter of city sparrows from the open sash window. That and the pounding of her head, a throb so intense it seemed audible.

Something else was wrong, she realised, still not moving. She was alone. Her memory of the night before was trickling back from behind the barrier of drugged sleep and she knew she shouldn't have been waking alone. Sophie! Sophie was in England. She had been there with her when the hospital painkillers had finally carried her over into what felt like a coma. But where was she now?

Lindsay rolled over, making the mistake of turning on to the side where a row of stitches held her face together. 'Shit,' she exploded, squirming swiftly up the bed and into a sitting position. Sophie, sitting by the window in a basket chair, looked up from the book she was reading.

'If it hadn't been for the snoring, I'd have started to think you'd died,' she said. 'How are you feeling?'

Lindsay's face twitched as another worm of pain snaked down her jaw. 'My face feels like it's wired for electric shock treatment and my body thinks it's been hit by a bus. My brain seems to have been connected to a bass drum machine and while I was sleeping, somebody stuffed my mouth with cotton wool, then left a dead reptile there for long enough to make my mouth taste of decaying lizard. Apart from that, I feel terrific,' she grumbled.

Sophie smiled sympathetically, closing her book and crossing to the door. 'I'll get you some coffee and a couple of painkillers.'

'Great. But just some paracetamol or aspirin, not those industrial-strength ones the hospital gave me. I've decided I want to put the zombie lifestyle on hold until I'm actually dead.'

'Wise move.'

'What time is it anyway?' Lindsay asked, looking around vainly for her watch.

'You broke the glass on your watch when you did your swallow dive into the asphalt. It's ten to twelve,' Sophie said on her way out.

'Ten to twelve? As in lunchtime? It can't be! You mean I slept through Helen greeting the world with Radio Four?'

'I made her leave the radio off,' Sophie shouted from the stairs.

'I have died and gone to heaven,' Lindsay said faintly. Kirsten could only get the radio turned off in the kitchen, but Sophie could still pitch Helen into starting the day without it altogether. If she'd had a suspicious mind, Lindsay would have wondered if there was still unfinished business between them. But six years with someone as dependable as Sophie had restored Lindsay's fractured trust in human nature. Helen's radio silence, she felt sure, was more to do with concern for her health than a desire to creep into Sophie's good books.

While she waited for Sophie to return, Lindsay shifted across the bed so she could see herself in the wardrobe mirror. Her right cheek was a patchwork of purple and blue-black bruising and brownish scabbed grazes, with her stitched scar running like a line of black thread up her jaw from the angle under her ear to a point level with the corner of her mouth. The bruising continued on her shoulder and down her right arm as far as the elbow, which sported an ugly scrape that still looked red and raw. As Sophie came back, Lindsay said, 'Really, you have to wonder if I'd have been better off with the baseball bat.'

'Not if you've ever worked a shift in casualty,

you don't,' Sophie said drily, depositing a mug of coffee on the bedside table and handing Lindsay two paracetamols and a glass of water. 'Believe me, if that bat had connected, you wouldn't be lying here. You'd still be in the Royal Free. Either that or in a drawer in the mortuary.'

'I don't think he was trying to kill me,' Lindsay objected. 'He gave up too easily. I think it was a warning.'

'So you think Helen's right? That it was Guy?' Sophie asked.

'Who else? I've dead-ended on the murder inquiry, so I'm no threat to Penny's killer.'

'But does the killer know that?' Sophie mused.

'If the killer is anybody I've met over the last few days, then they've seen me floundering around making an complete arse of myself,' Lindsay said bitterly, then winced at the effort of swallowing the painkillers. 'They're not going to feel threatened, they're going to be laughing their socks off. I've accused one person whose motive crumbled faster than an Oxo cube and another who had an alibi with thousands of witnesses. Well, hundreds. It was *local* radio, after all.'

Sophie gave a conciliatory shrug. 'Just a thought. So that leaves Guy. Funny, he never seemed like the violent type.'

'People do ridiculous things when they feel threatened.'

'Yeah, but . . .' Sophie frowned. 'I thought they'd seen you and Helen off with your tails between your legs.' She sat on the bed beside Lindsay, resting an arm on her lover's unhurt shoulder.

Lindsay cautiously drank some coffee. She closed her eyes as the rich flavour burst on her tongue and savoured the sensation of its warmth coursing down her throat. 'Heaven,' she murmured appreciatively. Then she opened her eyes and said, 'Guy's known Helen a long time. He knows she's not the sort to give in easily. I wouldn't be at all surprised if he'd decided to keep an eye on us. It would also explain where he disappeared to when I got away. He didn't follow me to the street; the taxi driver said he couldn't see anybody. But Guy could easily have slipped back inside the Watergaw building. He'd have keys and he knows the alarm code.'

'I suppose you're right. It is the logical answer,' Sophie sighed.

Lindsay drained her coffee cup and presented it to Sophie. 'I wouldn't mind another cup,' she said, looking up from under her eyebrows.

'Cut out the pathos and you might just get lucky.'

Lindsay forgot herself enough to smile, gasping as the pain kicked in again. 'Just get me some more coffee, or I'll find somebody that knows how patients should really be treated,' she growled.

Sophie chuckled. 'Did they give you a charm bypass before I arrived last night? Okay, more coffee it is.'

As she got off the bed, Lindsay said, 'Be a pal and pass me my laptop. It's over there on the chest of drawers. And if you could dig out Penny's last disks, then I can get stuck into the stuff she was working on when she died.'

Sophie shook her head. 'No way. Not today, Lindsay. You need to rest and recover. Doctor's orders. Believe me, you'll know exactly what I mean as soon as you get up to go to the loo. You'll have legs like rubber and muscles that are stiffer than a sergeant-major's salute.'

Lindsay scowled. 'Look, I know my body's cream-crackered, but my brain is working just fine. I'm not an invalid. It's not exactly going to strain me to hit the "page down" key every few minutes, is it?'

Sophie smiled. Lindsay's irrepressible determination was one of the things she loved about her partner, but there were times when it slid inexorably into stubbornness. This looked like being one of them. Sophie walked across to the chest of drawers and picked up the laptop. Turning back, she noticed a look of triumph on Lindsay's face. 'I meant what I said,' Sophie told her, walking out of the room with the laptop under her arm. Ignoring the howl of frustrated fury behind her, she carried on downstairs and put it in one of the kitchen cupboards before pouring another cup out of the pot.

'I don't believe you just did that,' Lindsay said, outraged, the moment Sophie walked back into the room. 'I do not believe you just did that.'

'One day is not going to make a blind bit of difference. If the cops were going to charge Meredith, they'd have done it by now,' Sophie said mildly, holding out the fresh coffee. 'Believe me, you'll feel so much better for it tomorrow, the day won't have been wasted.'

'Huh,' Lindsay snorted, grudgingly taking the mug. 'So what am I supposed to do? Play I-Spy with you?'

'Relax. Read a book. Have a bath. Watch some TV.'

'Boring.' Sulky as a teenager, Lindsay glowered at Sophie.

'Okay. So tell me about the investigation, all the things you didn't go into over the phone. Two heads are supposed to be better than one.'

'I thought I was supposed to be having a day off?' Lindsay grumbled. Sophie just stared her down. Eventually, Lindsay relented. 'All right, sit down and I'll tell you all about it.'

She'd got as far as Lauren's tale of being bribed by Penny to get into Monarch's offices when the phone rang. Sophie rolled off the bed and raced out of the room, calling, 'It's probably Helen. She said she'd check in to see how you were.'

At first, Lindsay could hear only a distant mumble from Sophie, then her voice grew clearer as she mounted the stairs, still talking into the cordless phone. '. . . quite a battering, so she's not in a fit state to do much . . . Yes, I appreciate that, and I know she'll want to know what's happened . . .' Sophie walked into the bedroom and held the phone out. 'It's Meredith's solicitor. The police have taken her in for further questioning.'

Lindsay grabbed the phone. 'Hello? Ms Cusack?'

'Ms Gordon. I'm sorry to hear about your injuries. No permanent damage, I trust?' Geri Cusack asked, her creamy voice as rich as a pint of Guinness on a winter night.

'I suspect I'll have to forget the modelling career,' Lindsay said drily. 'But never mind me. What's this about Meredith?'

'The police hung on to her this morning when she reported in under the terms of her bail. I've just had them on the phone. I'm on my way there now.' That explained the background noises on the line. She was talking on a car phone, Lindsay realised.

'Why have they pulled her in?' she asked.

'According to the custody sergeant, they've got a new witness. Danny King, the boss of Monarch Press?'

'A witness to what?' Lindsay demanded.

'It's something and nothing. He's given a statement saying he saw Meredith hanging around outside their premises the last time Penny was visiting. I'm sure it's nothing, but they're clutching at straws. Is there anything you've come up with I should know about?'

'As of now, I've got zilch,' Lindsay said, her bitter tone revealing exactly who she blamed for that. 'But hang on a minute,' she added, puzzled. 'How come it's taken till now for King to come forward with this statement?'

'I don't know. I agree it's odd.' The line started crackling, the static like emery board on fingernails. 'I'll tell you what,' she shouted. 'I'll call you back after I've spoken with Meredith.'

'Thanks,' Lindsay said. But the line was already dead, their conversation abruptly terminated. She looked up at Sophie and gave a lopsided smile. 'What was that you said about one day not making any difference?'

'I have this funny feeling we're going to have to forget about the day off,' Sophie sighed. 'I'll get the laptop.'

'Can't we print this stuff out?' Sophie complained after an hour of looking over Lindsay's shoulder at the laptop's tiny screen.

'I haven't got a lead that connects into Helen's printer,' Lindsay explained.

'So let's just stick the floppy into Helen's PC and print from that.'

Lindsay guffawed derisively. 'Helen's PC came out of the ark. She hasn't upgraded since before you two split up.'

Sophie groaned. 'Wrong size of floppy disk?'

'Got it in one. We're stuck with the migraine master here.'

With a sigh that made the mattress quiver, Sophie read on. 'It's very different from the first draft.'

'Mmm. It's better, too. More hard-edged, more economical with the language. I just can't get over how good it is,' Lindsay said without taking her eyes from the screen. 'One thing's for sure. Whoever tries to finish this has got a hell of a job on their hands.'

They carried on reading in silence, Sophie swept away by her first close read of *Heart of Glass*, Lindsay marvelling at the improvements that fury and heartbreak had brought to her friend's novel. They were disturbed twice, once by Helen inquiring after Lindsay's health and revealing that, as she spoke, VAT inspectors were going through every piece of paper in Guy and Stella's office, every file in the computer, and Watergaw's accounts. 'They're going to have to explain where that EU grant went as well,' she said gleefully. 'One of the inspectors stuck his head round the door half an hour ago to ask me about it. It turns out Stella was so sure of herself that she didn't erase the text of the forged letter from her personal section of the computer.'

'I like it,' Lindsay said, glad something she'd attempted had worked out. She didn't get long to bask in her success. Only minutes later, Geri Cusack had called back. Lindsay asked her to hold on while Sophie picked up the extension.

'Okay,' she said when she heard the click and

the line quality changed subtly, 'here's the meat. They're holding Meredith while they "develop their lines of inquiry" following Danny King's revelations. Apparently there's a supermarket opposite Monarch's offices and King's office overlooks it. He says he saw Meredith hanging around the car park, looking as if she was trying not to be conspicuous. She'd sit in one spot for a bit, then move and lean against a car, then move somewhere else again. This was when Penny made her last visit to Monarch.'

Lindsay clenched her eyes shut. 'This does not sound pretty,' she said. 'But how come it's taken him the best part of a week to "remember" this?'

'He claims he didn't know it was Meredith,' Geri said evenly.

'He didn't know it was Meredith? He's been publishing Penny for ten years and he didn't know Meredith?' Lindsay demanded. 'Shit, I know they were in the closet, but I can't believe he never met Meredith. Baz knew her. How come Danny didn't?'

Geri sighed. 'Meredith confirms she never actually met Danny. A couple of times, they were both at parties to celebrate Penny's books, but Meredith always kept a low profile.'

'Even so, her pictures were all over the newspapers after her arrest. I don't see how he can have missed that,' Lindsay protested.

'He says he only realised this morning. He claims Penny's editor was putting together the programme for a memorial service, and they were going through her photographs of Penny to choose which one they'd put on the front. Among the photographs was one of Meredith and Penny together. Danny immediately recognised the woman in the car park, he says.' Geri's voice was crisp, the warmth gone like a winter's day when the sun sets.

'You don't believe him either,' Lindsay said flatly.

'I can't think why he would lie,' she replied obliquely.

'To protect the killer?' Lindsay said.

'Or if he is the killer,' Sophie chipped in.

'Maybe it's nothing that dramatic,' Geri said. 'Maybe he just wants to keep the pot boiling so Penny Varnavides and Monarch Press stay in the news? You've met him – do you think he's capable of being that venal?'

Lindsay thought for a moment. Then she said, 'He's a wide boy. I'd say it's more likely than him taking a risk to protect somebody. How long can they hang on to her before they have to charge her?'

'Murder's a serious arrestable offence,' Geri said. 'So they have an automatic thirty-six hours. But if they need an extension, I suspect they won't have too much trouble finding a friendly magistrate to grant it. Fugitive risk and all that. Look, I have to go now. If there's any development, I'll be sure and let you know.'

'Thanks,' Lindsay said dully. She heard the double click as Geri and Sophie both hung up. Lindsay ran a hand through unwashed hair that was already standing up in a halo of spikes round her head. She felt impotent, trapped as much by her inability to think of something to do as by her physical incapacity.

Sophie appeared in the doorway. 'It doesn't sound good,' she said glumly.

'So we'd better get on with *Heart of Glass*.'

'It doesn't seem to be taking us much further forward,' Sophie sighed, coming back to squat on the bed beside Lindsay.

'I know, but what else is there?' With a profound sigh, Lindsay picked up the laptop and started to read again.

It was early evening by the time they'd finished the revised draft of Penny's final work. And nothing had leapt out at either Lindsay or Sophie to suggest motive or identity for her killer. Sophie stretched, thrusting her shoulders back and arching her spine, a soft groan escaping from her lips.

'See, I told you staying in bed was unhealthy,' Lindsay teased. 'Look at the state of you.'

'I blame the airline seats,' Sophie said, dotting a kiss on Lindsay's undamaged cheek and getting up. 'I'm going downstairs to start some dinner for us all. Helen and Kirsten should be home in a couple of hours or so. You fancy pasta with a Provençale daube?'

'I fancy you, but my face hurts too much. Not to mention the crucial damage to upper arm and elbow . . .' Lindsay smiled sadly.

'Not the pathos again, please, spare me the pathos! Do you fancy coming downstairs now?'

'In a bit,' Lindsay said. 'There are some other files on here that I want to have a look at. Look, these ones that end .LET. They're probably letters. And these other ones. God knows what they are. Probably nothing to do with anything, but you never know. I might as well finish while I'm stuck here.'

'Glutton for punishment,' Sophie said, rumpling her lover's hair and pulling a face. 'Perhaps a bath wouldn't be a bad idea later. Blood, sweat and tears is not a great recipe for hair care.' She went downstairs and investigated cupboards, fridge and vegetable rack. Half an hour later, she was about to deglaze the caramelized onions with balsamic vinegar when she heard Lindsay's voice shouting urgently.

Hurrying to the bottom of the stairs, Sophie called, 'What is it?'

'I said, I think I've found it,' Lindsay yelled.

20

Lindsay pointed to the screen. 'Look there,' she said, indicating with the cursor what she wanted Sophie to pay attention to. 'It wasn't the manuscript of *Heart of Glass* that the killer was after. It was the notes for the next one. "Structure: five sections, alternate POV between Sam McQueen and Martha Denny: *The Invisible Man, The High Cost of Living, The Ghost Road, The Information, Crime and Punishment,*"' she read out. 'One of the few pieces of paper left in the flat had those titles written on it. I thought it was a reading list when I first saw it, but she was obviously starting to think about a new novel. She was going to call each of the sections after a book.'

Sophie nodded. 'Yeah, so far so clear. But what's that got to do with Penny's death?'

Lindsay scrolled down further. '*Outline,*' Sophie read over her shoulder. '*Chicago??? NYC??? Sam McQueen: early thirties, Irish/Italian, third-generation respectable face of the Mob, has legitimate front business – ???magazine publishing??? Hits on a way of cleaning up the lives of serious criminals. He turns his publishing house into a money laundry. Step one – makes Mob figures respectable; hires them as commissioning editors on huge salary. Every month, the company pays their salaries into offshore accounts, then the money comes back into their US-based accounts from the offshore bank. But what really happens is Sam's firm pays the money into an account in Sam's name offshore. And the "employees" bring in their own dirty money from offshore into their domestic bank account, thus making dirty money look clean. Not only that, but they are legitimized in the eyes of the government – they pay taxes, they have Social Security numbers, they pay insurance, and they earn hugely inflated salaries because they are shit-hot editors – ho, ho, ho!'*

'My God,' Sophie breathed. 'That's bloody clever.'

'You're not kidding. It gets better, though,' Lindsay said drily, flicking the 'page down' key to bring up a fresh screen.

'In order to pay these non-productive, fake employees, the company has to have a much higher turnover. They pretend to produce fake magazines, which are sent to outlets that are Mob fronts. Outlet claims to have sold, say, 100 copies of computer magazine per week, thus legitimately putting an extra $500 through their till. They pay Sam's company for the magazine at wholesale, say $250 a week. And so Sam has, on paper, a string of highly profitable magazines with a team of commissioning editors. Only nothing is real.'

Sophie looked up and grinned admiringly. 'That is wicked,' she said. 'That is so clever. Where on earth did Penny get an idea like that? I never heard her show any interest in that kind of scam, did you? She was always much more interested in the psychology and sociology of lawbreaking than the mechanics.'

'Read on,' Lindsay said, gesturing towards the screen. Sophie scrolled down and carried on reading. *'Sam's a keen yachtsman, likes racing yachts. One weekend, he's sailing and he meets a woman who's crewing on the yacht he's helming. Martha Denny. Twenty-nine, undercover Treasury agent working on anti-racketeering crackdown. She's infiltrated Sam's social world to try and gather information on Mob-related activities. He thinks she's a photographer, and he falls for her. Soon, they're lovers – Martha battles with conscience as government agent, but figures he's clean, his company is clearly legit. Then odd things start happening. He gets his magazines to commission her to take pics, so she's around the office a lot. She notices a lot of calls come in for people who are never there; messages get taken, and presumably passed on, but she never meets the guys attached to those names. Then she finds out they all supposedly work on the mysterious tenth floor – in a nine-story building???*

'Martha's torn between love and duty. (Watch out – bit of a cliché? Or is that just men?) Sam realising early on that she's got suspicions, but he loves her too much to want to lose her, so at first he finds justifications and then has to cope with idea of ??Martha dead?? or

??himself dead?? if his Mob connections find out he's harboring a viper in their midst.

'Resolution???'

Sophie took a deep breath and exhaled slowly. 'Powerful stuff,' she said. 'I mean, it's a great story by any standards, but when you know what Penny could have done with it . . . it makes her death seem so much more tragic. I know that's a terrible thing to say, like saying some people's deaths are more significant than others, but that's how I feel about Penny.' She buried her face in her hands, feeling the prickle of tears in her eyes.

Lindsay pushed the laptop to one side and put her arm round her partner's shoulders, hugging her as close as her painful body would allow. 'You're right to feel like that. Penny was special. Most of us, if we make a difference to the lives of the people we care about, we're doing well. But Penny made a difference in a lot of people's lives, thousands of them strangers. She'll go on doing that for a lot of people, but all the books she still had to write won't get written now, and we're all poorer for it.'

Sophie leaned against Lindsay and smiled sadly. 'I'm really going to miss her. You know how it is with couples you spend a lot of time with – you tend to pair off crosswise as well. I always felt you were closer to Meredith than I was, and I was closer to Penny. I talked about things with Penny that I didn't discuss with many people.'

Lindsay sighed. 'You're right. I loved Penny,

but she could do my head in sometimes. When she got into her New Age meaning of life stuff, it was time for me to go and hug a PC. Or sneak off to Burger King with Meredith.' They sat together in companionable silence for a moment, each busy with their own memories.

Then Sophie remembered what she'd come upstairs for. 'You said this was it, the message that explained why Penny had to die. I don't understand. Are you saying it was a Mafia hit?'

'There's more than one kind of organised crime,' she said. 'Look at all the clues in the text. Who published Penny's novels? Monarch Press, owned by Danny King. Doesn't that sound a lot like Sam McQueen?'

'That's a bit thin,' Sophie protested.

'Is it? Let's not forget that Danny King is one generation away from the old-fashioned East End, where organised crime flourished. It didn't die just because they put the Krays behind bars. It's still going on. The gangland families are just as powerful as they ever were. More so, probably. They've spread out into Essex and branched out into drugs, but they're still basically the same mobs who have run London since Jack the Ripper was pulling the wings off flies. Just say, for the sake of argument, that Danny didn't use his pools winnings to set up Monarch – what if he used dirty money from friends of the family to get the business up and running and turning a legitimate profit?'

Sophie looked sceptical. 'Isn't this all a bit far-fetched, Lindsay? We're talking a London publishing house, not a New York casino.'

'You think publishers can't be crooks too?'

'Not like this, no. It sounds like a bad gangster movie script.'

'This isn't a gangster movie, it's a hi-tech thriller,' Lindsay replied, her voice bitter and sharp. 'One of those ones where somebody gets burned because they pick up too many pieces of the jigsaw by accident and suddenly they're looking at the whole picture. That's what happened to Penny.'

'But how? Penny wasn't an undercover FBI agent. She was just an ordinary writer.'

'She was an observer,' Lindsay pointed out. 'Penny was shrewd and sharp when it came to watching people. That's why her psychology was always so spot on, why her characters felt so real. Think about it. All those afternoons she spent at the mall or the bowling alley, hanging out, watching the teenagers, listening to them, absorbing everything about their culture. And she had that uncanny skill for identifying what was a nine-day wonder and what was a genuine trend that would still have resonance for her readers five or ten years down the road. You mean to tell me that if the jigsaw pieces were there for the grabbing, Penny wouldn't have gone for them with both hands?'

Sophie disentangled herself from Lindsay's

encircling arm and got up, fanning herself with her hand. 'Nothing personal, I was just overheating. I can't believe this weather, it's hotter than at home.' She sat down by the open window, trying to convince herself there was a breeze. 'So what were these jigsaw pieces you reckon Penny picked up on?'

'The phone messages. When I read that in her synopsis, I knew exactly what she meant. I didn't really register it at the time, but both times I've been at Monarch, Lauren the receptionist has dealt with phone calls a bit strangely. Some are totally routine – "Hold the line, I'll see if she's free", "Hold the line, I'll put you through to her secretary", that sort of thing. But there were others where she said straight off, "I'm sorry, he's not here, can I take a message?" Not, "Let me see if he's available." Or, "He'll be in later, can I get him to call you?" Or, "Would you like to speak to his secretary?" Just a flat offer to take a message. But if Danny King's operating a ghost-employee scam, that would be exactly what would happen!' Lindsay's voice was excited, her eyes sparkling for the first time since Sophie had arrived in the UK.

Sophie frowned. 'Okay, I grant you it makes a certain kind of sense if you reason it backwards. But how did Penny get from noticing a peculiarity in the receptionist's phone habits to working out the whole ghost-employee scam? I mean, you heard the same thing and it meant nothing suspicious to you until you understood what was really going on.'

Lindsay shrugged, then glanced at the bedside clock. 'I don't know the answer to that. But I know a woman who might. And with a bit of luck, I might just catch her.'

Sophie looked around the café with a critical eye. 'A bit gloomy, isn't it? You'd think she'd be glad of the chance to get a bit of sunshine on her day off.' Judging by the absence of other lunchtime patrons, everyone else was doing just that.

Lindsay shook her head. 'She doesn't want to risk being seen with me. Even on a Saturday. Lauren has the same relationship to Monarch as a flea has to a cat, which means she doesn't want to risk losing her meal ticket, though she's not averse to a nibble elsewhere as long as the price is right.'

'One look at you and she might think twice about opening her mouth,' Sophie commented, gesturing at her own cheek to illustrate her point.

Another night had spread Lindsay's bruises up and across her face to engulf her eye as well as her cheek and jaw. Time had rendered them more lurid shades of blue, with green and yellow making an appearance round the edges. The scabs covering her grazes had darkened, looking like mud that had been flicked over her skin and allowed to dry there. Under Sophie's gentle bathing, the dried blood had been cleaned from the long hairline cut along her jaw, leaving it looking far less serious than it had done the day before. The pain had subsided to a gentle throb, the ache dulled by the paracetamol Lindsay was still swallowing at four-hourly intervals. 'I'll just have to tell her the truth,' she said wryly.

'Let's hope she shows up,' Sophie said.

'Yeah. Before the cops decide they've got enough circumstantial evidence to charge Meredith,' Lindsay said glumly. 'They're not going to wait for ever, and they obviously think they know who did it. Which means nobody except us is looking for the real killer. Who thinks he's got away with it.' As she spoke, she saw Lauren walk in, and waved at the receptionist. 'Over here,' she called.

Lauren walked towards them. When she saw Lindsay's face, her double take was almost comical. Her face fell like a failed soufflé and her step faltered. Cautiously, she approached. 'What the fuck happened to you?' she said wonderingly. 'You look like you just went ten rounds with Freddy Kruger. I don't think I wanna be here.' She took a step backwards.

'I had an accident,' Lindsay said hastily. 'It's the truth. I took a header over a wall I didn't know was there and landed on top of a broken bottle. Nobody's had a go at me.'

'She's telling the truth,' Sophie butted in. 'I'm a doctor and believe me, her injuries are consistent with that explanation. Look at those grazes – you don't get skin damage like that in a straightforward beating.'

Lauren scowled. 'Who the hell are you anyway?' she demanded of Sophie, then rounded on Lindsay. 'I'm taking a risk, coming here to talk to you. What d'you want to bring a stranger along with you for?'

Lindsay sighed. 'Sophie is my girlfriend. She also happens to be a doctor, and on both counts she wasn't about to let me out of the door by myself this morning. It's okay, Lauren, you can trust her. Sophie was Penny's best friend back in California.'

Lauren looked uncertainly from one to the other. Something in Sophie's steady eyes calmed her and she sat down abruptly. 'You going to get me something to drink, then?'

'I'll go,' Sophie said, taking details of what everyone wanted.

While she collected drinks and food, Lauren said, 'You better be making this worth my while. Baz was having a right go about you yesterday, taking the piss something shocking. About how you was accusing her of murder, then Danny walks in and points out that she was doing a live radio show when it happened. And Baz says to me that if you turn up again looking for her, I'm to show you the door. So this better be good.'

Lindsay nodded calmly. 'I hear what you're saying. You'll be well looked after, I promise you.

First off, I've got a couple of questions, but if you don't mind, I'd rather wait till Sophie comes back.'

Lauren's eyebrows flicked upwards in bored exasperation. Her response was to take out her cigarettes and light up. 'What do you need her for?' she asked petulantly.

'Because my brain's still cabbaged from all the painkillers the hospital shoved into me when I did my swallow dive on to the asphalt. Chances are I won't remember all the things I need to know. Okay?' Lindsay said mildly.

'I suppose.' Lauren smoked furiously, her lips pursed between inhalations. When Sophie rejoined them with mineral water and sandwiches, she ostentatiously crushed out her cigarette. 'So how much are you offering me?' she demanded, all empty belligerence.

'How does two and a half sound?' Lindsay said. 'That's a final offer, by the way. Non-negotiable.'

'Two hundred and fifty?' Lauren squeaked, impressed in spite of herself. Then suspicion kicked in. 'What d'you want me to do that's worth that kind of money? I ain't putting myself at risk here.'

'Pretty much the same as you did for Penny. Let us in the building today and we'll drop the keys off with you later.'

'There'll be people there. Working.'

'On a Saturday?' Lindsay sounded incredulous.

'You've got no idea. Workaholics, some of them. Brown noses, the rest of them. Think just because Danny sometimes drops in on a Saturday that they'll get Brownie points if he sees them at their desk. Saddos.'

'So what time do they leave?' Sophie asked.

'Look, what are you going to do in there? I'm not going along with anything criminal, like trashing the place.' Lauren's voice was apprehensive underneath a superficial bravado.

'Nobody will even know we've been in there,' Lindsay promised. 'All I want to do is exactly what Penny did. There's something I need to check out for myself, just like she did.'

Lauren picked up one of the sandwiches and tore into it as if she hadn't seen food for a week. 'How do I know you're telling me the truth?' she said through a mouthful of sandwich.

Lindsay shrugged as Sophie leaned forward, pinning Lauren with her eyes. 'You have to trust us, Lauren. Lindsay told me how fond you were of Penny. Well, so was I. She was my best friend. I know we're asking you to take a big risk, but we're not asking for fun. This is as serious as it ever gets, Lauren. This is about my best friend's death, and I am absolutely determined to find out what really happened to her. Now, if you want to help, I'd be delighted to accept your assistance. But if it's too much to ask, that's okay too. We'll just have to find another way of getting at what we need.'

Lauren gave up trying to outstare Sophie and mumbled, 'All right. But this is the last time I take any chances, okay?'

Sophie reached out and touched Lauren's shoulder. 'Thanks.'

'Cash, mind,' Lauren said gruffly. 'Up front.'

Lindsay took out an envelope and pushed it across the table. Lauren paused for a moment, her eyes going from one to the other in a flickering gaze. Then she snatched up the envelope and ripped it open, revealing five new fifty-pound notes. Glancing quickly round her to make sure no one was watching, she held them up to the light to check metal strip and watermark. 'Oh, yeah,' Lindsay said with a tinge of sarcasm, 'I really look like a big-time forger.'

Lauren gave a sunny grin. 'All I know, you could be Al Capone. Right now, I couldn't care less. Be outside the office at half past five. They'll all have gone by then. I'll let you in.' She grabbed her bag and stuffed the envelope in an inside zipped pocket. Then, picking up the remains of her sandwich, she pushed back from the table, about to leave.

'Wait a minute,' Lindsay said. 'One or two questions, remember?'

Again the 'Oh, God' upward flick of the eyebrows, accompanied by the heavy sigh of the hard done by. 'All right, then, what do you want to know?'

'The couple of times I've been in reception, I've noticed you taking messages for people without checking if they were in. Is that a regular thing?'

Lauren frowned. 'Yeah. I've got a list of about

a dozen blokes. They never come in the office, but I get messages for them regular.'

'What do you do with the messages?' Lindsay asked. The hair on the back of her neck seemed to be standing on end and, in spite of the stuffy heat inside the café, she felt a chill inside. So much hung on Lauren's answer.

'I pass them on to Danny's secretary. When I started working on reception, I asked who they all were and she said they were business associates of Danny's. She said they were consultants who didn't have offices with secretaries of their own and it was convenient for them to be able to leave messages here. I thought they must be a right bunch of tossers if they couldn't spring for a mobile phone or voice mail or something.'

Lindsay let out the breath she hadn't been aware of holding. 'Thanks, Lauren,' she said softly. 'We'll see you tonight.'

She nodded and gathered up her bag, pausing to light a cigarette. 'Funny you should ask about the messages,' she said conversationally. 'Penny wondered the very same thing.'

21

Lindsay popped the last mouthful of strawberry tart in her mouth and carefully mopped her lips with the paper napkin. The movement of her jaw while eating still gave her twinges of pain, but she'd never been able to resist strawberry tarts, and those she'd found in California just weren't the same. Sophie was watching her with an air of bemused affection. 'I don't know how you can think about eating when the next thing on the agenda is burglary,' she said.

'S'easy,' Lindsay said, swallowing her mouthful of cake. 'Besides, it's not burglary. No breaking, no intent to steal or rape or commit GBH on the premises. It's not even criminal trespass.'

'You sure they haven't changed the law since you last covered the criminal courts?' Sophie said dubiously.

'They have changed the law. That's the current status. Which you would know if you actually read the *Guardian Weekly* instead of using it to put under Mutton's food bowl. That dog knows more about current British politics than you do.' Suddenly, Lindsay leaned forward and pointed across the car park to the front door of Monarch Press. 'Fuck! That's our man,' she said, indicating Danny King, who had just left his office with a tall man in shirtsleeves and suit trousers who carried a square sample case in one hand and a briefcase in the other. Danny was empty-handed, dressed in baggy cream-coloured trousers and a flowing dark blue long-sleeved shirt.

'The one who doesn't look like a sales rep?' Sophie asked.

'Got it in one. Oh, shit, they're headed this way!' Lindsay exclaimed, shrinking back from the window, as if that would render her invisible. For a taut moment, she was on the point of taking flight. Then the two men paused by a dark saloon.

'It's okay, they're only going to their car,' Sophie said, relief spreading across her face. The man in the collar and tie dumped his bags in the boot, then climbed into the driving seat, while Danny strolled further down the car park and climbed behind the wheel of a silver Mercedes convertible.

'Nice wheels,' Lindsay enthused as Danny shot out of his slot and headed for the exit. 'Shame about how he paid for them.'

'We don't know that for sure,' Sophie said.

'We soon will.' Lindsay checked her watch. 'Nearly five now, and anybody left will be out like greased lightning now Danny's gone and there's no one left to impress. I don't know about you, but I fancy another strawberry tart.' Sophie pulled a face. 'Hey,' Lindsay said. 'The night is young. My blood sugar needs all the help it can get. Like you said, it's a tough business, burglary.'

Forty minutes later, they stood inside the reception area of Monarch Press. Lauren had hustled them through the front door faster than a Royal aide helping the boss escape the paparazzi. Then she'd handed over a bunch of keys and a sheet of paper that provided Lindsay and Sophie with the instructions for setting the intruder alarms when they left, and Lauren's address so they could return the keys later.

'The list?' Lindsay demanded.

Lauren reached behind her desk and grabbed a scruffy sheet of A4 paper with a list of names. She thrust it at Sophie and, before they had a chance to ask her any more questions, was off.

The vertical blinds that lined the windows of the publishing house let in more than enough light for the two women to see where they were going and what they were doing. 'His office is upstairs,' Lindsay whispered, handing Sophie some latex gloves and wrestling her hands into her own pair.

'Why are we whispering?' Sophie hissed, efficiently covering her hands.

'Because burglars always whisper?' Lindsay

said in her normal voice as she picked a way through the open-plan office to the stairs.

'I thought we weren't burglars?'

'So sue me. I can't believe I'm doing this for the second time in the same week. Raiding offices, poking around in other people's data.'

Sophie shrugged. 'Synchronicity. You probably wouldn't have thought of this approach if you hadn't already been messing around with somebody else's computer. But let's face it, you dropped lucky with Guy and Stella. Do you really think we're going to find proof that Danny's running a ghost-jobs scam?' she said sceptically. 'Wouldn't a sensible man have destroyed all the evidence after Penny confronted him?'

'Professional criminals are convinced they're smarter than the police. They know they're never going to get caught. So they hang on to all sorts of incriminating stuff. Besides, Danny King can't get rid of the evidence without explaining to the tax people why it is his company has suddenly shed half its editorial staff when on paper they're the ones generating his profits.'

'Good point,' Sophie acknowledged.

They emerged in a corridor at the top of the stairs. On the first floor at Monarch Press, democracy and openness yielded place to hierarchy and privacy – or secrecy, depending on where the observer was standing. Lindsay was in no doubt which word she'd have chosen.

They walked to the far end of the corridor and

started working their way back towards the stairs. The end room was a boardroom that ran the full depth of the building, its centrepiece a vast antique oval table that must have used most of a mahogany tree. 'There's always something, isn't there,' Lindsay muttered. 'All these supposedly radical, right-on companies, they always have an Achilles' heel of good old greedy capitalist materialism lurking somewhere. Now why do I not believe that table's one of Danny's family heirlooms?'

'Because you're a twisted old cynic. Now come on, never mind the self-righteousness. We've got more important things to think about,' Sophie said, chivvying Lindsay out of the doorway and towards the next office, whose door revealed it belonged to the Sales Director. Opposite that was the Marketing Director, then Publicity, opposite Accounts. Finally, they came to an office with no nameplate on its door. 'I guess this is it,' Sophie said, turning the door handle.

They stepped into a small office with a modern desk and the usual array of electronic equipment. A buttoned damask Victorian *chaise longue* ran along one wall, beneath a framed photograph of Danny with a jeroboam of champagne surrounded by his staff under a banner that announced 'Monarch's Ten Year Reign'. This was clearly a reception area that doubled as his secretary's office. A second door led off it at right angles to the corridor. Lindsay opened it to reveal another room that ran the full depth of the mews.

One end of the room was arranged as a meeting space, with four grey leather sofas surrounding a glass and polished-granite coffee table. At the other end, two desks sat in an L-shape. The one facing out into the room was empty. The other held a computer. Between them was a black steel shelving unit that contained TV, video and a Bang and Olufson stereo that had probably cost as much as the average family car. A run of low-level black filing cabinets occupied the back wall below the window.

'Toss you for it,' Lindsay said, fishing a coin out of the pocket of her baggies. 'Call?'

Sophie groaned. 'Whatever I say, I just know I'm going to end up with the filing cabinets. Heads.'

Lindsay tossed the coin, caught it, slapped it on to the back of her left hand and revealed it with a flourish. 'Tails it is. I'll take the computer, you take the filing cabinets. Hang on, I'll get you a copy of the names on Lauren's list.' She disappeared back into the secretary's office, where, rather than wait for the photocopier to warm up, she slipped the sheet of paper through the fax machine. Giving the original to Sophie, she laid the flimsy fax paper on the desk next to her and switched on the computer.

'These are locked,' Sophie said, rattling the first drawer fruitlessly.

'Try these,' Lindsay said calmly, pulling a bunch of small keys out of the desk drawer to her right. 'Arrogant little shit deserves to be burgled.'

While Sophie searched for the correct key for the cabinet, Lindsay found her way around Monarch's computer software. It wasn't hard; they ran a network of PCs, an expanded version of systems Lindsay had worked on both in her university department and in small magazines where she'd contributed articles. It didn't take her long to find the personnel directory, where a database held files on all their employees. 'Yes,' she said softly, a sense of triumph surging through her.

'Got somewhere?' Sophie said, her voice muffled from kneeling on the floor with her head bent over a filing drawer.

'I think so. Look for personnel dossiers, see if they compare with what's in here.' Now that she was faced with the answer she'd been desperately searching for, Lindsay was almost superstitiously reluctant to start checking the individual files of the men on Lauren's list. Instead, she typed in a search request for Baz's file. Just for comparison purposes, she told herself.

The file listed Baz's title – Editorial Director (Fiction) – her work station number – 026 – her salary, date of birth, home address and telephone number, the names and job titles of staff she was responsible for, her starting date with the company and details of her pension fund contributions. Unable to resist, Lindsay called up Danny King's file. Publisher, work station 101, plus all the other details. What looked like an extremely expensive address in Holland Park. Plus a very healthy and generous pension. Now she had an idea what a file should look like, she typed in the first name on Lauren's list.

Paddy Brown was allegedly the Foreign Rights Acquisition Director at work station 201. He earned three times what Baz was paid, though he lived in what sounded like a block of flats in Bethnal Green. Like Danny, his pension arrangements looked well cushioned. The picture was similar for Bill Candy, the Translation Rights Director (work station 202), Paul Edwards, the Senior Commissioning Director (work station 203), Brian Hedges, the Promotions Controller (work station 204) and the other names on the list.

'It's just like Penny laid out for us,' Lindsay said. 'Look, he's even put the equivalent of an extra floor on the building.' Sophie stood up and looked over Lindsay's shoulder. 'That's what she meant with that cryptic note about the tenth floor of a nine-storey building. All the ground-floor staff have work stations beginning with zero, and everybody on the first floor begins with one. But all the shady staff's work stations begin with a two. That way, if there was ever a snap raid, all Danny King would have to say is that those members of staff work from home, or they have a roving commission or whatever.'

Sophie slapped a pair of files on the desk. 'Compare these. Legitimate employee files have copies of all the correspondence from when they applied for a job and were interviewed and had their references called in. Ghost personnel just have a letter of appointment. Bit of a giveaway, isn't it?'

Although she was eager for evidence to support her case, Lindsay was determined not to jump to conclusions again. 'I don't know . . .' she said. 'Couldn't he just say he head-hunted them?'

'I suppose so. That would save him having to forge letters and references. So does any of this actually prove anything?' Sophie asked.

'Taken on its own, none of it means much. But if we took this to the police, along with Penny's synopsis, plus Danny King coming forward at the last gasp to make a false statement about Meredith . . . well, it all adds up. It hangs together. This ghost-employment con couldn't stand up to any serious scrutiny, especially if he's supplementing it with a ghost publication scam. As soon as the cops start looking at it seriously, the whole house of cards is going to collapse.'

'And this is what Penny uncovered,' Sophie said dully.

'I think so. The phone calls made her suspicious, especially when she found out about Lauren's little list. My guess is that her main motive for getting into the computers here was to check out Baz's files, to see if there was any solid evidence for her suspicion that Baz was the one that Meredith had had her disastrous little fling with. But when she was actually faced with the prospect of uncovering the truth, she bottled it.'

'So she took a look at the mystery men in Danny's files as a way of putting off what she knew she had to do,' Sophie said. 'That would be just like her. She hated unpleasantness. She'd have done anything she could think of to postpone actually having to face up to the proof that she'd been betrayed twice over.'

Lindsay took a floppy disk out of her bag and slotted it into the computer, keying in instructions for it to copy the files in the personnel database. 'I think that's the way it happened. She had a devious mind, did Penny. She'd have realised right away there was something seriously dodgy going on. Even if she didn't work it all out at the time, she learned enough to figure it out later.'

Sophie turned back to the filing cabinets and started pulling out the files that corresponded to the list. For a few moments the only sound was the rattling of file drawers and the mechanical groans of the disk drive. Then Sophie said, 'But how did Danny find out she knew what was going on?'

Lindsay took the floppy out of the drive and zipped it into the back pocket of her organiser. She shrugged. 'I don't know for sure, but I think it went something like this. Penny, as Meredith found out to her cost, is a woman to whom honesty and integrity were paramount. The issue between her and Meredith splitting up wasn't infidelity, it was breach of trust. And Penny was ruthless, even though it cost her the woman she really loved. Agreed?'

'Oh, absolutely,' Sophie said. 'She wasn't a forgiving woman. She was absolute for truth and it made her judgemental. It was the side of Penny I liked least. You think she confronted him with what she suspected?'

'I'd put money on it. Remember that curious incident the day before she died? When she came to Monarch supposedly for a meeting with Baz, only Baz was out having lunch with somebody else and Penny kicked off? It wasn't like Penny to stand on her dignity like that. I reckon she was engineering an opportunity to get Danny on his own. And knowing Penny, she probably laid it out for him over the starters.' Lindsay slipped into a Californian accent. '"I know what you're doing here, Danny Boy. I know about the ghost jobs. I know so much about it, I'm going to put it at the heart of my next novel. And then people will ask where I got the idea from. They'll especially wonder if I change publishers at around the same time. Time you cleaned up your act, pal. Exorcise the ghosts or lose me."'

Sophie looked wide-eyed at Lindsay, rocked by the accuracy of her impersonation. 'Jesus! You gave me gooseflesh!'

Lindsay slid out of the chair and gave Sophie a hug. 'I'm sorry, I didn't mean to upset you.'

Sophie smudged a kiss across the top of Lindsay's ear. 'It was just a bit creepy. As if there aren't enough ghosts in here already,' she added with a nervous laugh, brandishing the files she'd extracted. 'We should photocopy these, so we can take them to the police, right?'

'Wrong.'

The voice came from behind the door. Deep, tight and angry. The two women swung round in time to see Danny King step out into the office. Lindsay's eyes swept over him, then swung irresistibly back to his right hand. Dull blue steel, just like in the movies. She didn't know what kind it was, but staring down the business end, the gun looked bigger than anything Clint Eastwood had ever relied on to make his day. The shock of it hurt her stomach and made her bladder burn. Years of journalism and messing with murder investigations had never taken her quite so close to her own mortality. It wasn't a place she liked. Instinctively, she moved closer to Sophie.

'Get away from each other,' Danny said. His cold control was almost more frightening than the black hole of the gun barrel. Without even considering the alternative, Lindsay obeyed, moving away from Sophie at the same moment as Sophie separated herself with a sidestep. That left Sophie in the inside corner of the L of the desks, with Lindsay a foot beyond the empty executive expanse that had stood between her and Danny.

Lindsay forced her eyes away from the gun to look at Danny's face. His expression was set, his jaw clenched so tight the muscles bunched under his ears. His creamy pale skin was flushed along the cheekbones, like two badly applied smears of a blusher designed for someone else's skin tones. His eyes glinted in the evening light like dark sapphires, hard and terrifying as the gun barrel. They carried about the same promise of compassion. 'It's over, Danny,' Lindsay said.

'I don't hear no fat lady singing,' he grated contemptuously, his veneer of cultured civilisation stripped away to reveal a savage gangster bent on survival. 'You're the ones that are over.'

'Killing us doesn't solve anything. It's just two more bodies for the police to investigate. This racket of yours – how many lives is it worth? Sooner or later, the trail's going to lead back to your door,' Lindsay said defiantly, praying her voice wouldn't crack or her bladder give up.

Danny made a sound like a dog coughing. Lindsay translated it as a harsh laugh. 'What fucking planet are you on? Do you have any idea of the people you've been messing with? This is not some cosy fucking TV series where the villain folds up in a heap and you get to be heroes. This is reality, and this is where you get to be dead.'

'There are people who know we were coming here tonight,' Sophie interjected, her voice low and calm. It didn't stop the sweat of fear running down Lindsay's armpits.

'I don't give a monkey's fuck if the Commissioner of the Metropolitan Police knows you're here,' Danny said, taking a couple of steps forward. 'The people I deal with, I don't have to give a toss about stuff like that. You don't understand a fucking thing, do you? Just like your stupid fucking friend Penny. She thought she could threaten me and my operation with her Goody Two Shoes mentality. None of you have the faintest idea of how the world works.' He ran his free hand over his sweating forehead. But the gun didn't even waver.

'How does the world work, Danny?' Sophie cut in, sounding as relaxed as a chat-show host asking him about his latest book.

'Money buys everything. Including love. And death. And it ain't love I'm offering tonight.'

22

Danny took another couple of steps closer to them, his eyes moving calmly from one to the other, making sure they knew he was watching them. 'So what happens now?' Lindsay demanded.

'I make a phone call, we wait for a little while and then it's "Saturday night and I ain't got no body" time, ladies,' Danny said sarcastically. He reached into the hip pocket of his fashionably crumpled linen trousers and pulled out a slim mobile, flipped it open and keyed in a number with his thumb. It looked like it wasn't the first time he'd used the technique. Lindsay wondered if he made a habit of holding a gun on people while he phoned his friends. Was this how it had been for Penny, the gunpoint hostage, then the setting up of the scene for murder made to look like accident?

A moment for the phone to connect, then Danny spoke, never taking his eyes off them. 'It's

Danny. I've got a waste disposal problem at the office. Two loads. I want a team round, soon as . . . Yeah, it'll have to be moved before it can be dealt with . . . See you.' He closed the phone, a smile thin as a filleting knife slicing across his face. 'Sorted,' he said contemptuously.

'Let's hope you make a better job of us than you did of Penny,' Lindsay said. In some strange way, hearing Danny transmit the order for her death had lifted the fear. It was inevitable now, there was nothing left to lose. It wouldn't take long for the hired guns to arrive and once they were there she and Sophie were good as dead. If there was ever going to be any hope, it was now.

'Oh, I think that went off all right, actually,' he drawled, his urbanity restored now he was convinced everything was under control.

'The freak accident line didn't hold for long, did it?'

A quick, careless shrug of the eyebrows. 'Accident, murder, what does it matter what the filth think? I could have had her shot or stabbed or strangled or battered to death. I know specialists, men who know what they're about. Professionals. But I thought, since it was costing me, I might as well get an earner out of it. So I took one of my boys along to her flat. She thought I'd come to talk terms. She never knew what hit her. But I had some great publicity for the new book. Which I figured she owed me, since I wasn't going to be getting any more books from her.' As he preened himself, his wariness was slowly receding, forced back by a tide of complacency. Lindsay wasn't the only one to notice it.

'It was a clever idea,' Sophie said. 'Utilitarian.'

'I hate waste,' he said. 'But I can't think of any way of making a shilling out of you two. Shame, really.'

'Another reason to avoid killing us,' Sophie said, still managing to sound as calm as a midsummer pond.

He snorted derisively. 'Don't give me that bollocks. I told you, this isn't like the telly. You don't get to talk me out of it. You're going to die. If you're a Catholic, I'm sorry, you're going to have to manage without the last rites.'

'Without these files, we haven't got a shred of proof,' Sophie said. 'The cops are never going to take us seriously. They'll realise Lindsay's a friend of Meredith, that she's grasping at straws to make it look like somebody else was responsible for Penny's death. All they're going to see is the money. Why would a millionaire publisher kill the goose that lays the golden eggs? Legitimate businessmen don't do things like that, not even ones who have a bit of a murky past.'

'You must think I'm a real punter if you think that bullshit cuts any ice,' Danny said, his eyes on Sophie. 'Anyway, if you didn't get any joy with the cops, you're just as likely to shop me to the taxman. Which is just as dangerous and probably more expensive in the long run.'

Sophie shrugged. 'All you have to do is send out redundancy notices and close the racket down.' She inclined her head towards the chair behind her. 'All right if I sit down? I've got a bad back, I can't stand for long. If I'm going to die, the least you can do is let me do it in comfort.'

Danny eyed Sophie suspiciously, then took a couple of steps forward to check there was no trick, nothing dangerous in reach once she was sitting at the desk. Lindsay instantly recognised the only opportunity she was likely to get. As he nodded and said, 'Okay,' she gathered her strength in a crouch and launched herself through the air at Danny.

She was slower than she anticipated, muscles still suffering from being crushed against asphalt. Worse, Danny was faster than she'd thought possible. He swivelled on the balls of his feet, his gun arm straightening without a jerk, his finger squeezing the trigger. A flash, a boom, the smell of cordite and her shoulder felt like it had hit a brick wall at something approaching the land speed record. The impact spun her round in a half-circle, but her momentum carried her crashing forward in an unintended shoulder charge.

They collided and crashed to the floor, Lindsay realising as she landed on top of him that only one of the screaming voices was hers. Beneath her, Danny gagged, trying to squeeze some air back into lungs that felt paralysed. The gun barked once, twice as Lindsay lay on top of him, incapable of struggle, beyond even wrestling for the weapon.

When they went down, Sophie threw herself across the desk, screeching like an express train, then crouched, panting, trying to stay away from the lines of fire as Danny's gun arm thrashed pointlessly around. Her eyes raked the room for any kind of weapon. But nothing suggested itself as a potential cosh.

Necessity mothered invention. Like a crab, she scuttled round the desk and ripped cables out of the back of the computer monitor, not caring that her fingers throbbed from the violence of her actions. All she could think about was Lindsay and the grunts and sobs coming from behind her.

The monitor came free in seconds that felt like weeks. Sophie slipped both forearms under it and lifted it clear of the desk. She turned to see Danny thrashing under Lindsay, his breath recovered. He was trying to free his gun arm enough to bring the barrel round to where he could blow a bloody tunnel through Lindsay's brain. She was incapable of stopping him, her body a dead weight leaking blood all over Danny's silk shirt and antique silk rug.

'Fuck you,' Sophie roared, standing over him. His panicked eyes rolled up in his head and he saw her standing there like a time-slipped Greek goddess of vengeance.

'No!' he yelled, his voice outraged, his face a

mask of astonishment that anyone could have the upper hand over him.

Sophie dropped the monitor.

Sophie crouched over Lindsay, a 9mm Glock sticking out of the waistband of her jeans. She was packing the hole in Lindsay's shoulder with the rags of the silk shirt she'd ripped from Danny King's unconscious body. She'd checked him for vital signs once she'd made sure Lindsay wasn't bleeding from an artery. He was unconscious, though not deeply so. She'd ripped his office phone from the wall and used the cable to tie his hands and feet behind his back in a vicious ligature that would guarantee he came round with excruciating cramps. It was, she had decided, the very least he deserved.

It was a long time since she'd worked in a casualty department, and even then she'd only ever seen one gunshot wound. It was a failure of experience that worried her, leaving her uncertain as to how life-threatening Lindsay's injury might be. She could gauge something from the blood loss, but when it came to assessing the actual extent of the injury or the degree of shock involved in such a wound, Sophie reckoned she might as well be a riveter as a doctor. She avoided mentioning that to Lindsay, settling instead for telling her that she was going to be okay, that Sophie would get her out of here and to a hospital just as soon as she had stopped her bleeding to death. She knew that even *in extremis*, Lindsay would appreciate the drama of that expression.

Lindsay lay still, curiously aware of the texture of the short silk fibres of the rug against the skin of her uninjured hand and arm. She felt strangely distanced from her pain, being more conscious of the shallowness of her breathing and the fat blobs of sweat running down her forehead and cheeks. The whole upper left quadrant of her body felt so strange, so alien, it might as well have belonged to someone else for all the connection she could make between it and her past experience. 'I love you,' she said, aware of Sophie's hands moving over her body. It came out as a croak, but Sophie understood.

'You're going to be all right,' she said gently. 'I love you too. Even if you are a complete head-banger.'

'Alive,' Lindsay croaked.

'Yeah, you're right. Better a live headbanger than a dead sensible head. Don't talk now, darling, save your strength. You'll need it if we're going to get out of here before the execution squad arrive.' Sophie wiped the sweat from Lindsay's face with a crumpled tissue, then stood up. 'I'm going to see if I can find a trolley or something that I can wheel you out of here on,' she said.

'No,' Lindsay grunted, forcing herself on to one elbow. 'Not time. For that. I can. Walk. If you just. Help me.'

Sighing in exasperation at her partner's refusal

to accept defeat, Sophie crouched beside her and pushed her into a sitting position. Then she slung Lindsay's good arm round her shoulder, held on to her wrist with both hands and tried to straighten up. It was a backbreaking job which Sophie would never have managed if the lie she'd told Danny about her back had been the truth. Lindsay's feet scrabbled uselessly under her as Sophie dragged her upright. Finally, they stood together in the middle of the room, Lindsay listing into Sophie, swaying slightly, but managing to keep her feet. The door seemed a very long way away.

'Okay,' Sophie said. 'One step at a time.' They managed a jerky movement in the right direction, then a stumble, a stuttering correction and, after what seemed an eternity, a few coordinated steps.

They had almost reached the door when the constipated quacking of a man's voice coming through a loudhailer split the quiet of the mews. 'Armed police. The building is surrounded. Come to the front door and throw out your weapons. I repeat, armed police. Come to the front door and throw out your weapons.'

The voice stopped them in their tracks. 'Oh, shit,' Lindsay mumbled.

'At least it's better than King's thugs,' Sophie said. 'Come on, let's get you through into the secretary's office.' She edged sideways through the door, supporting Lindsay as she staggered through behind her. 'Sit down a minute,' Sophie said, easing Lindsay on to the chaise. 'I'm going to call for an ambulance. I don't know if they'll have one, and you need to get to hospital as soon as possible.'

'Fine,' Lindsay groaned weakly as she slumped against the back rest. The initial physical blow to her system was deepening into a more profound state of shock, her mind a place where thought was as much of an effort as movement was for her body. Things were starting to look fuzzy round the edges of her vision. The focus of her world had narrowed till all she was aware of was the growing shriek of pain in her shoulder battling with the almost overwhelming desire to slide into sleep. Dimly, she heard Sophie speak. But the urgency in her voice was lost to Lindsay, as were her words. 'Soph . . .' she mumbled, her voice tailing off as unconsciousness absolved her from the necessity of decision or action.

'Oh, shit,' Sophie cursed, watching helplessly as Lindsay crumpled before her eyes. 'Ambulance? I'm a doctor. Two injured at . . . you've got the location? Fine. One just gone unconscious, GSW to the left shoulder, considerable blood loss. One unconscious, single blow to the head. How soon?' She compressed her lips at the estimate of seven to ten minutes, then realised it would probably take her that long to get Lindsay downstairs.

She replaced the phone and hoisted Lindsay

over her shoulder in a fireman's lift. It wasn't the most sensible way to carry someone with a gunshot wound to the shoulder, but Sophie didn't have a lot of choice. There was no way she was leaving Lindsay upstairs with Danny King, unconscious or not. Besides, she knew how important first impressions were to the police, and she wanted a clear separation in their minds right from the start between the two of them and King. It was going to be hard enough to convince them she and Lindsay were telling the truth, given the flimsiness of their evidence and the undoubted weight a corrupt system would place on the word of a rich and successful businessman. 'And he probably supports the Tory Party,' Sophie complained to her unconscious burden as she staggered down the stairs one at a time.

At the bottom, she paused for breath. The loudhailer invaded her ears again. 'Armed police. You are surrounded. Give up your weapons and nobody will get hurt. Throw your weapons out of the front door and show yourselves. I repeat, you are surrounded.'

'Yeah, fine, we get the message,' Sophie panted, bracing herself and heading across the open-plan office, grateful for the blinds that hid her from the police marksmen she had no doubt would be in place, fingers on triggers, nerves strung tight as a fishing line with a shark on the other end. She prayed nobody would be too eager tonight.

After what felt like half a lifetime, Sophie was

across the office and into the reception area. The muscles in her thighs were trembling, but she wasn't going to open the door until she knew the ambulance was there. Legs apart, free arm straight against the wall, she stood sweating for a full minute that stretched her patience near breaking point. Then she heard the swoop of an ambulance siren, growing closer, then abruptly silenced, like someone clamping a hand over a child's mouth.

Dry-mouthed with apprehension, Sophie cracked the door open a couple of inches. 'Don't shoot!' she yelled, reaching behind her to pull the gun free. She tossed it out underarm, giving it a flick of the wrist to carry it well away from her. The gun clattered on the road, then there was silence.

'I'm coming out,' she yelled. 'We're the victims here, understand? I've got a wounded woman here. We're the victims!'

'Come out slowly, with your hands raised,' the megaphone voice quacked.

Sophie curled her free arm under Lindsay's legs and let her slide down from her shoulder until she carried her in both arms across the front of her body. Then she slowly staggered out into the street, blinking the tears from her eyes. 'Get the paramedics,' she shouted. 'Somebody get the paramedics.'

EPILOGUE

The light in the seat-belt sign died with an electronic bong. Lindsay waggled her fingers at the window and said, 'Goodbye and good riddance.'

'You didn't enjoy your holiday?' Sophie asked.

'Two trips to hospital? Scarred for life in two separate places? Temperatures higher than California and not a room that has air conditioning from London to Loch Fyne? All the guns in America and I have to come to London to get shot?' Lindsay demanded, her voice rising to a squeak.

'We had a nice time in Scotland,' Sophie reminded her.

'You had a nice time in Scotland,' Lindsay said darkly, shifting in her seat to make her bandaged shoulder more comfortable. 'I had my mother acting like I'd been brought home to die and my father taking the piss out of me every night. And then when we did get up to Torridon, you wouldn't let me up any decent hills in case I wasn't recovered enough.'

Sophie shook her head, grinning. 'I don't think I was unreasonable to put my foot down about a Munro that involved an eight-mile hike just to get to the bottom of the mountain, followed by a 3000-foot climb and another eight-mile hike back to the car.'

'Well,' Lindsay grumbled. 'I've never done Maol Chean Dearg. And now I probably never will.'

'Maybe we could have a trip up there when the taxpayers pay for us to come back and testify against Danny King.'

Lindsay brightened up at the thought. It was the least she felt they deserved after the long hours – in her case, excruciatingly painful hours – of police interviews and making statements. After all that, King still hadn't been charged with Penny's murder. As a holding measure, they'd kept him in on attempted murder against Lindsay, conspiracy to murder and illegal possession of firearms. It was fortunate that the police had arrived when they did, alerted by a supermarket security guard who'd heard gunshots, still a rare enough occurrence in London to bring the police within minutes. Any later and King's sidekicks would have got in to destroy the evidence.

Lindsay had hit it off with the officer in charge of the murder inquiry, who had instinctively recognised a kindred pig-headed spirit. Privately, she had told them that they were never going to have more than a purely circumstantial case against King on Penny's murder and that it was up to the Crown Prosecution Service to decide whether they should go for it.

'Spineless tossers,' she'd confided over a cup of tea in the police canteen. 'I've tried to argue that the attempt on you only makes sense if you allow the previous murder, but they want more. They always bloody want more. Even against a toerag like Danny King. Trouble is, you put a toerag in an Armani suit and he looks like the frigging lawyers. It's the same as hostages starting to identify with their kidnappers. Suddenly all the briefs forget they're supposed to be on the side of the scruffy coppers and they come out in sympathy with the scrote in the suit.'

She'd sounded a lot more cheerful a few days later when she'd tracked them down by phone at Lindsay's parents' house. 'Your friend's neighbour. I think you met him? A Mr Knight?'

Lindsay cleared her throat. 'Might have done,' she said cautiously.

'I thought, what about putting Danny Boy in a line-up? Last resort, you know? His brief starts screaming, which makes us think it's definitely going to be a good idea. So we bring in Mr Knight and bugger me if he doesn't pick him out straight away. He remembers him because of his car. A Mercedes convertible. He noticed it because the arrogant little shit had parked it right outside our Mr Knight's house and he was just pulling away when our witness arrived home from work. Can you believe the conceit of the man? He thinks he's come so far from the East End that he's invincible. And our Mr Knight never thought to mention it because he didn't look like he was in a hurry and he didn't have any blood on him that he could see. Well, of course he didn't, did he? He's a professional. He knew he was going there to take part in a very bloody murder – he'd either have stripped or worn disposable overalls.

'Then our prize witness says, well, we can't blame him, can we? I mean, murderers don't drive around in top of the range Mercs like hospital consultants, do they?

'Soon as Danny Boy realises he's been fingered, he starts shitting it. He knows he's in the frame for murder. So he decides it's time to get out from under. He does nothing more than give us his sidekick, the thug who actually did the killing. King was just there to get him in and give the instructions about the stage setting. Can you believe it?

'Once he started talking, we couldn't get him to stop. His brief was practically in tears. We even found out you had a second lucky escape. You was attacked the night before, wasn't you? It wasn't some accidental trip over a wall that sliced your face up, was it? It was one of Danny King's little thugs, hired to scare you off.'

Lindsay couldn't prevent a dry laugh spilling down the line. 'Is that what he told you? Somebody's been winding him up. Yes, somebody tried to put my lights out with a baseball bat, but he didn't connect, so I legged it. That's when I really did trip over a wall. So if Danny got told I'd been cut, somebody ripped him off.'

'Couldn't happen to a nicer bloke,' the policewoman had said. 'Arrogant, vain, stupid as well. He doesn't even realise that he still gets charged with murder even though it wasn't him who did the actual killing. Joint enterprise, it's called. We've got him, nailed down at all four corners. Not even the CPS can walk away from it now.'

They'd celebrated that night, a double celebration since Helen had also called to announce that Guy and Stella would be facing charges of fraud and false accounting. 'I owe you,' she'd said. 'You gave me my professional life back.'

'You mean that?' Lindsay said.

'Of course I mean it. Why? What do you want?' Instant nervousness at the other end of the phone.

Lindsay let her stew for a few moments, then said, 'I can't think of anything off the top of my head . . .' Helen had exploded with laughter. It was a sound that cheered Lindsay even more than putting Penny's murderer behind bars. She wondered if she'd ever hear Meredith laugh like that again.

Meredith had left for San Francisco a few days before, her life in pieces. If it had been hard to contemplate life without Penny as a lover, it was impossible to imagine it without her very existence. Losing her job had been the final blow, a knockback whose impact had only really hit in the days since King's arrest, when the imperative of finding Penny's killer had been answered. The night before she'd left, she'd told Lindsay she wasn't going to make any decisions about her life for at least six months, displaying a strength and good sense that Lindsay envied.

The cabin steward's inquiry about drinks roused Lindsay from her preoccupation. 'To hell with sensible,' she said. 'I'll have a Scotch.'

When she'd taken her first sip, Sophie said gingerly, 'There's something we need to talk about.'

Lindsay turned her head and stared, a worm of worried fear stirring in her gut. Had she finally pushed Sophie too far? Was this the kind of trouble that altered lives beyond recognition? 'No more murders? That's not a problem, I promise.'

Recognising her apprehension, Sophie reached out and squeezed her hand. 'That would be nice, but that's not it. After we came back to London, while you were giving the cops the statement about your attack, I had coffee with somebody I used to work with in Glasgow. She's doing similar work to what I've been doing in San Francisco, and their consultant is leaving in the New Year to go to Australia. She's been asked to sound me out to see if I'd consider applying. What do you think?'

Lindsay looked aghast. 'British winters?'

'Proper curries.'

'No air conditioning?'

'Decent TV.'

'No sea?'

'Great theatre.'

Lindsay frowned. There had to be something that would clinch the argument against leaving California. Then her face cleared and she smiled triumphantly. 'Quarantine,' she said firmly. 'Six months behind bars. You couldn't do that to Mutton.'

It was Sophie's turn to look horrified. Then she nodded slowly, conceding defeat. 'I am reminded,' she said, 'of the joke about Jesus and the woman taken in adultery.'

'The joke about . . .?'

'Jesus stops the crowd stoning her and says, "Let the person among you who is without sin throw the first stone." And this little old lady pushes her way through the mob, picks up this massive boulder and throws it at the adulterous woman. Crash, bang, wallop, she's dead. And Jesus turns to the old dear and says, "Sometimes, mother, you really piss me off."'